Live; live; live

Live; live; live

Jonathan Buckley

Sort Of
BOOKS

Published in July 2020 by
Sort Of Books
PO Box 18678, London NW3 2FL
www.sortof.co.uk

Copyright © Jonathan Buckley 2020

The moral right of the author has been asserted.

A CIP catalogue record for this book is available from the British
Library

Typeset in Melior 10.2/13.5 to a design by Henry Iles.

Printed in the UK by Clays, Bungay.

272pp.
A catalogue record for this book is available from the British Library

ISBN 978-1908745873
E-ISBN 978-1908745880

For Susanne Hillen and Bruno Buckley

Freilich ist es seltsam, die Erde nicht mehr zu bewohnen
[True, it is strange to be living on Earth no more]

Rainer Maria Rilke
Duino Elegies: The First Elegy

Many of the things that have been said and are still being said are not true. People have arrived at conclusions without knowing enough. It has been said that I have misrepresented certain situations and incidents. We all misrepresent; we misperceive and we misremember. This goes without saying – which is not to say that truthfulness is never possible. I want to be truthful; I try to be truthful, and Lucas knew this. I did not dissemble. We were on good terms, though I could not be persuaded to believe. I made no attempt to refute him; beliefs such as those of Lucas are not refutable. I was intrigued, and this pleased him. I was interested in what he said and what he did, and in the people who turned to him. There were many conversations, some of considerable length, some revealing, on both sides. He was aware that I might write about our discussions. In fact, he encouraged me. This is to his credit. He knew that I would not be convinced, yet he confided in me. The modesty of Lucas should also be noted. He would not have wanted me to advertise his achievements, because he did not think of them as achievements. He simply happened to possess an unusual faculty, he thought. Having been blessed with unusually acute eyesight, likewise, would be nothing to boast about.

As for the archive – yes, I would have liked to explore it, to examine it. The files contain – or contained – many things that I would not be able to explain, Lucas assured me. But it was a question of confidentiality: he could talk about cases that had entered the public domain, and – changing the names – tell me something about a few others, for which absolute secrecy was not required, but he could not open the files. This was reasonable, and I accepted it. Erin's sister argued for their destruction: it would have been understood by his clients that nobody other than Lucas would ever read these documents, she said. Against her, I suggested that the documentation should be donated to a relevant institution or organisation. This may or may not have happened.

For a while, briefly, I was involved with someone called Magda. I mentioned her once to Lucas, and for some reason I supplied her surname – Adamczak. Lucas was delighted.

Several years earlier, he told me, he had been consulted by a family of the same name, in Walsall; the father was from Legnica, he recalled; his name was Jakub, and he had three 'extraordinarily beautiful and brilliant' daughters: Zoja, Krysia and Celina. 'The Three Graces,' sighed Lucas, allowing his gaze to become hazy. The mother, Marta, was the deceased. She had been an 'exceptional' cellist, and the daughters were talented musicians too: Zoja and Krysia played violin and Celina the piano. By profession, all three daughters were academics: Celina an anthropologist; Krysia a geographer; Zoja a musicologist. Zoja was working on a book about the musical life of Italian convents in the seventeenth century. It was to be noted that these highly intelligent young women had been grateful to Lucas. With Zoja, Lucas remembered, he'd had a 'fascinating' conversation about Chiara Margarita Cozzolani, abbess of the convent of Santa Radegonda in Milan, and a fine composer; when the plague struck Milan in 1630, the convent musicians had survived because they had effectively been in quarantine, Zoja had explained. Lucas had much to say on the subject of Zoja and the musical nuns; it was as though he had been with the Adamczak family only yesterday.

'I'll show you something,' he then said, getting up. I followed him upstairs, to the door at the end of the landing. The door opened onto the drabbest of rooms: off-white walls, grey carpet, a single bulb in the centre of the ceiling, enclosed in a globe of frosted glass, dirty. So at last I saw the archive. Against the long wall, opposite the door, six filing cabinets stood side by side – grey metal, identical, each with four drawers. To the left, a radiator. To the right was the room's sole window, with a Venetian blind, white. In front of the window, a four-drawer desk, black-topped, with thick steel legs. A pad of A4 paper, lined, occupied the centre of the desk; there was a pot of pens and pencils, beside a lamp, black. The chair, also black, was a standard item of bureaucratic furniture. Nothing mitigated the austerity of the room. The walls were bare. It could have been the workplace of a Stasi functionary.

From the desk he took a key, to unlock the nearest of the cabinets, which bore a printed label: A–D. A hanging file was extracted; on the tab was written 'Adamczak'. Lucas withdrew a yellow folder, and from the folder he withdrew a thin sheaf: 'Marta Adamczak' was the heading of the cover sheet. He showed me a page of notes on Jakub; Zoja, Krysia and Celina had documents of their own; another was marked 'Transcript'; another 'Report'. An envelope contained a cassette.

For every client there was a file, he explained, gesturing at the array: Abney, Adams, Adkins, Akerman, Alvin, Attwater, et cetera. His pride in the archive seemed more like that of an employee than of a creator. He impressed upon me that each file was the same in format: a document for every subject and for every participant; a recording, plus a transcript of every word that was on the tape; a report. I was permitted to extract one at random, not to read its contents but to verify that it was as thorough as the Adamczak file. I was being asked to appreciate the rigour of the system; his scrupulousness.

Lucas relocked the A–D cabinet. Taking a step back, he cast his gaze over these containers for the papers of the deceased. He smiled, as if seeing in his mind the ghostly ranks of the recovered dead, whose care was his responsibility.

There were stories in these cabinets that would make even the most hardened sceptic pause, said Lucas. He regretted that he could not prove this to me.

☞

Lucas had been reading a book about Helena Blavatsky. 'Have you ever seen anything more ridiculous?' he said, taking the book from the table, and opening it at a page of photos. Attired in a hooded and embroidered gown, resembling an end-of-the-pier fortune-teller, the figurehead of Theosophy, author of *Isis Unveiled*, *The Secret Doctrine*, *The Key to Theosophy* and *The Voice of Silence*, gazed off to the left, into the invisible. From the facing page, W.B. Yeats, with dandyish cravat and pince-nez, peered in the direction of the inspirational mystic. Lucas marvelled that so many supposedly intelligent people should have been duped by this character.

Yeats, Mondrian, Kandinsky, Malevich, Yeats, Scriabin – all had been fascinated by her. 'Incredible,' he said, as if they had been clients who had deserted him for the preposterous Blavatsky. 'I mean – just look at her.'

☞

The Showalter case – this has to be discussed. Online, 'Lucas Judd' + 'John Showalter' produces dozens of hits. Many of them credit Lucas with having solved the case in advance of the police. Here's one: 'Two weeks after the girl's disappearance, the police were getting nowhere.' Then, the story goes, Lucas arrived on the scene, and identified the killer in a flash of paranormal insight. Nobody believed him, of course. His powers were not recognised by the unimaginative officers of the law. Subsequent events, however, were to prove him right.

On several websites Lucas is compared with the more celebrated Doris Stokes. Doris Stokes, one will read, not only solved two murders in her native country but also made headlines in Los Angeles, where she was contacted by the spirit of the murdered Vic Weiss, who divulged to Doris crucial information about the circumstances of his demise. But Doris Stokes did not in fact solve the Weiss case: according to the LAPD, all of the information that she gave them had already been made public. The Lancashire constabulary likewise were adamant that the psychic had made no contribution whatever to their investigations, as Lucas told me, having rectified the misunderstandings that had arisen from some reports of what had happened in Tavistock, with John Showalter. It was true that Showalter was singled out by Lucas a full week before his arrest, but there was nothing uncanny about what Lucas had done. Lucas himself insisted that there was nothing uncanny about it. He had paid close attention to what was visible, that's all, he told me.

He had visited the parents of the missing girl on a Sunday afternoon, and followed the usual procedure: a long conversation, involving the parents and the older daughter and her boyfriend; he had spent an hour in the missing girl's room, absorbing. Nothing came of this procedure. There was no signal. The silence in itself, however, told him nothing. He had immediately ascertained that this was not a happy household. A show of harmony was maintained, but it was evident that there was friction between the mother and father, and that this friction had not arisen recently. Even more obvious was the parents's disapproval of the older daughter's boyfriend, and her resentment of this disapproval. And although nobody would admit to having argued with the missing girl, Lucas knew that there had been strong disagreements, involving everyone. In the climate of the empty bedroom, hostility was a powerfully present element. Therefore the absence of information in the air was not surprising. The girl, wherever she was, was not communicating with the house. But Lucas could not tell if she was alive or dead. He assumed the worst, as anyone would have done. A pretty teenage girl disappears; no sightings for two weeks – a happy ending was not to be expected. But there was no way of telling if she was living and uncommunicative or dead and uncommunicative, said Lucas. The living and the dead do not radiate different kinds of silence. Thus he did not know what had happened, not until he took a walk around the neighbourhood. An 'immersion in the environment' was often highly productive.

For many people, including the police, the sister's sullen boyfriend was the most plausible suspect. There were rumours, as Lucas had been aware before meeting the family, that there had been too close a relationship, briefly, between this young man and the missing girl. Jealousy and anger could be sensed during the conversation with the family, as could the boyfriend's belief in his own allure. He was known as a drinker; several tattoos were indicative of an aggressive personality. Lucas had not liked him, and the antipathy was reciprocated. But the boyfriend was wrong to think, as he clearly did, that Lucas had convicted him on sight. Lucas knew within seconds that he was innocent, just as he knew right away, on encountering John Showalter, that he was looking at the guilty man.

The encounter occurred at the end of the street in which the family lived. Lucas stood aside to let a man and his dog pass by. It was the beauty of the animal – a full-grown Bernese, a magnificent specimen, perfectly groomed – that made him speak to the man. It was impossible not to stroke this dog; Lucas asked permission, and did so. 'A handsome beast,' he commented. The man nodded, avoiding eye contact. 'What's his name?' asked Lucas. The dog's name was Mike. 'Really?' Lucas wanted to say; instead, crouching to peer into the eyes of the dog, he said 'Hello Mike.' Looking up, he saw the man glance up the street, in the direction of the house that Lucas had left a few minutes earlier. 'You are quite something,' he said to the dog, and gave its owner a smile of congratulation. The answering smile, said Lucas, might have seemed genuine to most people, but what Lucas saw in it was not friendliness: the smile informed him that this man was afraid – specifically, he was afraid that Lucas had been visiting the family of the missing girl.

Lucas stood up, to face the man. Feigning a mild puzzlement, he said: 'I think we might have met before.'

'Don't think so.'

'A couple of months ago, at the station?' Lucas invented a minor incident, of which he and the man had been witnesses. 'You didn't have Mike with you, but I'm sure it was you,' he said.

The man shook his head. 'Wasn't me,' he said.

Lucas increased the perplexity. 'You sure?'

'Hundred per cent.'

'I could have sworn.'

'Nope. Wasn't me.'

Lucas shrugged. 'My mistake,' he said. Then, having praised the dog once more, he turned on the man a final scrutinising look. Frowning deeply, he stated: 'But I know you from somewhere. Definitely.' And at this, he saw a flinch in the eye of John Showalter.

He asked the parents if they knew of a man with a large Bernese dog. They did: he lived three streets away; his daughter had attended the same school as the missing girl and her sister, but nobody could remember anything about her except her name. Lucas suggested that the police should talk to him. The police had already spoken to him, as they had spoken to everyone living within a half-mile radius of the house. It was hard to believe that anyone could suspect John Showalter. A family man; a quiet man; someone who 'kept himself to himself', as they all do. For more than twenty years he had worked for a local timber supplier. Every weekend, without fail, he went to see his mother, even though she was no longer sure who he was.

Two weeks later, after the discovery of the body, and the arrest and confession of John Showalter, a reporter rang Lucas, having spoken to the parents. Everyone was in shock. On John Showalter's computer the police had found photographs of the murdered girl, and many more pictures of much younger girls, which would have been enough in themselves to get him imprisoned.

Any competent investigator would have realised that something wasn't right with that man, Lucas told me. It amazed him that John Showalter had been interviewed by two officers, neither of whom had observed anything that had made them wonder if it might be worth talking again, at length, to this dull-seeming little man. 'It really didn't need a mind-reader,' said Lucas, shaking his head at the ineptitude. On several occasions, after the Showalter case, he had been approached by people who had lost faith in the instruments of justice. With apologies, he had declined most requests, urging patience and trust. Police work should be left to the police, he declared, to me. And Lucas had no desire to be a celebrity. 'In my – métier,' he said, settling on the noun as a label that would suffice for now, 'there should be no celebrities.' But he delivered the ruling as if I were interviewing him for a magazine profile.

It was an extraordinary coincidence, I remarked, that John Showalter had happened to be walking his dog in that street at exactly the minute that Lucas was walking down it. 'Quite,' said Lucas, meaning that it was not a coincidence at all. Killers often return to the scene of the crime, or to a locale associated closely with it. This is well known. It's often a compulsion, or a taunt, or a way of inviting arrest.

☞

'Who is that man?' I asked, on passing Mrs Oliver and Lucas in the street. I must have been seven or eight years old. My mother said that he was a relative, she thought. Later, when he was at Mrs Oliver's house almost every day, or so it seemed, she described him as a friend of Mrs Oliver's; this was puzzling, because Kathleen Oliver was so much older than him; friends were always the same age as each other, more or less. Some afternoons, I looked out from my room and saw him in the garden, in a deckchair, reading, as if he were on holiday. 'What does he do?' I asked. His job was unusual, my mother answered. He helped people who have lost someone from their family; a detective of some kind, was what I imagined. I had the idea of asking Lucas Judd to find my father; we did not know where my father was living. Then my mother had to tell me that she had come to think that my father did not want to be found.

Later, I could be told without evasion the nature of Mr Judd's profession. 'How does that work?' I asked. My mother didn't know, she told me, but she had some idea how other people did the sort of thing that Mr Judd did. She said something about séances, as if they were a special kind of experiment, organised by people who were trained to do what they did; I was not to think of it as nonsense. Mr Judd was a serious man; I could see that for myself. Then, at night, I would kneel on the bed and look at Mrs Oliver's house; over there, on the far side of the wall, Mr Judd was raising the spirits of the dead, like a wizard. Some nights, thinking of the ghosts that were swimming around in that house, I could not sleep. I looked at the windows, hoping, with dread, to see in one of them the eerie glow that I imagined the spirits would give off. Occasionally, I would see Mr Judd carrying something from the fridge, or standing at the sink, washing a glass. It was vaguely sinister, this pretence of ordinariness. He knew that I could see him from my room.

※

'She's going to live forever,' my mother remarked, on seeing Mrs Oliver in front of us, on South Street, walking alongside Lucas, arm in arm. Mrs Oliver, though the older of the pair, was still robust, whereas Lucas limped slightly, and used a stick. He might have been a man recovering from an operation or injury, and Mrs Oliver his mother, giving support.

It was the summer before I went to university. The memory of the moment is clear, and I know what I heard and saw when my mother said that. 'She's going to live forever.' I remember the tone and the smile. There was admiration for Kathleen Oliver, and something else, which was not quite malice – more a mild but surprising unkindness, which is perhaps why I have not forgotten it. It implied amusement at the failure of a plan, and could only have meant that my mother suspected, or was affecting to suspect, that Lucas's friendship with Mrs Oliver – if that is what it should be termed – was to some extent strategic.

Kathleen Oliver was not many years short of seventy when Lucas moved in; he might have thought that he should not have long to wait. Instead, he had now waited for seven years, and would wait for another three. Then again, those years would have enabled him to make certain of his claim. Yet, although I never understood what was going on with Mrs Oliver, it was evident that a true affection existed, at least, and was reciprocated.

※

At work in the house of Kathleen and Callum Oliver, Lucas had remarked on a bowl that had caught his attention; it was the first day of the job. The bowl occupied a ledge by the front door, and the manner of its display betokened value. The texture of the clay was rough; the colour was that of a drought-reduced puddle in mud. It was evident that the clumsiness and dullness were purposeful. Asked about it, Kathleen informed him that she was its maker. A conversation followed.

Lucas had questions about how the colours and the texture of the bowl had been achieved. He knew something of the tea ceremony. His intelligence was obvious, as Kathleen would tell me, one day around Christmas, after my first term at university; we were in the kitchen, and Lucas came in a couple of times, briefly, while we were talking; she spoke about him as if he were a favourite nephew, and she wanted him to overhear what she was saying. This intelligence, however, was not what had created the 'connection' that Kathleen had immediately felt; it was more an 'affinity of temperament', she said to me. Lucas too, another time, spoke of the 'connection' that was established by the conversation about the mud-coloured bowl. He was 'greatly moved', for some reason, by the way she handled the object, tilting it from hand to hand, as if it had life, as if it were a delicate animal. When she passed it into his hands, a certain trust was confirmed.

Callum came home before Lucas had finished for the afternoon. When her husband shook hands with the young man, something very strange happened, Kathleen told me. Callum was an imposing man; some found him intimidating, at first. And she saw Lucas glance away from Callum, downward, at the floor. But Lucas was not shy; he was not intimidated. Rather, it seemed, in facing Callum some thought had occurred to him that made it impossible to sustain Callum's gaze; it seemed to be a kind of embarrassment, she said. They talked for a few minutes, the three of them, and the conversation was easy. Then Callum abruptly excused himself. He had liked Lucas, it appeared, but he needed to remove himself from his presence.

Her husband suffered from migraines, she explained to Lucas; he'd had one that morning, and the after-effects were still with him. Only one third of that statement was true, and she knew – though Lucas gave every appearance of believing what she was telling him – that he had not been deceived. Then he surprised her, saying: 'He has lost somebody, very recently.' It was said as if he were the one giving the reason for Callum's departure. 'His sister,' he added. For the first remark, there was a simple explanation: the bereaved have an aura; we all can sense it. For the second: intuiting bereavement, one would have a reasonable chance of being correct by guessing that a sibling had gone. A parent would be most likely, but a sibling would be next. Another possibility: that Lucas knew who Callum was, and had heard what had happened, perhaps through somebody at the studios. But Kathleen knew that this would not be the case, as indeed it was not.

'How do you know that?' she asked.

In answer he shook his head, puzzled and apologetic.

They went out into the garden. The consternation deepened, because Lucas had understood more: the circumstances of the sister's death; the turbulence of her relationship with her brother; other things. His insight was appalling, said Kathleen, yet she was under a spell. And Callum, when this was reported to him, was unnerved – or further unnerved, as the first contact with this strangely intense young man had unsettled him immediately. The gaze of Lucas, though it had lasted but a second or two, had been acute and compassionate, he said. One encounter would have been enough for Callum, but Kathleen was caught, and Lucas had shown an interest in seeing more of her work. So Lucas paid a call to Kathleen's studio, and to Callum's, and it began. He became a visitor to the house.

When did it happen? In what year did those visits commence? This is a pertinent question. Erin would not know the answer. The only reliable sources are dead.

☞

I think I have an image of Lucas as he first appeared to me, but the image is as insubstantial as a figure remembered from a dream of many nights ago: a man high above me, standing on a stepladder, his face amid leaves. He has scissors or secateurs in his hand, I think. He speaks to me – this is certain. He says something, and smiles, and passes down a flower. Perhaps what he says is: 'For your mother.' This might not be Lucas; it could be a gardener. Whichever it is, the scene must be after the death of Mr Oliver; had Mr Oliver been alive, he would surely have done the job himself. The man on the stepladder is not Callum Oliver, I know that much. I think it is Lucas.

☞

Another scene: I am sitting on the floor of the living room of Mrs Oliver's house, on a red rug, in sunlight; there is a beautiful slope of sunlight coming from a window; Lucas is drinking from a heavy tumbler; the glass is cut into patterns like a crocodile's back; the adults are laughing; Mrs Oliver is known as Kathleen now; she has given me a book to browse through, in which there are photographs of a white wooden castle – a fantastical building, with roofs like wings. My father is no longer with us.

☞

I remember the first conversation of any length with Lucas alone; I think I do. It was perhaps a year and a half after he had moved into Kathleen's house; I would have been twelve years old, perhaps thirteen, just. Our paths had crossed in South Street; a fresh and bright afternoon. I had been to the bookshop, and I showed him what I had bought; he suggested that we should sit for a while, on one of the benches on the other side of the street.

Clamping the walking stick between his knees, he rested his hands on the handle, one over the other, and smiled at me in a way that suggested that this was to be the occasion for a proper talk. The stick, with its band of bright copper near the top, had intrigued me. From the way he walked, the stick often did not appear to be entirely necessary; its contact with the ground seemed light. It was sometimes more like an elegant prop; with the dark suits that Lucas favoured, and the prematurely silvered beard, the stick augmented the appearance of distinction.

Noticing the direction of my glance, he said: 'I could get along without it, some days. But it helps. I like to have it with me.' He let the stick topple into my hand.

The design on the copper collar, I could now see, was the image of a ship, embossed, with dates and some words below.

Putting a fingertip to the image, he told me about HMS *Foudroyant*, a story that involved Admiral Nelson. The stick was made from a piece of oak that had been salvaged from the *Foudroyant*. I read the ship's name on the copper band, as if it were a password that I had to remember. The

stick was a gift from a client, he explained; it had belonged
to her husband. I understood that the walking stick was a
form of commendation, of thanks. And I understood that
Lucas knew that I understood what was meant, though he
had not told me about what he did for a living.

At the end, he considered the sky for some time. Easing
back on the bench, he directed his gaze into the trees,
resting his interwoven fingers on the handle of the stick;
he might have been presenting his profile to a photographer. At the conclusion of his thinking, he rapped the
pavement decisively with the tip of the stick. 'Let us be on
our way,' he announced.

☞

At around that time, I remember, he asked me, in the
street: 'And how is your mother?' It was asked strangely,
as if she had recently been ill.

☞

The medium Hunter Selkirk seems to have specialised in
making posthumous contact with members of the armed
forces, and conveying to those who were in mourning
for them the news of the deceased's survival in spirit
form. An RAF officer, speaking through Hunter Selkirk,
complained of the difficulties that the dead often experienced in finding a conduit for their messages: 'There are
so many of us and so few mediums,' he said.

☞

Some weeks after the conversation about the *Foudroyant*
and the walking stick, I met Lucas again, by chance, at

more or less the same place. 'Shall we sit?' Lucas suggested, and we went to the bench – our 'bench of conversation', as he came to call it. The day was warm. The weather would have been remarked upon, I suppose; my progress at school; he would have enquired after my mother.

With the tip of the stick he stroked the shin of his outstretched leg. 'You want to know about the limp,' Lucas surmised, correctly. Then he told me about the crash. It had happened when he was just a few weeks past his thirteenth birthday – 'so your age,' he said, with meaning. It appeared that I should understand that some sort of affinity had been confirmed. He had spent the day at a friend's house, out in the countryside, and the friend's father had given him a lift home. It was late, and very dark. The father, it was evident, wished to be admired for his skill behind the wheel; his son encouraged him to go faster, and the father obliged – the roads were quiet, after all. An unlit car suddenly appeared in front of them, in the middle of the road. Foreseeing the collision, the friend's father turned the steering wheel sharply, so that his side would take the brunt of the impact – that was the intention, anyway. 'I am not going to wake up from this,' Lucas had thought, as trees whirled around the sliding car; though calamity was imminent, he was oddly calm, he told me. But he did wake up, some time later, as did the friend, who lost an eye, and the father, whose legs were broken, but not as badly as Lucas's. A year later, the friend's mother left her husband, taking their son with her. She had held her husband to be responsible, in large part, for the injuries that the boys had suffered; he had not been wholly sober, it turned out; and he had been driving too fast. 'No seat-belts in those days,' Lucas explained, whacking his shin with the stick. At first the doctors had thought they would have to amputate at the knee. 'So mustn't complain,' he said, with another whack.

Gazing up at the sky, he smiled — remembering something, it seemed. The recollection was a private thing, so I did not speak. He glanced at me, and returned to considering the sky; he nodded slightly, and smiled again, as if I had said something wise.

I thought of a question: 'Does it hurt?'

'Only when I hit it,' he answered, straight-faced; he whacked the shin again.

I laughed, and he grinned at me. But a few seconds later his expression changed, and he directed a different kind of look into my face — an attentive and complex look. 'I know it can be difficult, with just the two of you,' he said. His eyes doused me with sympathetic sorrow.

The crash was not, however, the low point of his early years, he told me. His father had died when he was only fifteen. Lucas was on a school trip that day, and he would never forget the face of the teacher who came to fetch him from the dormitory. 'Mr Courtney,' he said, and he tilted his head a little, half-smiling, as though now seeing the grim-faced ghost. 'A terrible day,' he said, looking skyward again, with an intensified gaze. Lucas had been immeasurably fond of his father. This was the phrase he used: 'immeasurably fond'. The words were spoken softly, as if great care were governing their selection; they indicated a precise measurement of affection. 'So I understand how hard it can be,' he said.

It was peculiar, that Lucas should confide in me; he seemed oblivious of the difference between his age and mine. I did not know what to make of it, as I told my mother. She answered: 'He's an unusual man.' To the best of my recollection, little more was said. Several times, over the years, she said the same thing: 'He is an unusual man', not with any suggestion of affection or admiration, but as if the adjective signified an objective category, akin to his height or nationality.

☞

Another moment on the bench of conversation: adopting what had become the customary pose (hands on the stick; eyes aimed cloudward), Lucas told me that his father had died of a subarachnoid haemorrhage. 'A stroke. A rare kind of stroke,' he explained, as though – it seemed to me – the rarity reflected well on his father. And the precise and difficult words were, I sensed, offered to me by way of flattery of my intelligence.

☞

Anecdote: from the Greek *anekdota*, meaning 'unpublished' / 'not given out'. Neuter plural of *anekdotos*, from *an-* ('not') + *ekdotos* ('published') – in turn from *ek-* ('out') + *didonai* ('to give'). Walking with me, Lucas once said: 'That would make a good anecdote.' The words, as I hear them now, suggest an anticipation of the current situation. 'I'm in good hands,' he said, perhaps on the same afternoon; the implication was that I might be his anecdotalist. But what the anecdote in question might have been, I do not remember.

☞

The death of Callum Oliver is central to the story of Lucas; perhaps more central than the life.

Callum swam in the sea throughout the year, before or after the working day. For an hour or more he would stay in the water. My mother once came across Kathleen on the beach, looking out, shielding her eyes from the sun with a magazine; though guided by the direction of Kathleen's gaze, my mother had to search for some time before she could distinguish the dark dot of Callum's hair in the midst of the water. 'He goes out too far,' my mother remarked. To which Kathleen replied: 'He won't listen.' As a boy, Callum had won trophies for swimming and been encouraged to compete at a higher level. He had not been prepared to make the necessary sacrifices. As a recreational swimmer, however, he was dedicated. When Kathleen had met him, he was going to the pool two or three times a week, doing fifty lengths per session, without a break. At sixty-two he was fitter than the average forty-year-old British male. Nonetheless, in conditions that were not difficult, he had drowned. While his wife waited on the beach, Callum drowned.

The sea was quite placid. There was a light wind, so the surface was slightly ruffled; no more than that. He was a long way out, at usual. Among the uncountable little cusps of water it was not easy to spot him; when Kathleen looked up from her book, it would take a few seconds to find him. Once or twice it took more than a few seconds; then she could not be sure that she could see him. He might have raised a hand to wave to her; it might have been a piece of flotsam. She put down her book and scanned the water. What she took at first to be his arm was in fact a floating bird. Movements of the water deceived her. As if it would make a difference, she ran down to the water's edge; standing knee-deep, she called his name, over and over. It took ten hours to find the body.

His heart must have failed, Kathleen thought; a cardiac arrest can kill even an apparently healthy person. It was established that his heart had not failed; neither had he suffered a stroke. Perhaps cramp had disabled him, or a sting. It was possible. And it was possible that he had intended to die.

Lucas could remember, 'as if it were yesterday', the shock that he had felt when Kathleen said those words: 'It's possible that he intended to die.' She was sitting in the damson-coloured armchair. Beside the chair, on a low table, stood a small stone head, of a young man, which Callum had carved. The fingers of her right hand, as her arm hung over the arm of the chair, stroked the stone hair. Looking at her fingers as they caressed the head, she told Lucas that she had come to think that it was probable that Callum had let himself drown. There was something that Lucas did not know, she told him; it was something that only she had known. From time to time, from nowhere, with no discernible cause, a 'massive darkness' would descend on her husband. 'Here we go,' he would say to her when he felt that it was beginning, as if he were about to be lowered into a cavern, and was both fearful and intrigued. It was a sensual experience, he said; he could feel the black bile, the melaina khole, flowing over his brain.

For Lucas, this disclosure required some readjustment of his thinking, he confessed to me. 'I had no idea,' he told Kathleen.

'Why would you?' she said.

(An obvious response: might a man of Lucas's abnormal sensitivity not have been expected to read accurately the character of a living acquaintance?)

Callum could often work through it, said Kathleen. He could not talk and he could not think, but he could work. The stone 'told him what to do'. The contentment that Lucas had seen in Callum was not a pretence. It was just that his contentment would sometimes be unavailable to him; he would be temporarily unavailable to himself. And Kathleen could protect him; she could ensure that he was left alone with his work.

But what had happened on that day? Had he been felled by something much worse than the usual influx of black bile? Had he, in an instant, been wholly engulfed by it? In a moment, could he no longer make the effort required to keep going? Perhaps, unable to think, he had suddenly decided – or it had suddenly been decided for him – that it would be best to die, or that there was no difference in being dead. She replayed in her mind what Callum had said to her before going into the water. They had barely spoken, but it had been a light silence. He had undressed, and kissed her, and walked down to the water. She loved him; he knew this, and he loved her. He could not have set out with the intention of never coming back to her. She had seen, she thought, a slight shadowing in his eyes – one of his lighter clouds, which the water, or work, or music, or her company had in the past been able to disperse. It had not been the onset of the black bile; the black bile was something quite different. It had not been that; she would have seen; he would have said; he had always told her when it was starting – the announcement was an aspect of his love for her. But perhaps, when she was out of sight, his mind had ceased to be his own; unable to think, he had not known that they loved each other. An avalanche of despair. It was all improbable, but possible. Even after thirty years, there could have been some part of his mind that her husband had withheld from her. There might have been a secret.

There was no secret, Lucas told me, as he had been able to reassure Kathleen, when she turned to him. Callum's death was accidental, he promised her. What else he had learned posthumously from Callum, he could not reveal to me.

☞

When depressed, Callum would often take himself off to a quiet place on the shore, to look and to listen, Kathleen told Lucas. The lapping of the sea was a lesson in mortality. Sometimes the corrective would work, and his turmoil would recede. The sound secured him, as the contemplation of a skull might make a penitent secure. And sometimes it was more than a corrective: it brought elation. It made him rejoice, Kathleen said. 'Live,' it urged, with each whisper of the water. 'Live; live; live.' Leaning forward, Lucas repeated the words with too much fervour, to make sure that the lesson was not lost on me. This was his mission: not to help people to keep hold of the past, but to help them to live.

☞

Lucas cited the case of Swedenborg – the great thinker, Emanuel Swedenborg. He was a hero to Lucas. 'A genius. A man of the highest integrity,' he would say, as though providing a personal reference. Swedenborg was brilliant, certainly. In 1724 he was offered a professorship in mathematics, but he declined the post, because he was not truly a mathematician – metallurgy, geometry and chemistry were his subjects. But he had many subjects. His mind was boundless. After spurning the professorship, he turned his attention to physiology and anatomy. His studies of the nervous system and the brain were groundbreaking, Lucas informed me. The concept of the neuron was first formulated by Swedenborg. A genuine scientist, then. A mighty intelligence. In later life, however, he swerved towards the spiritual, the mystical, the theological. Psychic powers were manifested. One night in July, 1759, at dinner in Gothenburg, Swedenborg had a vision of a fire, in Stockholm, the city in which he lived, the city in which he had been born. Stockholm is about five hundred kilometres from Gothenburg, but Swedenborg saw that Stockholm was in flames. And a fire had indeed broken out, while Swedenborg was having his vision. A few hours later, in his mind, he saw it stop, very close to his house. It took several days for reports of the fire to reach Gothenburg. It turned out that Swedenborg had described the conflagration with uncanny accuracy. And once, asked by Queen Louisa Ulrika to tell her what he knew of her brother, Prince Augustus William of Prussia, who had recently died, Swedenborg whispered to the Queen a secret shared only by the Queen herself and her sibling. This proof of Swedenborg's clairvoyance 'caused the blood to drain from her face,' whispered Lucas, as if he had himself witnessed the Queen's astonishment.

The fortitude of Kathleen, in the years following her husband's death, was admired by all who knew her, and quite rightly, said Lucas. One could not imagine a woman less inclined to self-pity. The day after the funeral she returned to her workshop. She worked long hours, as before. She talked about Callum to anyone who wanted to talk about him, but she seemed to have no need of commiseration. She had always been a somewhat taciturn character, and that did not change. To those who did not know her, she would have presented no symptoms of bereavement. The physique seemed to emanate both outer strength and inner. The crop of grey hair was helmet-like. For some, perhaps, she appeared a little too resilient, too self-sufficient, suggested Lucas. It was as if one's sympathy were being rebuffed in advance. But what people were seeing, or creating, was an inaccurate image. (A recurrent motif in his conversation; Lucas too had often been mis-seen.) Kathleen was more fragile than she appeared to be; of an evening, with Lucas alone for company, she talked and talked. She was haunted, he said. For more than thirty years Callum had been her companion; more than ten thousand days. And of all those days, just one of them now occupied the foreground of her memory. A single hour of that day stood like an insuperable gate in her mind – the hour of his disappearance. Beyond that gate lay all that could be remembered of their life together. There was much that could be remembered, but in order to see it she had to open that gate, and the door was so heavy that she was unable to push it aside. This, it seems, is what Lucas enabled her to do. The death of Callum, he proved to her, had been a mishap. 'We brought that door down,' he told me.

☞

The posthumous entity undergoes a process of disintegration, Lucas explained. Freed from the labour of maintaining a coherent self, a labour that is necessary in order to live in the terrestrial world, it becomes what one might imagine as a nebula, in the universe of spirits. Its individuality, ultimately, is surrendered. For us, the bereft, the departed person also becomes a nebula, a cloud of memories. 'The dead begin to evaporate from the earth immediately,' said Lucas. 'But I can prolong the process. I can delay the inevitable,' he said. 'I keep them in view for a while longer, but that's all,' he said, as if that explained anything.

☞

A day after the crash, in the small hours of the night, the teenage Lucas had come 'as close to death as it is possible to get without dying,' he told me. A nurse was talking to him, and suddenly it was as if his mind had withdrawn into a place that was impossible. His body had become a huge thing, and he was occupying a small part of it. It was hard to describe the experience. It was like being in a deep cave within a mountain; that was the best image he could think of. The nurse was at the mouth of the cave, peering into the darkness in which he was lying, and she was speaking a language that he could not understand. Some of the words were familiar, but the more she spoke the fewer words he recognised. He was sinking away from the world of language, and the nurse was sinking back into the air, falling away from him, very slowly. 'I am dying,' he heard. No thinking produced the phrase. 'It simply arose,' said Lucas. There was no fear in it. 'So this is dying,' he said to himself, as though arriving in a great city, where a new life would begin. His blood pressure had plummeted; his oxygen levels too. Nurses were at work on his body; a doctor arrived, and the word 'critical' was spoken. Lucas heard this word and understood it. He saw the doctor, but not with the eyes of his body. The Lucas who was observing the doctor did not have a body; this Lucas was a consciousness that occupied no definable location within the room but had an awareness – a precise awareness – of what was being done to the body that had hitherto been its residence. He saw his injured body; he saw the ruined leg, and all the other injuries, with nothing more than curiosity, as if it were an exhibit in a medical museum; he saw everyone who was in the room, and he heard what they were saying, although 'heard' was only an approximation of the sense that he had now acquired, said Lucas. More than that: he heard words that were being thought but not uttered. It was as though he were hearing half a dozen radios simultaneously, each tuned to a different station, but what he heard was not a cacophony – every voice was absolutely clear.

For some time his consciousness observed what was happening; there was no sense that time was passing, however; he was suspended in a perpetual moment, in a condition of absolute contentment; it was like the non-time of a dream. As the people attended to his body, his consciousness moved away, like a vapour drawn by a current of the air. It entered other rooms, seeing everything, hearing everything. Then, as if pulled into a slow and gentle whirlwind, it fell back into the body of Lucas. His consciousness descended on a slide of light, he said. He was borne back on 'a great wave of love' for all the people who had striven to rescue the body. When he awoke, the first person he saw was a doctor who had not been at his bedside when the crisis had begun. His eyes had never seen her before, but he knew her name. He knew everybody's name and exactly what they had done and said in the preceding hour. As if revisiting a scene in a film that he had watched that very afternoon, he gave an account of what had happened when he was on the brink of death. This was uncanny, but there might have been an explanation that would satisfy the sceptical, Lucas conceded. Patients have, after all, endured operations in a state of awareness that the anaesthetics should have made impossible. Though apparently unconscious, he might have been able to see and hear. He might have guessed correctly which of the nurses had thought he would not pull through. As for the sensation of leaving the body – a benign flood of endorphins might account for it. Perhaps we are all ushered out of life in a festival of hallucinations. But how could hallucination explain the fact that Lucas could describe, in detail, the disposition of the adjoining room? What explanation could there be for his knowing what precious little item had been put into the hand of the patient in that room by his wife? How could he have known her name?

This, said Lucas, was the day on which it was shown to him that we do not die with the death of the flesh.

'Science tells us' – wrote Wernher von Braun, creator of the V-2 ballistic missile, later of the Saturn V – 'that nothing in nature, not even the tiniest particle, can disappear without a trace. Think about that for a moment.' His conclusion: 'everything science has taught me – and continues to teach me – strengthens my belief in the continuity of our spiritual existence after death.' Death was of course something that SS-Sturmbannführer von Braun knew a great deal about.

An example of Lucas's generosity must be remembered: the gift of the bowl, on my birthday. It is an object of much more than pecuniary value, but the pecuniary value is not trivial. Kathleen, deceased one year previously, had been 'impressed, and touched' by my appreciation of what the bowl signified, when she first showed it to me, said Lucas; a less 'receptive' boy would not have seen past its misshapenness. 'She wants you to have it,' he said. I remember this – the present tense was used, pointedly. Facing me, Lucas held out the bowl with straightened arms. He spoke as the ambassador of the deceased creator. Her teachers had taught her that the spirit of the maker – the kami – persists in the objects that are fashioned by the maker's hand; the spirit of Kathleen was in the substance of the bowl. From the window seat, in sunlight, Erin observed the presentation. Evidently he needed her to be present, to witness what he was doing. Does this reduce its generosity?

☞

The tips of my thumbs meet on the nearside of the bowl, and the tips of the middle fingers come together on the other side. This is how Lucas held the bowl to transfer it to my ownership, as Kathleen had held it, showing me how the span of the hand was the measure that had been employed. This was the measure that was always employed, she told me. Things were understood differently in Japan, she said, and I considered the bowl, imitating the concentration of her gaze. It was an ugly object, one might think. Its skin was like a toad's back. The warts were clots of milky glaze; there were runnels of the stuff, like ooze, and towards the base it was streaked with red, as though it had been lifted out of blood. Other parts were raw, the tone of soil. The rim was uneven, and the walls were of irregular thickness. Kathleen passed it into my hands, with care, entrusting a treasure. I looked down on the imperfect circle of the rim; the bowl lay in the imperfect bowl of my hands. A great satisfaction came from the weight of it, the curvature, the surface. I knew not to grasp it, but to let it sit, like something that breathed.

The colours of the bowl were colours one might see in a river bank, Kathleen proposed. The white might be melting snow; the red a leakage of iron from the earth. Mud, to us, is a category of dirt; the crudest of materials; not quite a solid, not quite a liquid, it has no beauty and no worth; it has no place in art. But in Japan she had come to understand that there is no validity to our categories of 'the beautiful' and 'the ugly'. In nature, there is no such distinction. 'In nature there is only nature,' she said. I was fourteen years old; I received Kathleen's words as wisdom. What I was holding was an image of nature, an image transmitted by the maker of the bowl – transmitted, not invented. Its blemishes were not blemishes: they signified decay, the never-ending breaking down of everything that surrounds us, and of ourselves. The bowl was a celebration of things in decay. And she talked about the thrill of the moment at which she discovered what had happened in the kiln – the appearance of the bowl was to a large extent accidental, Kathleen explained. There was no way to predict what the 'whims of the ash' would do to the glaze. It was beyond her control. She had made the bowl quickly, 'without thinking', and then she had surrendered it to the kiln, to let the fire do its work. With her thumbs she gouged at the air, at an imaginary piece of clay, pressing a clod rapidly into shape.

☞

Then there was the difficulty of understanding the role of Lucas. He was there while Kathleen talked to me about the bowl – or rather, he passed through the room. This I remember: she told me a story that was to be taken as a parable, about a master of the tea ceremony, making ready to receive his guests. Everything inside the tea-room was in its rightful place, and the floor had been polished so that it gleamed like glass. The garden around the tea-room had also been prepared: the ground had been raked over and over again; the stepping stones had been scrubbed. It was autumn, and the leaves of the maple tree were ablaze. The master cast his gaze over the tea-room and the garden. The setting was immaculate. So then he took hold of the trunk of the maple and shook it, dislodging several leaves, which he left where they fell. 'The imperfection is what makes it perfect,' Kathleen instructed. The conversation bewildered me, I am sure. I was being taken into the confidence of an artist and was being given a lesson by her, but I had no idea what I was to do with this lesson. Lucas passed behind me at the conclusion of the tale of the maple leaves, and there was an exchange of glances between himself and Kathleen, whose glance suggested that I was being approved, that I was being taken into their company in some way. And there was something else that I saw in Kathleen's glance – a teasing quality. The relationship was strange. To Kathleen, Lucas was the son whom she and Callum had never had, Erin would later suggest. Yet the look that passed across me, as I held the bowl that Kathleen had made, was not the look of a mother. Perhaps what I told myself was that she was an artist, and that artists do not think or talk as we do; it is in their nature to be miscomprehended.

She was an artist of a grandmotherly age, yet she insisted on being addressed by her first name, like a friend. But she had been our neighbour for years, and not until Lucas became her companion did I get to see inside the house. When I was invited, on my own, the invitation came from Lucas, as if the house were now as much his as Kathleen's. Was I invited in order that she might have some other person to engage her, in compensation for the loss of her husband? Lucas had spoken to me, on the street, several times. Perhaps he had reported that I might be of interest to her now. Perhaps as a younger child I had been of no interest.

☞

The toad-bowl glows on my desk, on its lamp-lit stage. At the base, there are three small black marks: the prints of two fingers and a thumb, left there when she held the bowl upside down to dip it into the glaze. Holding it, I see something of the moist lime-coloured light at the windows, and the brown-red tones of the Anatolian rug, at which I stared, listening to Kathleen.

☞

In his foreword to the autobiography of the medium Ena Twigg, the Right Reverend Mervyn Stockwood, Lord Bishop of Southwark Cathedral, writes: 'If we were to take psychic studies seriously, we would learn to appreciate that our experience in this world is not the consummation; instead we live now *sub specie aeternitatis*. There are other worlds and dimensions, and this should be taught in our schools as part of our general education.' Distraught at the sudden death of her daughter Sally at the age of twenty-four, the novelist Rosamond Lehmann turned to Ena Twigg, who was able to console her client with the news that Sally was in heaven, and had been befriended by Saint Francis of Assisi. Having become aware of Sally's musical talents, the saint had assigned her the task of teaching unborn birds to sing. Eighteen months after her daughter's death, Lehmann wrote: 'often I have more peace of heart and soul than ever before in my life – in spite of all the grief.'

I remember the afternoon when Kathleen talked about the game of *go*. The board was doused with sunlight in the bay window. The amber gleam of the wood was remarkable, and I remarked on it. Kathleen's hands glided over the surface, a steady inch above, as if the substance were a liquid that must not be disturbed. Had she been able to afford it, she would have bought a board made from a single piece of *Hyuga kaya*; this was a composite of three. 'But delicious, don't you think?' she said. This would have been some time after the day of the bowl; I had been approved. 'Inhale,' she commanded. A sweet and subtle fragrance arose – this was one of the special qualities of *Hyuga kaya*; of greater importance were the durability and the fineness of the grain, which ran from player to player. The direction of the grain was significant, as was the delicacy of the sound made by the stones on this exquisite wood. The wooden bowls of lens-shaped stones were then produced: the black made from *nachiguro* slate, the white cut from clam shells; they had cost even more than the board. Kathleen displayed a single white stone on the palm of her hand; it was *yuki* grade, snow grade, the best, and she held it up so that I could take note of the narrow straight veins. She placed it on the board, and smiled at me, and at the soft click of the little stone against the wood.

This tiny sound was an aspect of the pleasure of *go*, Kathleen told me, as were the fragrance of the wood, its grain, its weight and density, the colour of it, the colours of the stones. With chess there was no such satisfaction in the materials of the game. Chess was hand-to-hand combat, whereas *go* was an engagement of much greater subtlety. I accepted readily the implicit compliment.

Instruction now began. In a game of chess, you begin with the two armies facing each other; here, however, you begin with emptiness, and the potential for any number of games, Kathleen explained. 'The possibilities are infinite,' she said, gazing into the board, as if through a window, onto a landscape of thrilling wildness and extent.

'You play not so much to win as to learn, to become a better player,' said Kathleen. 'You endeavour to create an interesting thing, with your opponent. The game is more important than the players.' Whereas each piece in chess has a specific role to play, a particular way of behaving, in *go* every stone is equal. There are no hierarchies of kings and queens and foot soldiers. At one point in a game, a stone might be strong; later, the same stone might be weak. 'Every stone is vulnerable, and every stone can cause damage,' she explained.

'It's all very metaphorical,' Lucas heckled from the armchair, from behind a newspaper; he could have been a long-married and affectionate husband.

'Well, it is,' answered Kathleen. The rebuke was mock-headmistressy. She went on: in chess the focus is upon the enemy's king, and three or four pieces might gang up to trap him, but in *go* there's no focal point – the whole board is alive. 'Everywhere, the situation is constantly changing.'

'As I said,' Lucas intervened.

'Lucas is useless at it,' said Kathleen.

'I am,' he said happily. Then he warned me: 'It's like bleeding to death. Very, very slowly.'

'I'll show you how to play,' said Kathleen. 'The rules are simple.'

'The rules aren't the problem,' said Lucas.

Regarding him over the rim of her glasses, she enquired: 'Lucas, wasn't there something you were going to do?'

He lowered the newspaper and gazed at the facing wall, slack-mouthed, failing to remember. He turned his clueless eyes to Kathleen. A mimed word gave him help. 'Ah yes,' he recalled, and bowed in apology. It was a routine for my amusement.

Lucas left us, to run his errand for Kathleen, to the chemist, and she instructed me in the rules of *go*. We began to play. There was a fluctuating wind that afternoon, and an upstairs window clattered in a gust. Kathleen looked up. 'It's the one on the landing,' she said. 'Would you mind?'

I went up the stairs, into a part of the house that I had not seen before, a part that belonged to Kathleen and Lucas, in a way that the rooms downstairs, where I was often a visitor, did not. Something might be revealed, I thought. The arrangement of this household was strange. Usually she spoke to Lucas like a mother to her son (sometimes a son of fifteen, rather than a man of middle age), but on occasion there was a deference in Lucas's manner, as if he were the live-in assistant of a famous person, and sometimes – even before her frailty – I observed a dependency, as though Lucas were more a nurse than an assistant. And once in a while I would notice a glance that seemed to expose a sentiment that was of quite a different order. That made me uneasy, as when Lucas came back and Kathleen said 'Thank you, dear,' with the inflection of a private joke, as if they were allowing me a glimpse. The

creak of the stairs augmented an atmosphere of secrecy
and intrusion. Nothing that I saw bore any trace of Lucas;
the glassy dark wood of the floorboards, the threadbare
rug, the sun-bleached burgundy curtains – it all signified
Kathleen. On a wicker chair at the top of the stairs stood
a huge glass bowl of dried petals, from which a weak and
dusty scent arose. All four doors along the landing were
shut. There seemed to be some meaning to this. In any
other house, I thought, one door would have been ajar, at
least. They had made a point of closing every one. On two
other occasions, while Kathleen and Lucas were living in
the house, I went upstairs: once to fetch a book from the
shelves on the landing; once again for the window. All the
doors were shut.

'Let the game take you in,' Kathleen encouraged me,
and I did. She handicapped herself, yet always won. But
I learned, and improved, and was happy to lose. Kathleen
considered placidly the terrain of the board; she placed the
stones quickly, as if intrigued to see what the consequence
would be. Often Lucas watched for a while, admiring, and
perplexed, both by what was happening in the game and,
it seemed at times, by the invincible Kathleen.

The evening of the swim clarified nothing. About to
turn back, having walked east for some time, along the
beach, I saw a man sitting on the sand, reading amid
bags and towels, and recognised him as Lucas. A late
September evening; the sun had just gone – so, about
7pm. It was cool, but not chilly. In the moment that I
realised that the reading man was Lucas, Lucas saw that
the walker was me. He beckoned me to approach. This
was some time after the episode of the bowl; I was one

of the chosen few. Kathleen's clothes were strewn about. Lucas pointed to where she was, neck-deep in the placid water; wading rather than swimming, it appeared. With Lucas I would have talked about school, I imagine. We admired the sky: clouds of charcoal ash, as I recall, with a lower stratum of pomegranate. The tide was low. The distance from us to Kathleen would have been thirty yards or so. Seeing us marvelling at the horizon, she turned to do the same; and then she returned. I can see her, pushing through the water, striding out. Her pallid shoulders emerged; she emerged to the waist, entirely naked. The birth of Venus did not come to mind. The flesh was chicken flesh, blotched with violet from the coldness of the sea. Not knowing who it was, one might have mistaken the stocky body for a man's – an unfit man, and elderly. Half-revealed, she turned away, not abashed at seeing me there, but to look back over the water. It occurred to me that this was an act of remembrance; that this was the time of day at which Callum had died, in these waters. Another thought: that with Callum gone, Kathleen, never conventional, no longer cared what anyone thought. For perhaps a minute she stood in the shallows, then turned back towards us and walked out, in no hurry. This is when Lucas stood up, lifting the towel. He went down to the water's edge, arriving as she reached the sand. There was no urgency; no need to protect her modesty. Like the attendant of a grand eccentric, he held out the huge white towel at full stretch, at shoulder height, and Kathleen turned into it, with a smile of gracious thanks. It was not a sexual scene; but she had decided to be naked in Lucas's presence; she must have undressed in front of him. I did not know what to think of it. She sat down, swathed in her towel, to the side of her clothes, and we talked as she watched the light disappear. What we talked about, I can't remember. It was a weightless little conversation, such as we might have had upon meeting in the street. Her nudity had been of no account. While she dressed, I looked away, but not at her request or suggestion. This must be the strangest widow in England, I decided.

☞

Kathleen talked to me about life without Callum, once, in the year that was to be her last. I had returned from university; our conversation had a new frankness, warranted by the elevation of my status – I was now semi-independent, a young adult, a proto-scholar. After the death of her husband she had fallen into 'an abyss of grief', she told me. Too weak, too badly injured to climb out, she had seen everything as if from the floor of this abyss; people were all at a distance from her; she could barely see them or hear them; the light was far away. It was Lucas who had guided her back to the upper surface. And yet, the climate of her life was no longer what it had been with Callum; it never could be. 'It's colder now,' she said. A posthumous reunion of the spirit, such as Lucas envisaged and promised, could not be a perfect reunion, she seemed to be telling me. I thought, without speaking, of Achilles in the underworld, telling Odysseus that he would rather be the living slave of a dirt-poor farmer than a king among the dead.

☞

Some people seem to believe that there was a disagree-ment about the scattering of Lucas's ashes. There may well have been, but there was no disagreement in which

I was involved. The brother and sister, I know, would have preferred a burial and a stone. They told me so; or the brother told me that his sister found cremations too squalid, and he sympathised with her point of view. 'At least the waste disposal element is a bit less obvious with the church option,' he said to me, after the funeral. Erin noticed that I was talking to the brother, and did not care for the way he seemed to be taking the day. The smirk was objectionable, she said to me afterwards; and I was implicated in it. But a cremation is what Lucas had wanted, Erin said, and there is no reason not to think that this was true. And whatever my relationship with Lucas might have been, it was for Erin to decide what should be done with the ashes. She chose not to make a ceremony of it; exactly what was done, only she and her sister know. Golden Cap was a place of particular significance to Lucas, Erin told me, and I can only make a guess as to the nature of that significance, as he never made any reference to it, and neither did she. I did not ask. Obviously it must have played some part in the story of Erin and Lucas. My view is that what was done was entirely fitting: the body reduced to dust in the shortest possible time, and cast into the air, the spiritual element. But had an equivalent of Callum been on hand, Lucas once told me, he might have considered commissioning a stone: a quiet monument, in the style of Wittgenstein's gravestone; name and years, and nothing else. 'Something gloriously humble,' he sighed, in a parody of self-importance.

A Saturday afternoon; I was alone in the house, and Lucas called to me over the wall, inviting me to join them; Kathleen had made a rhubarb and apple pie – a speciality. This would have been some time after I had seen them on the beach.

The three of us ate in the garden, before Kathleen took a nap. 'I'll leave you two to talk,' she said, leaving us, and I heard the implication that Lucas had something significant to say to me – something, perhaps, about his life with Kathleen, which was still opaque to me.

And Lucas was indeed in expatiating mood, but his subject, after some preliminaries that are now forgotten, was not his current life; it was his family – in particular, his mother. I should count myself fortunate in being the son of my mother, he told me, and for a moment I wondered if I had given him some reason to suspect that I lacked gratitude. What he meant, however, was that he had not been so fortunate.

With the death of his father, Lucas had been left alone with his mother; the brother and sister – of whose existence I was only now made aware, I think – were somewhat older than Lucas, and were living elsewhere. 'I was an addendum,' he told me. As a child he had often felt, he told me, that his mother had been 'less than wholly delighted' by his conception. The hardest years of motherhood were behind her, she had thought, but then Lucas arrived, surprisingly, and the drudgery recommenced. His mother was never 'the warmest of women'. She was 'an efficient mother, but not a cuddler,' he said. Young Lucas had come to feel that his mother regarded him as something of a project, a test of her child-rearing skills and stamina. His father contributed to the work of raising the boy no more and no less than was customary for fathers of that period. Of course, there had been episodes of tension between the parents, but no arguments within Lucas's hearing. Sometimes, however, and with increasing frequency in later years, he had sensed that a disagreement might have recently occurred, or been in the offing. When his father died, his mother's demonstrations of grief were soon over. She was unhappy, as went without saying, but it seemed to Lucas not so much that his mother was bereft at the loss of her husband, but that she was burdened by all the work that she now had to do on her own. 'The household was understaffed,' as Lucas put it.

He admitted that he had thought that his mother should have observed a lengthier period of full-blown widowhood. To his way of thinking, she had been a little too hasty to fill the vacancy. She was a good-looking woman and not yet fifty when widowed; in time there would be another man, in all likelihood, but a two-year pause was not long enough for Lucas. He might have found it easier to accept that his mother had found a new object for her affections so soon after her husband's decease had she accepted a replacement other than the one she chose. Malcolm ran a company that offered 'Logistical Solutions' – Lucas relished the absurdity of the slogan. 'Translation: he owned some lorries.' There were signs that the business was doing well. He was also few years younger than Lucas's mother, and played a lot of squash – as she told Lucas one evening, by way of presenting her admirer's qualifications, prior to introducing him to her son. It was impossible to understand the attraction: the man had no apparent interests other than his business and, now, Lucas's mother. He wore a watch that had half a dozen pointless dials within the main one; it might have been permissible if worn by an astronaut. The watch, one felt, told the world what Malcolm felt it needed to know about him. It was not inconceivable that he had never opened a book since leaving school. Yet Malcolm's imperceptible magic did its work. One night, a conversation was convened in order to clear the air. It ended with his mother telling him, with rather fetching and youthful vehemence, as if defying the wishes of a parent: 'You will have to get used to it, because we're getting married.' At least she had delayed the announcement until Lucas had left home.

The newly-weds moved to a large house, with extensive grounds, several miles removed from the old neighbourhood. A room was set aside for Lucas's use during the university vacations; Malcolm had no offspring to accommodate, which, as Lucas put it, 'might or might not have been an aspect of his allure'. The room was three times the size of his boyhood bedroom and had a fitted wardrobe that could have held the uniforms of an entire platoon. After graduation, for a few years, he occupied this room half a dozen times a year, at most, for weekend visits. He was the most welcome guest. 'It wouldn't have been a surprise to find complementary chocolates on the pillow when I arrived,' he said. At best, his relationship with Malcolm was one of reciprocal indifference. Lucas acknowledged that his mother's new husband had occasionally made an attempt to reduce the distance between them. He recalled, with embarrassment, an evening during which Malcolm solicited the aesthete stepson's appreciation of a recently acquired artwork – the head of a racehorse, life-size, in solid glass. Lucas feigned admiration impeccably, he thought, but – 'for once' – he felt ashamed of himself, he told me – ashamed of the pretence, and ashamed of his snobbery, because Malcolm was doing his best, after all. An antique table was bought for the display of the horse's head; it was the first thing one saw on entering the house. A staircase curved around it, a wide staircase that Lucas's mother would descend, 'as if appearing in the film of her own life,' said Lucas.

Yet he admired his mother, he insisted. Above all, he admired her honesty. 'I like this life,' she stated, as though asserting a philosophical principle. She liked not having to worry about money, she told him. Lucas was unaware that there ever had been any reason to worry about money before. She liked the house and the enormous garden and the holidays, and she liked no longer having to work full-time. 'And she did seem happy,' Lucas conceded. 'She seemed to love Malcolm, perhaps more than she had loved my father,' he said, appearing to find some sweetness in the mystery of it, and he sighed, as if exhaling the smoke of an invisible cigarette.

If I were to see Lucas with his mother, he told me, I would not think that they were related. 'Which, in a way,' he added, 'we no longer are.' There was little affection between them, but no rancour, either; and no physical resemblance that he could see. Under the influence of Malcolm she had perhaps become the woman she had always wanted to be; unencumbered. 'Perhaps I could have been a better son,' he said, and for a few seconds seemed to give the proposition some thought. 'You're a very good son,' he told me, is if conferring upon me a certificate of quality. They were not close, but he wished his mother well. 'I do,' he assured me. 'People should not be alone,' he said, looking me in the eye, with too intense a kindness, to ensure that this most important of lessons should be remembered. From time to time he visited his mother. She was nearing eighty, and no longer in good health.

Three years after this conversation, his mother died. It was some time after her death that we became aware of it, when Kathleen, talking to my mother, made reference to the funeral. It had happened a fortnight before. We wondered: leaving aside the fact that, according to Lucas, he and his mother had become to some extent estranged, was it appropriate, given what Lucas believed, to pass on our commiserations? Had any real loss occurred? It would be strange to call on him in order to express our sympathies for a misfortune of which he had chosen not to inform us, and which might not, to his way of thinking, have been a misfortune at all. His mother was now an occupant of the higher realm. Nonetheless, next time she saw him, my mother offered her condolences, and he accepted them, with thanks, as one might accept an unexpected but very small gift. He said nothing about his mother, then or ever again, to either of us.

In fact, I later learned, she had not seen her younger son for several years. 'Estrangement' was not the right word, his brother informed me – rather, there had been a 'cessation'. Money was the immediate cause; Lucas had been in need, the brother believed, and their mother had not been as generous as she might have been, possibly because Malcolm would not allow it. Malcolm had little respect for Lucas's line of work, and his wife's point of view was more or less the same, said the brother, whose sympathies did not need to be made more explicit. Malcolm was not at the funeral of Lucas. Having nursed their mother in her dwindling years, he had declined abruptly once she had gone, and was no longer occupying the house. When I asked if Malcolm knew that Lucas had died, the answer was: 'I doubt if the name means much to him any more.'

I too was 'unexpected', my mother told me, eventually. We had one conversation on the topic; a brief one. After seven years of trying, she told me, she had almost given up hope. Adoption was something that she would have considered, but not my father. Childlessness began to seem to be her fate, and she was getting used to the idea when Anna Bramber, then a colleague at the clinic, gave her the news about her sister. The sister, Belinda, married happily to a 'lovely man', very successful, and with a good job herself and a 'lovely house', had a life that would have been perfect if only there were children in it. She and her husband were 'desperate' to have a child, but had conceived only three times in the decade of their marriage, and each of those pregnancies had failed. Tests were done, and no physiological explanation was found. Belinda was approaching forty; the odds were lengthening. A few months before Belinda's fortieth, Anna moved in with her boyfriend; within weeks, a baby was on the way. Not knowing how she could tell Belinda, she postponed the announcement for two months, then three. Every week the sisters spoke on the phone, and the deception was making Anna miserable. When the pregnancy became unmistakeably visible, she could no longer keep it a secret. She rang Belinda. 'Bel,' she began, 'I have some news.' And Belinda answered: 'So have I.' Relaying the amazing story to my mother, the next day, Anna proposed that a greater power was at work. 'I'll pray for you,' she said; Anna often prayed, sometimes to give a little bit of extra help to those who came to the clinic.

For a while, a few years after my father went, a young couple lived at number 17. An attractive pair, as I recall. She had an old-fashioned grey-green gabardine coat, and I have an image of them walking arm-in-arm in the rain, with the man – Gareth? – holding the umbrella, like a stylish couple in an old film. They were often to be seen arm-in-arm; their happiness was remarked upon. Then the baby arrived, and every Saturday morning the glum husband could be seen, steering the pushchair around the streets; he had the face of a bolt-tightener on a production line, six hours into his shift. Some men do not like the idea of no longer being the sole beneficiary of a woman's affection, my mother remarked, after we had passed him. This I took to be an allusion to my father, just as I had taken the husband of Belinda to be an envied paragon of love and patience and success.

☞

'If it weren't for Lucas, I wouldn't last a month,' Kathleen told me, in her room at Belmont Court, after what would be the last operation. 'I read and I fall asleep, and when I wake up I've forgotten everything. I'm just pouring words down the plughole.' Her laugh was a single small puff of air. Her left hand was no longer obedient; she looked at it as if it were a pet that she was obliged to look after. 'I wait for Lucas,' she said, 'and for the light to go out.' Every day, when Lucas was not on the road, he visited Kathleen. Every single day. This should be known. 'How is she?' I would ask him, and he would answer: 'OK. She's OK.' His demeanour was more mournful in the weeks before her death than after. Fifteen weeks she survived in Belmont Court.

One afternoon my mother, looking out of an upstairs window, saw Lucas standing in the garden, wincing into the sunlight. She knew what this meant. He looked like a prisoner who had been released that morning, refamiliarising himself with his home. She went outside, and Lucas called to her: 'She has left us.' That was all he said; he went back into the house. Later she saw him writing at the garden table. We were invited to the burial. No more than a dozen people were there. His speech was brief and simple, and touching. He spoke quietly, and as though the phrases in praise of her spirit, of her mastery, of the selflessness of Kathleen and of her art, were occurring to him as he spoke. 'But words are superfluous,' he concluded, touching an eyelid. 'We shall miss her, always.' I sat beside a woman who turned out to be the owner of a gallery through which many of Kathleen's pieces had been sold. It was interesting, the way she listened to Lucas, and the way, later, she addressed him. His status, evidently, was unclear to her. He might have been a secretary whose influence she knew to have been rather greater than that of an employee.

I remember a Saturday afternoon, with my mother, in Dorchester; my father had been gone for five years or so. We entered a shop, a large shop. A sharp shower had started, and my mother pushed the door open with urgency. A woman in an emerald green coat was leaving; she had her head down, and was unclipping an umbrella. My mother, also head down, wiping rainwater from a sleeve, bumped into her. She looked up, to apologise, but the apology was cut short: my mother and the woman in the green coat stepped away from each other, and seemed to be embarrassed in a way that the small collision did not explain. The woman – younger than my mother, but not young – performed a sort of bow, then swerved around us, hurrying, and my mother watched her leave; her expression was a glare, as if the woman had said something rude. Following my mother's lead, I too looked at the woman. With the umbrella held low, screening her face, the woman in the green coat trotted up the road.

A comment was required. 'She worked with your father,' said my mother. And then: 'A nasty piece of work.' The woman had not looked at all like a nasty piece of work; and why would my mother talk about someone from my father's workplace in that way, as though she knew her well? She had not known the people he worked with, I had thought. There was only one way, it seemed, to connect the woman we had just encountered, who was not nice, with my father, who had gone, and was always referred to as 'your father'. My mother intended that I should make this connection; this is what I understood, though no further mention was made of the woman in the green coat. And the fact that this woman was not to be mentioned was proof that I was right to make the connection that I had made.

A couple of years later, also in Dorchester, with a friend and his sister, I saw the green coat again. The hue was unmistakeable. There it was, on the opposite side of the road, but the woman wearing it was perhaps not the woman we had seen at the shop. She seemed heavier, but shorter; her hair was different, in cut and in colour. With my friend and his sister I crossed the road, and woman crossed too. Having only a few seconds to make sure, I looked at her bluntly; she was looking directly at me, but not, I saw, to ascertain if this might be somebody she had seen before – she knew who I was, and, under the influence of her certainty, I saw that the woman's face, though changed, was the face that I had seen before. Passing me, observing that the recognition was mutual, she surprised me by smiling, slightly; what the smile said to me, I thought, or came to think, was that she would have liked to speak to me, and was sorry that this was not possible. I looked back, from the other side of the street; she did not look back. The green coat flashed once or twice within the crowd, then was lost. I never saw the woman again, or was never aware of having her in my sight.

It required self-control to withhold a report of what had happened. My mother might even have been pleased, I thought, to hear that the woman had become plump. 'Let herself go' was a phrase my mother had used, of someone else of whom she did not approve. But silence could do no harm, so I said nothing. The woman in the green coat was, or had been, my father's other woman, I believed; as perhaps she was.

☞

On the bench of conversation, Lucas said of my father: 'I liked him.' As I recall it, the statement implied that, in saying this, Lucas was taking a position that was not unanimously held. I had not been aware that Lucas had ever spoken to my father; I doubt that the possibility had ever occurred to me. 'I met him, a few times, when I was visiting Kathleen and Callum. In the street,' Lucas explained, answering my thought. Kathleen and Callum had liked my father too, apparently. 'You remember Callum? Mr Oliver?' he asked; the suggestion was that I, though only a boy, must share his evident affection for Callum. For me, Mr Oliver was a figure rather than a person; he was the man who had lived with Kathleen. I replied that I remembered him well; a liking could be inferred from my voice. 'A good man,' Lucas pronounced, definitively.

'What did Dad think of Lucas?' I asked my mother, perhaps that evening. To which the reply was: 'I don't think he had a view.' My father was not to be spoken about.

At 3am on a Wednesday night, in a hostel in north Wales, more than two hundred and fifty miles from home, young Lucas awoke from a dream in which his father, in the shadow of a huge church, on the moonlit central square of a town that did not seem to be in England, shook the hand of his son, firmly, but with tenderness, and some sadness, then turned his back and strode away, along a track of white stones that designated the central axis of the square, swinging his arms as though he were one of a marching company of whom he was the only visible man. Lucas woke himself up, having cried out, in reality, as his father – without once looking back – vanished under the arcades that bordered the square in front of the church. The air in the dormitory was colder than it should have been. A window had been left open, he thought, but it had not. He lay back, closing his eyes. His bunk seemed to have become unmoored from the floor; the air of the room was changing and then he saw his father, through the skin of his eyelids, with a clarity that was greater than that of any dream. Lucas was in the air, at ceiling height, gazing down on his father, who was lying on the floor of his bedroom, staring up at his son; his father's face was motionless.

At that moment, at home, his father was lying on the floor of his bedroom, with his eyes open, staring into the face of his wife, not seeing her.

The anguish, Lucas told me, did not arrive immediately; it overwhelmed him only when he returned to his mother. Instead, what he felt, at first, as he lay in the hostel bed, in the hinterland of full wakefulness, was a 'great surge of compassion'. Then, a sensation of 'extraordinary well-being' suffused his body, even though he knew – or 'almost knew' – that his father was dead. This is what he wanted me to believe. He had been 'immersed in understanding', he told me. What he had understood was that 'all was well', and no sooner had this understanding taken possession of him than he became aware that his father was with him: it was no longer a vision that he was experiencing but a presence, the presence of his father's consciousness. They communicated with each other. It was not a conversation, however – it was an 'exchange of feeling'. There was 'a mingling' of himself and his father. A metaphor came to mind: imagine two liquids flowing together, urged Lucas; one an oil, the other not; of different colours. They do not dissolve into each other or undergo dilution; each remains distinctly itself, in its essential self, but their forms, as they circulate around and through each other, are constantly changing. They modify each other, in ways that are immensely complex, and yet they stay the same substance. Thus it was with the spirit of his father and his own.

The analogy was approximate, necessarily so, Lucas apologised. It was not possible to represent the phenomenon in a way that the rational mind could readily accommodate, just as it was impossible to reduce the world of quantum physics to simple images. We cannot visualise how something can be both a wave and a particle, or how that particle/wave can be in two places at once, or how the behaviour of a particle can depend on whether or not it is being observed, or how particles can become entangled in such a way that they continue to mirror each other, even when separated by huge distances, by light years. These things are real, nonetheless. The science seems to make no sense, but if it were not correct our computers would not function. The world in which we live our lives seems to obey certain rules. It is dependable. Tomorrow morning, our surroundings will look much the same as they do today. Houses will still be standing; trees will not have disappeared; our neighbours will not have vanished into another dimension. But on the smallest scale, nothing is stable. Within the atom, uncertainty reigns. This is a great mystery, said Lucas. How can our world of solid and law-abiding objects be constructed from particles that behave so unpredictably? We do not know how this can be. The two realities seem to be irreconcilable, and yet both are true. So it was with the experience of which Lucas was telling me. His consciousness and his father's had become removed from the world of stable forms. They had achieved a communion of spirits. This was very hard to imagine, and yet it was true, Lucas assured me, as true as the unimaginable tumult of the particles of which our bodies are made, and every other thing.

☞

Ludwig Wittgenstein, no less, once spoke of an immensely interesting spiritual experience, Lucas told me. Regaining consciousness after an operation, he had become aware of his soul as something quite separate from his body. It was a 'black ghost in the corner of the room'. Slowly this ghost approached the body from which it had removed itself, and again 'took possession of it'.

☞

At the moment of death the deceased – or the spirit of the deceased, or the soul – embarks on a journey. As the body shuts down, the spirit-soul floats away. It is a process akin to evaporation. Or a sort of refining – the corrupted residue of the flesh is left behind. So far, so Christian. But whereas the Christian soul is transported immediately to heaven, or hell, or purgatory, according to which variety of the faith one espouses, the liberated soul in Lucas's system, if we can call it that, ascends to the supra-physical dimension with less urgency. Having been evicted from the corpse, it lingers for a while, in a zone from which it can, should it feel so inclined, make contact with those whom it has been obliged to leave. Separation can be as difficult for the dead as it is for those who mourn, it would appear. It takes some time to loosen the multifarious threads of memory and sentiment that bind the soul to the world in which it had lived its embodied life.

Think of the spirit as the occupant of a little boat on an ebbing tide. Before long, it will be lost to us. The sea will bear it away, to the vastness of the open ocean. As they drift off, the dead concern themselves less and less with what is happening back in the place where their bodily existence occurred. They are caught up in deeper and higher things. From time to time, before reaching the horizon, they might cast a reminiscent gaze upon the world; their mood is usually wistful, but rarely regretful. They have acquired the perspective of the wise, no matter how unwise they might have been while they lived among us. But for a while the boat remains in the shallower waters, and its passenger is close enough to communicate with us – or rather, with those of us who have ears to hear. For some reason, not many of us have been given the necessary apparatus. Lucas was one of the blessed. In the interval between the death of the body and the disappearance of the soul, Lucas could be of service. For several months after the departure of the departed, or longer, in some cases, Lucas was within range for them. The tides of the afterlife operate to a more generous and irregular schedule than those of the terrestrial seas.

☞

Had I asked him the question that so often presented itself – 'Is this what you actually believe?' – I might have been banished from the house. Lucas was capable of bearing a grudge, as he said himself. I had witnessed his contempt for a journalist who had interviewed him two or three years before; she was a 'sanctimonious idiot' who had made up her mind long before meeting him; his anger was still strong. And there were people he had snubbed because of their less than friendly attitude towards Erin, which was taken by Lucas to be an insult to himself as well. I had seen the snub in action on the street – it was as though he were walking behind a private front of frigid air. The offenders might as well have been invisible to him. And I would not have asked the question anyway. His seniority was a consideration, as was his manner. The entire style of the man made such a question impossible. Having asked myself why this should be so, I answered that it would have been like asking an artist – an artist of established reputation – for a justification of his work, for a paraphrase of his 'ideas'. The analogy is inexact.

☞

There was no confrontation, but there were discussions that roamed around the periphery of the question.

'Where do these spirits reside? Where are they going?' Lucas wondered. 'Why do they communicate through me? I don't know.' But it could not be denied that he heard them. Things that were true had often been revealed to him; items of information of which he could otherwise have had no knowledge. 'So many things are incomprehensible to us,' he pronounced. People of great intelligence – 'much greater than mine' – have struggled to understand the mysteries of the spiritual world. Many eminent men of a scientific cast of mind had come to concede the reality of spirit presences, without being able to explain what those presences were. The great Alfred Russel Wallace – biologist, naturalist, explorer, geographer, anthropologist, co-conceiver of the theory of evolution through natural selection – had stated that he knew (I can hear that *knew*, as spoken by Lucas – the word had colossal weight) that 'there are minds discon-nected from a physical brain – that there is, therefore, a *spiritual world*', Lucas insisted, as if passing on an asser-tion that he had heard Wallace make. Other authorities were cited as required. The philosopher Henry Sidgwick, 'no fool', had been the first president of the Society for Psychical Research; even mightier figures – William James and Henri Bergson – had followed him, and nobody had ever accused William James and Henri Bergson of being gullible. Lucas invoked them as though the names were proof in themselves.

☞

The cosmos confounds us, Lucas said. Because we stand on what feels like solid ground, we believe that we live in a world of solidities. In reality, however, everything is insubstantial. Atoms consist mostly of empty space.

Particles are not particles at all. That's the reality, but it's not a reality that we can live with. We have to believe that things are as they appear to be, on the surface. 'The sky, when you really look at it, is unbearable,' said Lucas. We were sitting in the garden, on a summer evening, two years ago. He raised a hand, as if the stars were a spectacle that he had arranged for educational purposes. Out there, a billion light years away, there are black holes that are thirty, forty times more massive than the sun, and they are revolving around each other two hundred times per second. 'Two hundred times, every single second. Can you even begin to imagine such a thing? Can you imagine the distance of a billion light years? A single light year – that's six trillion miles. So a billion times six trillion. It's just words. The reality is inconceivable. It's beyond what our minds can accommodate.'

'Unbearable' and 'incomprehensible' were not the same thing, I suggested. Something that could not be imagined was not necessarily something that could not be understood. One could understand the physics of the whirling black holes without being able to picture them.

'We understand nothing,' Lucas pronounced, taking pleasure from the inadequacy of human intelligence. 'How did this all begin? How did something come out of nothing? The Big Bang – how could there have been such an event? How could there be an explosion in a void? How could there even be a void?' Question after question was released into the air; there was no end to them; the debate, such as it was, would invariably end with one of Lucas's questions. 'How can we know that we are not living in a simulation of reality?' he asked himself, and Erin looked at me, with a placid but challenging gaze, as if she doubted that I had the strength of character to become a true pupil.

☞

The last day of my father's life with his family: it has a date, but for me no reality. A Thursday in April; nothing of that Thursday can be recalled. Once a month his work would take him away from home for two or three nights; there had been no indication that his departure on this occasion would be permanent; perhaps the decision was made abruptly, on the first or second night in whatever hotel it was. This is possible. I have no memory of the car being loaded with more than the usual suitcase. He was going to stay in Birmingham; he had often had to stay in Birmingham.

At the weekend my mother talked to me: my father would not be back with us that night. In fact, he would not be back soon. It was not certain when he would be back. I think I remember the tone: something had gone wrong, but it was no emergency. My mother was not weeping; I know that. There was no great sense of upset, or of anxiety. We sat at the table, on opposite sides, as though we were about to play a complicated board game and she had to explain the rules to me. The sun was bright inside the house. On the sill above the kitchen sink, yellow flowers stood in very clear water, in a milk bottle; my memory tells me that I looked at the flowers for a long time.

Later, another conversation, this time sitting side by side. The television had been turned off so that my mother could tell me what she had to tell me. At the end, there were tears; both of us. 'Your father and I cannot live together,' she said, as if the reason that he was going to live somewhere else were a fact that was not personal, as if somebody had come to the house and told them that they could not live together, and she had accepted it because there was nothing they could do about it. 'But you'll still see him,' she promised. What I remember: looking at our reflections on the murky dark-green TV screen, when we had stopped crying. I went to bed late, and the house was so quiet I had to get up and look into what was now my mother's room. Not finding her there, I called out; she was downstairs, and none of the lights were on. This might have been a different night.

The wardrobe in what was now my mother's room was no longer full. But in the rooms in which we lived there were few signs of my father's absence. On the wall, near the front door, a small wooden plaque, with a colourful metal shield attached to it, hung on a hook; three little ships were on the shield, and their hulls were strangely shaped, like horseshoes. The meaning of the shield was unknown to me, but the three golden ships were a detail of the house that gave it character, like a signature. One afternoon, coming into the house, I saw, in place of the shield, a framed photograph of the harbour, as it had been a long time ago. My father had been in the house, it seemed, and I had not seen him.

But I did see him again, for a while. He said the same thing as my mother had said: 'We can't live together.' The words were different when he said them: he seemed to be accepting that the failure was his. This, I think, was the day at the museum in Dorchester, when a feeling of point-lessness overcame me, at the thought that, when I was back home, I would not be able to talk to him about what we were seeing, and so the day would be incomplete, and the hours at the museum would fade out of my memory. Every two weeks I had a day with my father, before he moved to a different town. It was more than a hundred miles away, but he might not be there for long, he said; I would stay with him, soon. I did not stay with him. He moved house again, but not nearer. Then my mother did not know his address any longer, she said. That he was living in Manchester we knew from the postmark on the cards that came to the house at Christmas and on my birthday, for several years. Some money was enclosed, but there was never any proper message.

'I don't know,' my mother said, when I asked her what had happened; she shook her head, gazing out of the window, as if a message were written in the sky but the letters were as vague as clouds, and it was not important anyway. 'He doesn't love us,' she said; we were to harden ourselves.

☞

Two years after his father's death and the mingling with his father's spirit, Lucas was granted proof that the scope of his talent would not be confined to his family. The revelation occurred at the house of a woman called Laura, a colleague of Lucas's mother, a few years her senior, divorced. Laura had been a steadfast support in the months following the death of Lucas's father. She was the most frequent visitor; sometimes the two women went shopping together; later, there was the occasional trip to the cinema. Bit by bit, Laura was drawing her friend back into the world. One evening, shortly before Christmas, she held a gathering at her house – a few friends and neighbours, and a selection from work. One of the neighbours, a man called Malcolm, at least separated and maybe divorced, had started to interest her, Laura confessed. She had seen signs that the interest might be reciprocated, though he was perhaps slightly younger than she was, and it was therefore probable that he was on the lookout – if he were on the lookout, that is – for a companion more youthful than herself, Laura aknowledged. 'As is generally the way,' said Lucas, submitting a guilty plea with a rueful twist of the mouth.

Lucas was invited too; other teenagers would be present, he was promised. Two other teenagers were present: a vapid and lumpen girl who never left her mother's side; and a boy who talked loudly and at length about football, the only subject about which he was capable of talking. Lucas spent much of the evening on the outskirts of the event. Permitted a bottle of beer, he withdrew to the stairs to drink it; he took a second bottle.

It was while he was finishing this second bottle, waiting for his mother to conclude her goodbyes, that the extraordinary thing happened: he heard a word, whispered, so clearly that the sound made him turn. Nobody was near enough to have been the whisperer. But he sensed a presence, an obstruction of the air such as a body would make, though there was no body. Again he heard the word, quieter than before, but more urgent. Initially he had heard it as 'Really', but on its repetition he was less certain. The third time, though, he heard the two syllables clearly – the word was 'Reenie' or 'Reaney'. The name meant nothing to him, and he did not know what it was that he had heard. The sound had not arisen in his brain; it had come into his ears from outside. It was a whisper, and the voice was male. Perhaps, he decided, there was something strange about the acoustics of the staircase; perhaps what he had heard was a person speaking in a room at the top of the stairs. This was improbable. And why would the syllable have been repeated twice? Then came another whisper. 'Letter Finlay' was what he seemed to hear. It made no sense;

perhaps it had been a fragment of a phrase or a sentence. He waited. A minute later, there was another repetition: unequivocally, simply, the phrase was 'Letter Finlay'. The voice had an accent of some sort, he could now hear; it was not English. He was left with those two words, and an accent, plus 'Reenie'.

Walking home, he told his mother what had happened on the stairs. She was sure that 'Really' was what he had heard, rising from the hubbub of conversation. As for 'Letter Finlay': the obvious explanation was that the words had popped into Lucas's head, and his brain – perhaps tired, perhaps a bit blurred by the beer – had made it seem that the words had been spoken. 'No,' Lucas insisted. 'I heard them.' He insisted just once. His mother was not receptive. She had other things on her mind – Malcolm, for one, it turned out.

Lucas knew that he had not misheard. A few days later, at work, in response to Laura's remarking that Lucas had seemed preoccupied – upset, even – at the end of the evening, his mother told her about the words that had seemed to be whispered to Lucas. 'He says he heard something like "Reenie"', she said, and Laura smiled. Her middle name was Irene, a fact known to few, but known to one person at the get-together – a woman called Joan – who had known Laura since their schooldays, and from time to time would use the diminutive that they had sometimes used at school: Reenie. That's what Lucas must have overheard, she said. But then Lucas's mother revealed the nonsensical phrase: 'Letter Finlay'. At this, Laura's expression changed in an instant: tears appeared, and the frown and the set of her mouth suggested that she had taken offence.

She had not taken offence, Lucas informed me. Laura's reaction was one of consternation and distress and fear.

She had once known a young man called Moray; he had fought in the war, and when he came home, injured, she had realised that she loved him. Moray had always called her Reenie, never Laura. He was 'the love of her life', she had come to understand, as she confided to Lucas's mother. For reasons she would not talk about, they had not been able to stay together. Neither would she say why Letter Finlay, a tiny place in Scotland, in the Highlands, had been of such importance to them.

It had not been impossible for his mother to explain what had happened with Lucas on the day his father died. We all imagine, at times, our loved ones in peril. For all she knew, Lucas – a boy who was given to morbid thoughts – had worried himself constantly by picturing his father stricken. In the end, his imagination had coincided with reality. That's all there was to it, his mother persuaded herself. With Laura and the lover she had lost, however, coincidence – though not absolutely out of the question – was less convincing as an explanation. His mother was disturbed by the incident in Laura's house, said Lucas, and it was rarely spoken about again. For the following year's gathering, Laura implemented an adults-only policy. And Lucas knew better than to tell his mother anything of his other moments of uncanny intuition: the weeping woman alone at the traffic lights, whose daughter's voice Lucas could hear, for instance; or the man on the bus who stared out of the window as if under hypnosis, who was seeing all the time something that Lucas too could see, and nobody else. After what had happened on the stairs, a distance opened up between Lucas and his mother, he told me. His mother could not accept the truth of it. Her son had carried off some sort of trick, but how he had done it, and why he had done it, was incomprehensible. Sometimes, in windows or mirrors, or on the periphery of his vision,

Lucas would see his mother looking at him, as someone who was not to be trusted, or resisted all comprehension.

☞

After the funeral, I asked Lucas's brother what he knew about the story of Laura and Moray, and what Lucas had experienced at Laura's house. The brother knew nothing of this episode. He remembered a supportive colleague, but thought that her name had not been Laura. The sister likewise knew nothing. This may or may not be significant.

☞

We can disregard what Father Brabham has said. Of course, he could never have approved of Lucas's domestic arrangements. Not that he knew anything about the relationship between Lucas and Erin, other than that they occupied the same property. But that was enough. There was a whiff of sin. A similar whiff comes off at least two participants in Father Brabham's ever-dwindling congregation. I could supply the names. Adulterers both, I know for a fact. But Father Brabham finds them more congenial, it seems. Bear in mind, too, that Lucas was in competition with Brabham's business. One could argue that Lucas was the more successful. More people attended Lucas's funeral than one would find in Brabham's church of a Sunday. Many more satisfied customers over the years, I should think.

And there was a philosophical disagreement. In Lucas's afterworld, everyone is saved. We float away into the eternal haze, all of us. Nobody is punished. The idea of hell, Lucas believed, was what had first attracted Father Brabham to the organisation. But if Father Brabham had read the original script more closely, he would have discovered that the lake of inextinguishable fire, supervised by Satan and his punitive battalions, is not in the Book, as Lucas once told him, or so Lucas told me. After hearing, from a woman of the Brabham flock, that Father Brabham had made, to her, an extremely disobliging remark about Lucas's enterprise – having learned that another member of the flock, perhaps failing to find in Father Brabham's sermons the solace she required, had decided to consult 'the imposter' – Lucas took the opportunity, on next encountering Father Brabham in the street, to request that he should refrain from passing slanderous judgement on what Lucas was doing. Father Brabham denied the charge of slander, but did not deny that he thought that Lucas's ideas were incompatible with the tenets of Christianity. In reply, Lucas doubted that Father Brabham knew much more than nothing about the ideas that Lucas espoused, but did not deny that those ideas were opposed to certain aspects of Christianity, if by 'Christianity' one meant the doctrines propounded at Father Brabham's place of work. Some of these doctrines, Lucas argued, were misrepresentations of the Word. In particular, the notion that sinners were doomed to never-ending torment and pain is not to be found in the New Testament. Lucas quoted John at him (And I, when I am lifted up from the earth, will draw all people to me), and Corinthians (For as in Adam all die, so in Christ all will be made alive). If you care to look, said Lucas, you'll find that Jesus said nothing about the devil and his lake of eternal fire. Father Brabham, reported Lucas, did not appreciate the lecture.

☞

'I think Callum really liked you,' Lucas once said to me. This was a couple of years before I left home. I was to understand that I should be proud of having secured Callum's approval. But why, I wondered, to myself, could Lucas only 'think' that Callum had liked me? Given that we were to believe that the spirit does not die, and that Lucas had been in contact, repeatedly, with the spirit of Callum, why was it not possible to ascertain Callum's opinion of me? Why not a straightforward: 'Callum liked you'? Lucas seemed to hear the unspoken objection. The spirit of Callum, now bodiless for several years, had journeyed too far to be audible, he explained.

☞

The voice of Lucas – this is something to be considered.

I was in the kitchen, preparing the meal with my mother, when Dean Martin's voice came out of the radio, and a few seconds later my mother joined in. This would have been during my second year at university. The song was 'Sway'. My mother started to hum-sing, *sotto voce*. At the instrumental break she smiled, and the smile was of a sort that required a question. Lucas, she informed me, could do a perfect impersonation of Dean Martin, singing this song.

The story was as follows. Did I remember when the Websters left the house across the street? I did. And did I remember that Lucas and Kathleen had invited them round for drinks, with a few other neighbours, so everyone could say goodbye? I remembered. No other children were there, so I was allowed to go home. I climbed over the wall, I remembered; from my room I watched the adults for a while. They talked in the garden; Mrs Webster cried on Kathleen's shoulder. Towards the end of the evening, I now learned, Lucas did his Dean Martin number, with props: a tumbler of whisky and a cigarette. It was, my mother assured me, 'very funny'. This I found hard to imagine.

Lucas, it was later revealed, could not sing. In the kitchen, on Erin's birthday, he stood beside me as my mother brought in the cake. We sang, and the sound he produced was an untuned baritonal rumble. The final line had only one note. His tunelessness seemed to embarrass him. Why would he have pretended to have no singing voice? For Erin's birthday he would have done his best. Are we to conclude that Lucas as himself could not sing, but as a mimic of Dean Martin he could? 'Perfect' was no doubt an exaggeration, but the performance could not have been like the groaning of 'Happy Birthday'. Pretending to be Dean Martin, he carried a tune. Perhaps the alcohol explained it, I think I thought.

When the instrumental break was over, my mother resumed her hum-singing. At the end, again, she smiled.

As I recall this scene, an image occurs to me: a shape in the depths of cloudy water, a shape so nebulous that it might be imaginary, but for a moment it seems to be rising towards the surface, then disappears. Did the possibility of my mother and Lucas rise in my mind in this way, then vanish, being scarcely credible?

'This is the living, breathing man – the man in full,' Lucas recited, from the back of the biography he was reading. It was a good book, he told me, but it was not 'the man in full'. Though the subject was not long dead, and the writer had interviewed many people who had known him, the book was no more than a portrait, and a portrait is not a person. A portrait, he instructed me, was an image of the portraitist as much as it was an image of the person portrayed, no matter how 'accurate' it might be.

It would be possible, if one were of an unsympathetic cast of mind, to present certain episodes from what some might call Lucas's career in a way that would create an image that was not at all to Lucas's advantage. Those episodes might be constructed from facts, but they would not be 'true'. The case of the girl he called Claire Vaness, for example.

He had found her too late; this was a fact. The mother had insisted on paying him, though he had failed; he had tried to refuse the payment, but he had relented; this too was a fact. Subsequently, something more than a professional relationship had arisen; some time had passed between the child's death and the commencement of his relationship with the mother, but it could not be denied that some might have found this relationship questionable; he himself had come to regret it; these were facts. They were facts, however, comparable to unattractive features in a depiction of a face, Lucas proposed. The lineaments are not the essence; they are only the surface. The truth of the Vaness case – what was essential, what nobody but those involved could know – was what had happened between Lucas and the mother in the days that followed the finding of the daughter. He had helped her to achieve what he would call 'a quietness' – not acceptance, but the beginnings of acceptance, as the trickle of a spring might be the beginning of a river. Her 'soul', he wanted me to understand, was like a field of battle on the morning after the cessation of fighting. 'A great deal of suffering was still to come,' he conceded, moved by his own eloquence.

☞

But what do I know of my parents' marriage? At night, sometimes, I could hear them talking in their room.

Rarely words – usually just the rumble of my father's voice, and the less frequent and barely audible murmur of my mother's, in the pauses. The voices would go on for many minutes. I might fall asleep in listening, or wake up and hear them, and be comforted. It was one of the sounds that were to be heard in the night, like cars at a distance, or the drone of the wind in the chimney, or the skirmishing of foxes, or the jostling of the leaves in the Olivers' garden. The voices, never loud, each succeeding the other in a tone of agreement, made a sound that meant marriage. All parents talked at night.

But after my grandmother died, the talking went on for longer. One night I came awake after midnight, and I heard them still. Another night, soon after, was the same. It was to do with my grandmother's death. Now my mother had no parents. When she put me to bed, we cried together. In the night I heard her crying while my father talked to her. I still heard her crying weeks later. One afternoon, we drove to the house in which her parents had lived. It was not the house in which my mother had lived when she was my age; there was no upstairs, only a loft. It was warm in the loft, with a thick sweet perfume of rot and dust; boxes were filled with old clothes and books. I was allowed to stay there on my own. I found a dressmaker's dummy, the colour of a lion's fur, with writing on its chest. When I came back down, my mother was sitting where I had left her, in the garden, looking at the house. My father was not there. My grandmother would always hug my mother, but never my father, I had noticed. We stood side by side at the gate, my hand in hers. 'Goodbye,' she said to the house, raising a hand as if to a person standing in the doorway, and she gave me the key to hold.

There was a lot of night-time talking around the time of the visit to my grandmother's house. I heard no arguing, but something happened then, something that I saw, that struck me as forcefully as any argument could have done. I came into the living room, where something had been broken; I had been in the kitchen, and had heard the crack. From the door, I saw my mother kneeling to the side of the fireplace; a gap had appeared on the mantelpiece, the place that should have been taken by the porcelain shepherdess with the lamb in her lap; the shepherdess had come from my grandmother's house. Swiping the carpet with her hand, my mother was gathering the fragments; she cupped the blue bonnet in a palm and looked at it. My father was standing at the table, with his back to me; his fingers were resting on some sheets of paper, and his briefcase was open alongside. It was as though he had noticed nothing; he could have been alone in the room. 'It's all right,' said my mother, or something like that; we could fix it with some glue, she promised. Perhaps knowing this was not true, I went back to the kitchen; going, I glanced back into the living room, and in that moment my father, unaware that I was still there, looked aside, at my mother. He aimed his sight at the back of her head, and his face changed, for less than a second. For a moment, his face was convulsed. He became somebody who was not my father. It was so sudden – as if he had cut himself badly, or been shocked by electricity. I could not understand what I had seen, and tried to believe that my eyes had made an error.

☞

Many men of my father's generation, and of preceding generations, became fathers primarily because fatherhood was a role that a man was expected to assume at a certain age, Lucas wanted me to understand. This was not so much the case nowadays. A man who elects to be childless will not necessarily be deemed irresponsible or immature. For women, however, the situation has not changed so much, still. Convention is a powerful influence. The female body is a childbearing apparatus, and a woman is held to have an obligation to obey that biological imperative. The childless woman has to justify herself, unless there is a medical excuse, or she has failed to attract an acceptable mate, or finds no man attractive. Then Lucas said again: 'My mother should not have had children.' It was said as if his mother were not his mother. He speculated that my father might have been like her in this respect. 'But I can't say that was the impression he gave,' said Lucas, and I remember wondering why, given that the mind of Lucas was so sensitive an instrument, he could not have known for certain if my father had been a man who had not wanted to be a father.

'But you look quite sensible,' remarked a woman whose name has not been recorded, on being introduced to the celebrated medium Gladys Osborne Leonard. Perhaps the most famous of Gladys Leonard's many clients was Radclyffe Hall, author of *The Well of Loneliness*, who first consulted her in 1916, in the hope of making contact with her recently deceased lover, Mabel Batten. Over a period of eight years Radclyffe Hall consulted Gladys Leonard on an almost weekly basis, and so detailed was the information thereby obtained that she felt compelled to hire a private detective to find out if the medium might be making use of some non-supernatural source. The detective discovered nothing untoward, apparently.

☞

The ones who run away generally don't want to be found, and thus do not direct their thought-beams homeward, as Lucas explained, if not in exactly those words. In the rooms of some of the missing, the silence was the silence of final abandonment. It was sometimes extremely difficult to tell the family that he was detecting nothing. Though it would have eased their distress for a while, he would never pretend that he had received information when none in fact had been received.

Some of those who run away, however, maintain an ethereal connection with those they have left, and these are the ones whose transmissions Lucas could conduct. Numerous states of mind could explain why these people could not simply pick up a phone or send a postcard, to set at rest the minds of those they had deserted. Anger is one. Lucas on more than one occasion intuited a great anger directed at one or more members of the family. Stepfathers and stepmothers sometimes, of course; most often, though, fathers of various degrees of moral corruption – who could not, as goes without saying, be told everything of which Lucas had become aware. Where the father turned out to be the cause, Lucas conveyed only the gist of the message: 'Your daughter is alive.' Fear is another explanation; frequently fear of the man they have fallen in with, who now claims exclusive rights. Confusion, depression, drugs – these too, separately or in combination, can create impediments to direct communication, as in the case of the young man from Telford, whose thoughts turned often to his sister, though he could no longer remember where she lived, and had lost his own name and history. 'And shame,' he added – as in the case of Katie Burtenshaw, whose recovery had given Lucas the deepest satisfaction of all.

Here a stepmother was involved: a woman somewhat younger than the deceased mother of the girl, and a believer in certain theories of parenting, theories in which the enforcement of boundaries and rules featured prominently. No sooner had the replacement mother been installed than the rules were applied to the two stepdaughters she had acquired. One proved compliant, one not. Katie, the latter, began to hang out with 'a bad crowd'. Before going to the house, Lucas walked around the town – a humdrum place, in south Wales. Had he lived there, and been Katie's age, he would have found a bad crowd to hang out with, he told me. 'No country for young people,' he pronounced. On the morning of Katie's flight, there had been an argument; she had come home at three o'clock in the morning, long after the agreed curfew, to find the stepmother waiting in the kitchen, like a policewoman. At eight she left for college, and at some point before lunchtime she came back home, crammed a bag that belonged to her father's wife, and took a bus out of town. Three years passed, and not a word. An investigator was hired; the trail went cold in the Liverpool area; Katie had not touched her bank account, nor visited a doctor, it seemed; there was reason to believe that she no longer called herself Katie.

Lucas followed the usual routine: first the conversation with the family, then the missing person's room. The bedroom had been left in the state in which Katie had left it, except for the bed. Pictures were stuck chaotically on every wall, some of them drawn by Katie – fantastical landscapes, mostly; some with castles and towers. She leered in photographs, spoiling for a fight, or grinned, madly happy, with an arm around a friend. A collective preference for black clothing was evident. On a shelf, a pale photo of young Katie with her father and mother was propped against a small stack of sci-fi novels, amid miscellaneous tickets, a scatter of polished pebbles, figurines of polar bears, an empty perfume bottle, a miniature torch. 'An oasis of unruly life,' was Lucas's phrase. The room spoke of the girl's 'yearning and unhappiness'. Lying on her bed, he heard her voice – or rather, he heard a voice that he knew would turn out to be Katie's. The words of the dead, he elucidated, do not often have a sound 'as such' – they arise in the recipient's mind like 'strong thoughts or memories'. In the case of Katie Burtenshaw, however, there was an audible voice. It spoke of her father; it called to him. For perhaps half a minute Lucas listened, then the voice faded away, and at the moment of its vanishing Lucas knew certainly where she was. His mind for a moment had become the girl's. He saw what she was seeing.

That night he stayed in Bristol. In the evening he walked the streets of the city centre, not expecting to find her at once, but doing what had to be done as preparation for the encounter. He was 'introducing' himself, as he put it. The next day, at noon, he took up his position at a café that he sensed she would be passing. Within the hour, a bedraggled young woman appeared, in black jeans and sweater, sauntering from one side of the street to the other as she approached, pleading with shoppers, with little success. She reached the table at which Lucas was sitting. For a few seconds he studied her: she was thinner than the girl in the photos; the hair was a different colour; she seemed ten years older, not three; but it was Katie. She recoiled from his scrutiny, and when Lucas held out a five-pound note she looked at it as if it constituted a proposition. He pushed the note across the table, and as she picked it up he said to her: 'Hello Katie.'

There were people to whom she had to say goodbye, but the following morning she was in the car with Lucas. He bought her some new clothes for the homecoming. When they drove into the street, her father was outside the house, waiting. Lucas parked at a respectful distance. 'When she was yet a great way off, her father saw her, and had compassion, and ran, and fell on her neck, and kissed her,' Lucas recited, becoming tearful. 'It was very gratifying,' he told me.

At the start of the month a cheque would arrive from my father. My mother did not know his address, she told me, and she was not inclined to make enquiries. There would have been an address on the divorce papers, but I did not know that the divorce had happened until some time after the fact, and I never saw the papers. Around that time, the postmark changed: the cheques were now coming from Newcastle. On my birthday, I would receive a card, signed 'Dad', with a banknote inside, and a couple of words. The last one came when I reached sixteen; two banknotes were enclosed.

For a long time it troubled me. Whatever the state of his relationship with the child's mother, how could any man reject his son in this way? Could his guilt explain it? Had my parents, hating each other, agreed that it would be best if my father were to remove himself from my life? I could find no evidence of hatred, other – perhaps – than the glance that I had seen, when the figurine of the shepherdess was smashed. Might that have been the one moment in which the truth had become visible? There had been evidence sometimes of a coolness between them; and the woman in the green coat appeared to be part of the story. And yet, there seemed to have been some proof of affection, even in what were to be the final months, the months that I could remember most securely. My father putting an arm around my mother's shoulder, as she stood by the sink; I remembered that, and a smile from my mother, for my father, as he came into the house. Or did the touch and the smile signify nothing? Was it their intention that I should observe them, and be misled? Would I have been able, at that age, to distinguish a performance of affection from affection itself? For that matter, was what I thought I remembered the same as what I had actually seen?

Some time in my fifteenth year, I spoke to Lucas about my father. Was it true, I asked, that he could find missing people?

There had been cases in which he had been able to help, he answered.

In that case, could he tell me where my father was living?

And Lucas replied: 'Not if he doesn't want us to know where he is.' He explained: no matter how much a person might want to make contact with someone who had gone away, the crucial factor was not the strength of the first person's feelings – it was the strength of the second person's.

Think of it as being stuck in the bottom of a pit, Lucas suggested. 'You want to get out, but the pit is too deep and steep. You can't throw a rope out, but someone can drop a rope in. The rope can only come from outside,' he said. Seeing that I was puzzled, he offered an alternative image: what mattered was the incoming signal. With the naked eye we can see a star in the Cassiopeia constellation that is around three thousand light years from Earth – that's three thousand multiplied by six trillion miles. The world's most powerful beam of light is visible, on a clear night, at a range of 275 miles. 'This is what you have to understand,' said Lucas. 'The outgoing signal is just a searchlight, the incoming signal is the light of a star.'

But if that were so, I said, didn't it follow that my father should be in some way visible?

'Ah,' Lucas replied, 'but there are billions and billions of stars, aren't there?' Being visible was not the same as being conspicuous.

I think I considered this proposition for a while, before venturing an objection: how, then, was it possible to find anyone at all?

It had to do with intention, Lucas explained. The idea of the star and the searchlight was not an absolutely exact analogy. It served to clarify an aspect of the situation, but not the situation in its entirety. Now I had to think of the star as a kind of searchlight, albeit a searchlight of inconceivable power. The missing person, to make contact, aims his or her thoughts in our direction, like a beam of light.

So if my father were thinking of me, I would be spotlit – was that it?

Not quite. The light would be sent towards me, but one should bear in mind that – like the star in Cassiopeia – the light might be so faint as to be visible only in perfect conditions, with perfect eyesight. I was to understand that Lucas was the creator of perfect conditions, and that his vision was of a special order. And that a metaphor is only a metaphor.

Because I was not yet an adult, Lucas would of course have to ask my mother's permission before making any attempt to trace my father, he said to me. That evening, I told her that I had been talking to Lucas. She vetoed the proposal. 'We have to move on,' she said. 'If your father wanted to be with us, he would be here.'

☞

Another time, as if relating a parable, Lucas told me about the woman who had been his neighbour before he moved into Kathleen's house – a single mother, with a daughter who was thirteen years old when Lucas first met them, sixteen when he left. The girl's father had left when she was not quite one year old. He was not a good father, the woman confided to Lucas; people – women especially – have always tended to confide in him, I was to understand. The bad father had liked a drink, and it took only a few months of sleepless nights with the baby to make his drinking dangerous; dope was involved too – a lot of it. He resented more than he loved his child; at times had hated himself for this resentment, a hatred for which the treatment was yet more drink and dope. The man was a mess. Volcanic arguments became a regular event. Two or three nights a week he would come home in the small hours, sometimes with friends, all of them unruly. In the whole of that year, the mother had only one night off. She went round to a friend's house, leaving the father in charge. She hadn't told him that there was going to be a party at the house, but somebody who had never liked her was at the party and this person made sure that he found out about it. The bad father was led to believe that the mother had been getting too friendly with someone else that night. This was not true, the woman assured Lucas, but she had not told her child's father the whole truth about what was happening at the friend's house, so that had made her a liar as well as a whore. There was a fight, involving fists, then the father packed his bags and walked out, the same day. That was the last she had seen of him.

Left alone with the child, she found that life soon improved. If you'd seen them together, said Lucas, you would never have guessed that the start of the girl's life had been such an ordeal. Mother and child had moved to a different town, and were happy in their man-free household, in the same street as Lucas. Not perfectly happy, however, because the daughter, in her sixteenth year, had become 'obsessed' with the missing father. What had begun as curiosity became a need. She talked of having a 'phantom pain', the mother told Lucas. So often did the girl dream of her father – whose face she knew only from a single photo – that she had become convinced that he was trying to reach her. 'But I really don't want to see him,' her mother said. 'He might be dead, for all I know. And I wouldn't care.' She wanted to know what Lucas would do in her situation.

The man was not dead, Lucas knew. Sitting beside the woman, on a bench in the small park near where they lived, he could sense that the girl's father was alive. 'Wait a while longer,' was what he advised. If the girl felt the same way when she passed sixteen, the mother could then take steps to find the man; she would not have to meet him, if he were to be found, as Lucas was sure he would be. The woman did what Lucas had counselled.

A few months later, walking through the park, Lucas saw, ahead of him on the path, the woman and her daughter, with a man of the woman's age. Only the woman was talking; the man, at her side, nodded as he listened; the posture was penitential. This, Lucas understood at once, was the errant father; he had been forgiven, albeit not absolutely. For some time he had been living with another woman, but the love of his daughter and of her mother – a love that he had done his utmost to deny – had been doing its work in secret, as Lucas put it. Of course, Lucas had an image for it: the man's new life had been a shoddy house, raised on land through which water had been flowing constantly, deep underground, undermining the foundations. And suddenly the house had collapsed, and the man had found himself standing in the light.

Such things happen sometimes, Lucas concluded. It could happen for me. But if my father did not come back, that wouldn't necessarily be a worse outcome; sometimes one parent is better than two. My father had not been at all like the man in the story, as went without saying, he added.

☞

A woman in Guildford confessed her sins to Lucas, at length. This was before he had set to work on making contact with her sinned-against husband. No sooner had Lucas taken his place at the table than the adulteress began to disburden herself; she seemed to think that the self-purging was a necessary preparation for exposure to supernatural scrutiny. She had been repeatedly unfaithful. Her work had taken her to trade fairs in distant cities, regularly, and she had availed herself of the opportunities for illicit pleasure that these gatherings always present to the participants. None of these liaisons had been of any significance beyond the immediately sexual, she insisted. After the birth of their second child, her husband had come to find her body unappetising. Eventually they had consulted a counsellor, but their physical intimacy remained desultory, then became non-existent. Her body's appetites, however, had not dwindled; if anything, the opposite was the case. This was an inadequate excuse, she knew. She had despised herself after each encounter, and now she despised herself even more, even though her husband had never suspected anything, she was absolutely sure. From looking at her, said Lucas, nobody would have thought her sluttish. It was hard to describe her effectively, so bland and proper was the appearance. She had summoned him because, having never believed in ghosts 'or anything of that sort', she had recently come to feel that the house was inhabited by a presence that could only be the presence of her husband. It wasn't that she had seen him or heard him – no, what she was talking about was a presence like that of a person who has just that moment left the room. 'An invisible shadow' was how she put it.

It was ridiculous, she knew, but she had come to feel that her husband might now know of things that had been unknown to him when he was alive. She needed to submit to his judgement, to confess to him as she should have confessed years ago.

Lucas asked her: 'Are you certain that he never suspected?'

She was as certain as it was possible to be. Had he suspected, he would have confronted her, she said. He had not been a secretive man, she told Lucas, unaware that the statement made no sense. Her husband would not have believed that she could have been capable of such behaviour, she said. At times she herself found it hard to believe. But in certain situations she had become a different woman – someone she barely recognised and did not like.

Lucas understood her remorse, but confession, he advised her, was not necessarily a good thing. He deployed a metaphor: life as a vast lake, across which we are constantly moving, in the small vessel of the self. Think of our secrets as stones; the guilty secrets are heavy stones. They slow the vessel down; they increase the risk of foundering. In confessing, we drop these heavy stones overboard. The impulse to do this is especially strong as we approach the far shore, at the end of the voyage; the boat, made lighter, is more easily brought to land. Sometimes it is best to jettison the stones, but sometimes it is not, Lucas advised his client. In offloading the unwanted cargo, we might unsettle the boat, or even capsize it; when the stones strike the silt of the lake-bed, the water becomes muddied. It was an elaborate metaphor. Lucas, evidently, was pleased with it. And it seemed to have worked for the Guildford sinner; she was comforted; her guilt was made less burdensome.

Neither should she be fearful of the judgement of her husband, Lucas reassured her. Forgiveness was more likely than condemnation, because the perspective of the dead is so much wider and wiser than that of the living. Their vision partakes of the eternal, whereas ours is merely local. The dead rarely reproach, he told her. And indeed he detected no anger in the spirit of the husband. There was some sorrow; Lucas could not pretend otherwise. But sorrow was a thing of the flesh, and would soon fall away. He understood the temptation that had overcome his wife. The lapses were not even affairs; they were not of the essence.

The woman cried when Lucas and the husband were finished. People often cry when the contact comes to an end, but this woman's weeping was operatic, said Lucas. She couldn't tell Lucas how grateful she was. She insisted on making a meal for him – she was an excellent cook, she promised. Having been granted absolution, she seemed to give no further thought to the husband. A 'terrible woman' said Lucas, but he pronounced that adjective as if trying to put into words an unusual taste, a taste that might have been both pleasant and not. There might have been a slight smile. This was before Erin.

☞

'One can easily imagine a religion in which there are no doctrines, so that nothing is spoken,' said Lucas one afternoon. 'As Wittgenstein said,' he added, though he knew, I'm sure, less of Wittgenstein than I do, which is not much. 'The essence of religion can have nothing to do with what can be said,' he pronounced.

☞

When in her trance or dream state, Geraldine Cummins would transcribe the dictation of the dead at an extraordinary speed – on one occasion she wrote two thousand words in just seventy-five minutes. It was taken to be proof of the authenticity of her mediumship that Geraldine ordinarily wrote very slowly – it could take her as long as seven or eight hours to compose a mere thousand words.

☞

In the depths of her trances, Catherine-Elise Müller – more widely known as Hélène Smith, the Surrealists' 'muse of automatic writing' – received visions of life on Mars, and messages in the language of that planet, which she transcribed into her Martian script. This script was in fact a coded form of French, her native language. Each letter of the Martian alphabet corresponded to a French equivalent; the Martian syntax was the syntax of French. Hélène/Catherine-Elise maintained that she was the reincarnation of Marie Antoinette; her current low-level life was a punishment for misdemeanours committed when she had been the wife of Louis XVI. In yet another existence she had been an Indian princess named Simandini. Why, Lucas wondered, did nobody ever claim to recall a previous life as a disease-ridden peasant in some benighted one-donkey village in the middle of nowhere, circa 1300?

☞

The state of high sensitivity that was necessary to receive a signal often lasted for many hours after the conclusion of the session, Lucas informed me. It was an uncomfortable condition: the nerves had been exposed by a kind of wound, and it took time for the skin to thicken again. He had come back from Hereford, where a consultation had turned out to be especially arduous. Contact had been achieved, but this was one of those instances in which Lucas would, in retrospect, have preferred to fail. The client was another widow. It seemed that fear was primarily what had compelled her to ask for Lucas's help. This woman, he knew within moments, had lived a life of complete subservience to her husband, a subservience in which violence had been involved. Every day, since the day of her husband's death, she had been aware that he had not left, she told Lucas. She had not seen anything. Rather, she was the one who was being seen, as if there was always a camera hidden somewhere, she explained. Now that her husband had been raised to the heights of the spiritual world, she was being subjected to his constant scrutiny; she needed to know, via Lucas, that her continuing obedience was being recognised and approved.

Two sisters and two daughters were also in attendance; the fearfulness encompassed them as well. As soon as he started, Lucas was in the presence of a spirit of unusual malignity. What he detected was a fulmination of ill-will aimed at one of the wife's sisters, and – even stronger – a despotic rapaciousness directed towards one of the daughters. 'It was foul,' said Lucas. For the wife, there was almost nothing – just a virtual wave of the hand, as she disappeared from his sight. It was difficult to find anything to say that would do the client any good. 'He is glad that you are thinking of him,' he reported. 'There is nothing to worry about,' he said to the widow – which she could choose to take as a message from the husband. What he wanted to say to them all was: 'You're finally off the hook.'

To recover, he went for a walk. By the river he found a bench to sit on. It already had an occupant – an elderly woman who said 'Hello' as he sat down, and then resumed her watching of the water. Smiling slightly, she watched the river as if seeing a procession in the distance, and Lucas, still 'raw', then felt himself to be struck by a 'deluge of love', in the centre of which sat the woman, who was thinking, he knew, of her son. Simple proximity to a grieving person sometimes was enough to make him conscious of a signal, albeit rarely one of such strength. It was an effort to remain silent, but he did not speak. One should never impose. Once, when he was young, he had been in a similar situation. In a park in London, he had found himself standing close to a woman who was weeping. So powerful had been the words that he had heard, and so powerful the impulse of compassion, that he had said something to her. The woman looked at him as if she had been poisoned, and screamed at him, and ran. At the time, he had only recently come to make use of his gift, but his trust in it was not yet robust. And so, suddenly presented with a message, he had immediately passed it on, without thought, in order to console, yes, but also to put his gift to the proof. 'Inexcusable selfishness on my part,' said Lucas.

☞

Some half a million people expire in this country every year. And Lucas maintained that the dead typically remain within range for twelve months or so; the figure varied. Yet whenever Lucas tuned in, he did not hear a pandemonium of the dead. He heard – when he succeeded – only the voice, or the words, that he had been commissioned to hear. He never mentioned any problem of interference. One voice came through clearly. How did this work? It would appear that the spirit with whom contact was sought emanated a signal that was directed at the person or persons who had issued the summons to Lucas. We might think of the signal as being carried by a cable of some sort. The cable can be connected only to certain categories of people: spouses; lovers; close friends; relatives; occasionally, colleagues. We must surmise, however, that the voltage of the spiritual cable is so low that the communication arrives at its destination with insufficient power to be understood by the recipient. This is where Lucas and other such adepts give assistance. Positioning himself near the terminal, Lucas absorbed the signal and boosted it. He was a step-up transformer of the psychic network.

☞

In 1918, Arthur Findlay, a stockbroker and justice of the peace, and recipient of the OBE in recognition of his work for the Red Cross during the war, attended a séance given by John Campbell Sloan in Glasgow. After participating in many more of Sloan's seances, Findlay became convinced of the reality of spirit voices. In his book, *On the Edge of the Etheric, or Survival After Death Scientifically Explained*, which was published in 1931 and reprinted thirty times in the year that followed, and is still in print, Findlay proposed that recent advances in subatomic physics gave support to the claims of spiritualism. The universe is an immense complex of vibrations. Individual consciousness consists of the interaction of the vibrations of the mind and the vibrations of the body. At death, the vibrations of the mind enter a different environment, in which 'etheric vibrations' provide the matrix. The reviewer for *Nature* magazine was not persuaded by Findlay's proposition, writing that Findlay 'seems to have no appreciation of the implications underlying many of his remarks; no desire to see the phenomena described in accurate and scientific terminology.' In addition to his books on spiritualism, Arthur Findlay also wrote a two-volume *History of Mankind*, and a survey of human development, *The Curse of Ignorance*, also in two volumes. As for John Campbell Sloan, he claimed that the voice in which he spoke during his trances was that of an American Indian named White Feather, who for some reason preferred to be addressed as 'Whitey'. In discussing the uncanny accuracy of some of the things that Whitey relayed to him, Findlay assured his readers that an 'eminent mathematician' had calculated the probability of Whitey's answers being the result of mere guesswork, and had arrived at odds of '5,000,000,000,000 to 1 against'.

☞

'But to talk of these things is like trying to play Bach while wearing oven gloves,' proclaimed Lucas. His repertoire of similes and metaphors was extensive. They were presented to me like jewels on cushions. 'Words pass through these mysteries like bullets through fog,' he told me. 'When I try to explain these things, I misrepresent them, necessarily. They require a language that none of us could speak.' Or: 'This is like trying to draw a diagram of the universe.' Or: 'I am not transposing these ideas into words – the ideas are the creation of words. The truth lies above the words, outside them.' Cradling the infant Kit, he talked about the inadequacy of talk, and gazed into the eyes of the blissful speech-free baby. 'We are slaves to words and the reason that proceeds from them,' he said.

☞

Much has been made of the Attwater case.

Having reason to believe that her husband, deceased eighteen months previously, was making attempts to contact her, Mrs Attwater, seventy-four, decided to avail herself of the services of Lucas Judd, whose name she had discovered in the course of an hour's research at her local library. Various disturbances at home could be explained only, she had come to think, as incomplete transmissions from the Beyond. In the morning, certain objects were found in places other than where they had been left the night before; nothing major (a cup, a book, et cetera), but objects do not move themselves, do they? At night, and sometimes during the day, whispering could be heard, as if from the other side of a thin wall. The whispering became more frequent; the movement of the small domestic items was now occurring every two or three days. She was unable to make sense of what was happening; a professional was needed.

With Mrs Attwater's husband, the signal was as powerful as any he had experienced, Lucas told me. Such was to be expected, when the marriage in question had been so long and so strong. Muriel's cottage was a dilapidated old place, but of a decent size and with a fine view of St Michael's Mount; she and Jack had lived there for more than half a century. They had few friends, she cheerfully told Lucas; the company of each other was all they needed. 'We were always happy,' she told him, serving tea in a burrow-like room that was as warm as a bakery; she would be even happier if Lucas were to confirm that Jack lived on in spirit, and was not suffering. This was what caused her such anxiety – that the disturbances might be a sign of some kind of torment. Her anxiety was erased within hours: the spirit of Jack was in torment only in so far as he was impatient for their separation to end, as it would, before long.

Once every two or three months, for more than two years, Lucas would drive to the cottage, and there, for an hour or more, through him, Muriel would commune with Jack. Such was the strength of their love, he had remained within range somewhat longer than was usual. Those afternoons, Lucas told me, were among the most rewarding experiences of his life.

Material reward ensued, but with consequent trouble. The happiness of Jack and Muriel was exclusive; neither had felt inclined to introduce any children, having observed too many fractious or imperfect families. So, there were no children, and no close friends, and a family of limited extension: one unmarried brother for Jack, resident in Germany with a male companion, and rarely seen; and a nephew – Melvin Dodd, property developer, father of Matthew and Rachel – for Muriel.

Melvin, on being informed, after the death of his aunt, that almost the entirety of her estate was to pass to this Lucas Judd character, and none of it to himself and his family, as he claimed he had been led to believe it would, decided to take action. His aunt, he maintained, being of fragile health and fluctuating mental capacity, had been coerced by this conman into disinheriting her natural beneficiary. The chief instruments of this coercion, he alleged, were the 'séances' that Mr Judd had conducted in the home of Mrs Attwater. In the final week of her life, Melvin Dodd submitted, his aunt had revealed to him that many of the 'messages' from Jack Attwater that Lucas Judd had supposedly intercepted were extremely critical of her nephew. It was Melvin Dodd's contention that these supposedly posthumous utterances had been invented by Mr Judd in order to enrich himself by forcing his aunt – who would never, as Mr Judd had quickly ascertained, have done anything contrary to the will of her husband – to remove her family from her will and replace them with Judd himself. On her deathbed she had promised her nephew that she would do the right thing and pass everything on to her family. The concept of *donatio mortis causa* was invoked.

Staff at the nursing home in which Muriel Attwater had passed the last weeks of her life confirmed that her nephew had been with her in her final hours. It was noted, however, that Mr Dodd had rarely been at his aunt's bedside until the very end. Mr Judd, on the other hand, had been so regular a visitor, and been regarded by Mrs Attwater with so much affection, that he was assumed to be a favourite relative.

Matthew Dodd, the nephew's son, had put in a single appearance; with his business commitments, he had barely had a spare hour. His sibling, Rachel, had accompanied him; she too had been unable to visit her great-aunt more than once; this was because, as Lucas told me, she had a 'phobia' of hospitals and any other places in which one stood a risk of being obliged to observe the sufferings of the infirm and the ailing.

According to Melvin Dodd, his aunt had been 'particularly fond' of Rachel. On her deathbed, apparently, she had made repeated reference to her affection for the young woman. And of all the family, Rachel had been the one who had been most attentive to the elderly Muriel. This was not disputed. The motive for this attention, however, was not a charitable one, Lucas reported. Rachel was the family's 'scout', Muriel told him, or 'the advance guard'. Her solicitude was entirely tactical, Muriel believed. Always there would be a little gift for the old lady: a scarf, perhaps, or something exotic and edible. They came from airport duty-free shops, Muriel was sure; Rachel and her boyfriend – a dealer in vintage sport cars – seemed to take a remarkable number of holidays. 'I can see right through that one,' said Muriel. 'I can see through the lot of them. Dirty windows, the whole bunch.'

Rachel's father did not deny that there had been some friction between himself and his aunt, and that this friction had not been a passing episode. It was, however, a thing of the past, as its cause had been the hostility of Muriel's husband, a man who, as he approached retirement, with a paltry pension in prospect, had seemed, increasingly, to take the nephew's prosperity – anyone's prosperity, for that matter – as some kind of personal affront. But with Jack's passing, a rapprochement with Muriel had been effected, Melvin maintained. Bygones could not entirely be bygones, of course; there were still some 'issues', on both sides. But aunt and nephew had both made considerable efforts to repair the relationship, and these efforts had been largely successful. Which was why the bequest to Mr Judd had been such a shock. There was only one possible explanation: her hand had been forced; her mind had been befuddled by the messages that Mr Judd had plucked out of the air.

The rapprochement was a fiction, Muriel insisted. True, Melvin had driven down to see her half a dozen times since Jack's death, which was approximately half a dozen times more than in any preceding year. But whatever Jack had thought of the ethics of property speculation, Muriel agreed with him. The 'friction' may have been less noisy, with Jack gone, but it had not ceased. Melvin liked to think of himself as a sharp operator, but he was 'just a very little shark' in the ocean of filthy money, she joked with Lucas. As soon as Melvin stepped out of his ridiculous car, she could see him measuring up the house; coming through the door, he was imagining what he could do to the place. And Melvin's wife was even worse: formerly a model, she had no discernible interests other than consumer durables, and her contentment seemed to be entirely dependent on Melvin's ability to underwrite the perpetual refreshment of her wardrobe. Engagements of a vague nature tended to prevent her from visiting the old woman with her husband; the squalor of the cottage was too much for her, said Muriel, who had reasons to suspect, as well, that her nephew's business was no longer thriving as it once had. She sensed that the wife was ruffling her feathers; her first husband, Muriel had learned, had been promptly ditched as soon as his revenue stream had begun to dwindle.

As evidence of the worrying deterioration of great-aunt Muriel's intellectual faculties, Rachel Dodd spoke of an increasing forgetfulness: for example, Rachel had turned up at the house at lunchtime one day, as arranged, only to find that Muriel was not at home; she had forgotten all about it. But in fact she had not forgotten, Muriel told Lucas; she had pretended that it had slipped her mind. The truth was, she had been unable to face the unlovable Rachel, and the pretence had amused her, just as it had amused her to feign an inability to remember certain simple words. Rachel was a dull child, and 'not as good an actor as me,' said Muriel. Similarly, with her nephew she had affected some moments of absent-mindedness; she had repeatedly been unable to recall his wife's name; it was a way of making the time pass more agreeably.

No neighbours could be found to support the assertion that Mrs Attwater's mind had been in decline. Lucas produced a letter, dated three weeks before her death. The handwriting was tremulous, but the writing was cogent. 'I will soon be with Jack,' Muriel wrote. There were remarks about the Dodds – 'the vultures', she called them. Most importantly, she informed Lucas that she had instructed her solicitor to amend her will. Whereas it had been her intention to leave the entirety of her estate to a variety of charities, she would now be leaving much of it – the house included – to Lucas, 'my one true friend'. The charities would still receive a decent percentage. There was no suggestion in the letter that it had ever been her intention to bequeath anything to her wretched nephew, and it seemed clear that Lucas had hitherto known nothing of the terms of Mrs Attwater's will. The solicitor confirmed that the subject of Mr Dodd and his family had never arisen in any conversation between himself and Mrs Attwater; indeed, for many years he had been unaware that a nephew existed. At no point in his dealings with Mrs Attwater, the solicitor testified, had he observed anything that might have caused him to question her intellectual competence. Neither had he had any reason to think that she had in any way been coerced into altering the document; Mrs Attwater was not a woman on whom coercion would work, he ventured.

The judge was of the same mind. Although Mrs Attwater's faith in Mr Judd's paranormal talents might be taken by some people as being indicative of a certain degree of credulity, he had heard nothing that might incline him to think that Mrs Attwater's testamentary capacity had been in any way impaired. As for the accusation of coercion, there was no reason to believe that it had any basis in fact. It may well have been the case that the communications that Mr Judd purported to be relaying from the deceased Mr Attwater had played some part in persuading Mr Attwater's widow to modify the terms of her will, but persuasion should not be mistaken for coercion. All the evidence supported the conclusion that Mr Judd had shown 'immense kindness' towards Mrs Attwater. The relationship between Mrs Attwater and Mr Judd had, furthermore, been entirely a professional one, contrary to an insinuation made by Rachel Dodd. There was no merit to the argument that the doctrine of *donatio mortis causa* should be applied in this instance. Had the claim of Mr Dodd been upheld, the greater part of Mrs Attwater's estate would have passed to someone who had never been named as a beneficiary in her will. Accordingly, the claim was dismissed.

Rachel had been an interesting case, Lucas told me. She would have become a much better person had she removed herself from the intimidation of her appalling parents. Muriel had not been entirely fair to her, he felt; perhaps there had been some envy of the attractive young woman. Though Rachel had dressed too 'operatically' for his taste, turning up for her day in court in an outfit that would have been more appropriate for a bout of shopping in Knightbridge, she was an 'extremely presentable girl', Lucas told me. But Rachel's parents were dreadful people; 'heartless bastards', the pair of them, the father particularly; he had 'the personality of a hammer', and Matthew Dodd was just as bad – he was nothing but the clone of his father. A letter had arrived that very morning from Matthew Dodd. He showed it to me, directing my attention to the word 'chancer', underlined twice. Lucas pushed the letter deep into a bin, as if cramming a fist into the gullet of an aggressive animal.

We came to the beach. Wielding a bat of driftwood, he tossed up pebbles to himself, and smashed them into the water. 'Bastards!' he cried, and smacked a stone. A dozen stones were dispatched, in a dozen strokes. The indignation had become comedic by the ninth or tenth stone. Another newly revealed aspect of Lucas: the remarkable hand-eye co-ordination. Every stroke was sure and strong. I asked him if he had played cricket when he was younger.

'But of course,' he answered. 'What a loss to the game,' he lamented, and another stone went arcing into the deep water. 'Give it a go,' he said, passing the battered length of wood. 'It's tremendously therapeutic.'

He lobbed a pebble; I swung at it, and missed. I missed twice. The third one flew half the distance of his worst shot.

'Good man,' he said, applauding, as my stone hit the water.

☞

When giving my speech at the funeral, I noticed, seated near the back, a woman who did not quite seem to belong to this congregation: for one thing, she appeared to be in her twenties, and thus of an age well below the median; for another, her demeanour did not suggest that her interest in Lucas had been that of a client. She looked more like an observer than a believer. As if aware of my curiosity, she approached me, back at the house. She had liked the speech, she told me, then she remarked that it was a pity that the ceremony had not taken the form of a Quaker gathering. Her sister had married a Quaker, and their wedding had been, for her, a rather wonderful event, because at one point in the proceedings there had been an opportunity for any guest who felt so inclined to stand up and say something about the couple who were about to become married. Had this been possible during Lucas's funeral, she would have spoken, she told me, because she knew something about Lucas that she would have liked everyone present to know. Her story concerned something that had happened three years ago. She had been involved at that time with someone she should not have been involved with. On this particular night, they were on their way back to her flat when they started arguing. The boyfriend was drunk, and had decided that she had been giving the eye to another man in the pub, a man who in fact didn't interest her in the slightest. The argument quickly turned nasty, and he slapped her. At that moment, a car swerved across the road and stopped ten yards away, with its headlights aimed squarely at them. She was dazzled, and then, out of the glare, came this gentleman, not young, with a stick in one hand. The boyfriend warned him to back off, but the white knight was not to be deterred. 'Are you all right?' he asked her, and on being told that she was not, he offered her a lift home. The way he brandished the stick, when the boyfriend took a step closer, suggested that he might know how to use it. Another car now pulled up, and the boyfriend retreated. Not only did Lucas give the young woman a lift, he stayed with her for a while, just in case the boyfriend decided to call round. The next day, and a few times after that, he rang her to check that she was safe. So that is something I learned about Lucas, and it should be recorded. And would I have done what Lucas did? I think not.

☞

My mother was impressed that Lucas could admit that he was sometimes unsuccessful. As many as one consultation in four produced no satisfactory result, he once told her, it seems. In Middlesborough, for example, he had failed to achieve contact with the father of nine children, six of whom had convened for the attempt, with their mother. The chances would have been good, one would have thought, with so many targets for the mind-beam of the deceased to hit. But the size of the gathering might have been a hindrance. Some diffusion or dilution of the signal might have occurred, somehow. Another factor to be taken into account: two of the siblings, it quickly became apparent, were not in accord with the others. Two of those who were present, that is. Of the absentees, two were overtly hostile to the endeavour, and the other was not prepared to travel up from Kent. Lucas suggested that the resistance of the non-attenders could have reduced the chances of success. Certainly the presence of the sceptics made things difficult for him. Emanating suspicion throughout the evening, they polluted the environment with a kind of white noise, Lucas explained. It was almost impossible to achieve receptivity in such circumstances. One would not ask a musician – a master of a delicate instrument; a flautist, say – to perform in a tin-roofed shed in a downpour; this situation was comparable, he said. All that came through – but it came through strongly – was a sense of something unresolved, a disagreement of some seriousness, involving the father and one of the daughters and 'perhaps' one of the absentees. Lucas said nothing to the group about the discord that had come to his attention. In the absence of any countervailing good news, he had thought it better to report that nothing had come to him. Further proof of his kindness and honesty. 'It would have been so simple for him to lie,' my mother said to me, overlooking the fact that, by Lucas's own account, he had in fact lied to his clients. But what she meant is that Lucas could have easily and convincingly feigned the transmission of an uplifting message from husband to widow. A benign untruth would have made the woman happy, and secured a good payment. The woman, despite the disappointment of the outcome, had wanted to pay Lucas for his trouble, as did some of the offspring. He had, after all, driven a long way and paid for a hotel room. Lucas would take nothing, not even a contribution towards the cost of the petrol. He had been unable to help; therefore, there should be no reward.

Lucas's self-denying attitude towards remuneration seems to have enhanced his prestige with those who called on him. He never charged anyone for his services. If people wished to make a voluntary donation, he might accept, according to circumstances. Sometimes, if he thought the offered sum too generous, he would take only part of it, I was told. It was ungenerous of me, my mother said, to point out that Lucas himself was the source of this testimonial to his virtue. His pricing strategy was a canny one, I suggested; after all, none of his customers would want to be thought miserly. The word 'customer' was inappropriate, said my mother.

The humility was beneficial to Lucas's image. He seemed to have taken some vow of poverty. This was indicative of integrity, an integrity akin to that of the priest, and of the scientist, as opposed to the presumptuousness of some who lay claim to spiritual distinction. Each session was an exploration, a test, an experiment. As with any true experiment, the outcome could never be certain. Making a connection with those who have left us was not like attaching a hose to a tap, as some would have us think.

The faith of Mrs Pedley, for example, seemed in no way weakened when Lucas failed to hear anything from Mr Pedley. Though he had been provided with a variety of items that had been of acute significance to the departed husband (pen, watch, mother's locket, photo of Mrs Pedley in her wedding dress), these conductors did not attract a single strike. Lucas became conscious of an aura of love and happiness, akin to a change in the air pressure before a storm, but no words. The aura appears to have been enough for Mrs Pedley. For a full four hours Lucas had made himself available, and she was grateful for the effort. She seemed to imagine the afterlife as some sort of celestial grassland of perpetual mild sunlight, on which the dead all milled around, in a stupor of contentment. What were the odds of finding one face amid that unimaginable multitude? Mr Pedley had died three years earlier, so was almost certainly too far back from the foreground by now. Three hundred million people had followed him into the hereafter in the intervening period. That is one hell of a crowd.

'Sometimes,' Lucas said to me, 'I look at the words that have come to me, and I cannot work out what they might mean. Sometimes nobody in the room can make sense of it. It happens,' he said, opening his hands in acceptance of the mystery. There were several ready explanations:

playfulness on the part of the deceased; obstructiveness; or Lucas might have misconstrued. 'And sometimes,' he said, 'the message really isn't worth reading.' The deeply obtuse do not suddenly become perceptive people after being translated to the beyond. 'With some people, you could send them on a tour of China, and when they got back you could ask them what they had made of it all, and they'd say: "Big place. Didn't much like the food." And that would be it, pretty well. Nothing to say. Same with some of the dead,' he said, laughing. 'Being dead is lost on them.'

☞

Arthur Conan Doyle, writing in 1924 to his friend Oliver Lodge, enclosed with his letter a photograph taken at the previous year's Armistice Day ceremony at the Cenotaph. Lodge, like Doyle, had lost a son in the Great War. A fog of some sort was visible in the picture. Within this fog Doyle could discern the faces of some of the fallen. 'My son is certainly there and, I think, my nephew,' he wrote. Lodge, a key figure in the development of wireless telegraphy, was a Christian Spiritualist, and for two years served as the president of the Society for Psychical Research. After the war he attended several séances in the hope of receiving messages from Raymond, his son. Messages were duly received. In 1916 he published *Raymond, or Life and Death*, which became a bestseller.

☞

At the séances conducted by Marquis Carlo Centurione Scotto, in his ancestral castle, the spirit voices addressed the gathering in several different languages: Latin, Spanish and German, plus five dialects that were said to have been unknown to the Marquis – Piedmontese, Romagnolo, Neapolitan, Venetian and Sicilian. It is widely agreed, however, that the medium's most impressive achievement occurred on the night of July 18, 1929, when he vanished supernaturally from the chamber in which the séance was being conducted. The following year, the journal of the Society for Psychical Research published Theodore Besterman's review of *Modern Psychic Mysteries*, an English translation of reports on the paranormal activities of Marquis Carlo Centurione Scotto, written by an investigator named Ernesto Bozzano. Besterman had some doubts about the phenomena that Bozzano had supposedly observed. In protest at Besterman's unwarranted scepticism, Sir Arthur Conan Doyle resigned from the Society for Psychical Research.

☞

In order to achieve the most accurate 'tuning' possible, it was sometimes necessary for Lucas to spend some time in the home of the deceased before attempting to achieve contact. In the case of the Binfield client, it was evident immediately that tuning would be difficult. Anger, as we all know, is commonly an aspect of grief, but this woman's anger was not of the common variety. The husband had died, of heart failure, at the side of the local swimming pool, aged sixty-two, five months before Lucas received the call; in each of those five months, the widow had made distressing discoveries of a financial nature. Her husband's bank account, she found, contained less than she had expected to find – considerably less. The almost-new car, bought a year ago, for cash, much of which had come from a bonus paid by his employers, had not in fact been bought for cash; there had been no bonus. The credit card statement was a shock. He had spent an absurd amount of money on a pair of shoes. There was a payment to someone who turned out to be a dealer in sports memorabilia; the husband had paid hundreds of pounds for a box of Arsenal match-day programmes, which she had found under a blanket in the loft. In another box she found autographed shirts and photographs. Substantial amounts of cash had been withdrawn from his account, inexplicably. And he had been betting on horses, two or three times a week; he knew nothing about horses, as far the wife was aware. 'I'd have preferred an addiction to pornography,' the wife told Lucas. 'At least I could have understood it.' Every time there was knock on the door, the widow had an attack of dread – this time, would it be the bailiffs?

She wanted explanations and apologies, and she needed to know what other revelations might be in store. Lucas, she believed, would be the means of obtaining justice. Of the reality of an existence beyond the one we call life, she had no doubt. Her mother, who had known someone who had been cured by Harry Edwards, had been a 'deeply spiritual woman', and had raised her daughter with constant guidance from the girl's father, who had remained at her side long after his too-early death. 'She spoke to him every day,' said the Binfield widow, 'and he told her what she should do.' Lucas was shown some of the books that had sustained his client's faith. She had read every word that Raymond Moody had written, though her husband had not found it possible to believe.

Despite the woman's commitment, Lucas could find no signal. The room in which they tried to make contact was not conducive to the procedure, he told me. It was as neat and clean and inert as a museum installation showing a suburban domestic interior of two decades ago. He came out of his receptive state in order to talk to the woman again. Anger, he explained, could be a barrier.

The preparatory conversation with Lucas had rekindled and redoubled her grievances. They should pause, he advised. The woman went for a walk, leaving Lucas to extract what he could from the air of the house; it was 'spiritually refrigerated', he told me. At the resumption, he again received nothing. 'All I heard,' he said, 'was the silence of indifference. The dead do not often apologise, Lucas told the widow, endeavouring to console. 'Their eyes are turned to higher things.' But he had a suggestion: could others who had known the husband be brought into the circle? He likened the hypothetical gathering to a radio telescope – the larger the dish, the more sensitive the instrument. Calls were made, firstly to a cousin who was more like a sister. Resistant at first, the cousin was persuaded into compliance by Lucas. She lived thirty miles away, and consented to give up an hour of the following evening. Two friends – husband and wife; former neighbours – were also recruited, along with a current neighbour whose cats the client would feed whenever their owner was visiting her son. The social network was not extensive.

That night, Lucas slept in the dead man's room. The couple had not shared a bedroom for 'a long time', he had been told; the marriage had produced no children. It was, said Lucas, 'the deadest room in Britain'. On opening the wardrobe, he saw a row of suits under plastic, and above them a row of shirts, all of them white or blue. The shoes, on the floor of the wardrobe, were aligned with such precision that a ruler might have been used to position them. Lying in the bed, looking around the room, Lucas saw nothing that signified a person of flesh and blood. He could have been in a two-star hotel.

The next day, at 8pm, the group convened. As soon as they were seated, the environment was changed. It was, as Lucas put it, as if a single cloud had formed above a landscape of absolute desert. And now there was a signal. Information was coming in, but the information had nothing to do with money. By the time the session was concluded, Lucas knew no more about the husband's illicit expenditure than he had already understood. Neither was anything like remorse directed towards the wife. The signal encompassed the wife, as Lucas told me, but it struck her as the beam of a car's headlight strikes whatever lies ten feet to the side of the verge. At the centre of the beam was the cousin who was more like a sister, whose lack of enthusiasm for the undertaking now took on a different meaning.

In the circumstances, it was best to offer some palliative. As far as he could tell, there were no further financial irregularities to be unearthed, he told the wife. There was something, however, that he would have to discuss with her in private. As the guests made ready to depart, Lucas discreetly took aside the cousin who was more like a sister and asked if she could stay for a little longer. 'One rarely sees a woman of that age blush,' he said to me. When he left, an hour later, the widow gave him a sum much larger than he could have expected; but she shoved the envelope into his hand 'as if paying off a blackmailer'.

☞

One afternoon, Lucas came to the door. I was home from university, and alone in the house. Holding his arms wide, in a gesture of submission, he said: 'I am taking a walk, and was wondering if I might have your company for an hour.' This was in the interval between the loss of Kathleen and the arrival of Erin; just before or after Easter.

He wanted to hear about the essay I was writing; we talked about Jeanne d'Arc; the horror of her death, he told me, had given him nightmares as a boy.

After a morning of heavy rain, the streets now had the shine of fresh steel, and there was a glitter of droplets in every tree. Overhead the sky was lucid; in front of us, over the hills, there were floes of mussel-coloured cloud, against a backdrop of Uranian blue. Sunlight ebbed then struck again, spreading a white-gold varnish quickly onto the fields, and we stopped at the sight of it. 'Glorious,' said Lucas, raising his stick in salute. For two or three minutes we admired the scene, not speaking, until the grass had darkened again. Lucas turned back towards the town; a smile informed me that the spectacle had given rise to a thought. A glance from me was sufficient to extract it. 'We are sentimentalists,' he said, in a tone of rueful conclusion. 'Not just you and I. Everyone,' he clarified, again making use of the stick, swirling it in the direction of the town, as though to include a whole classroom in his accusation. 'We are sentimental because it is not possible to be naïve.' Naïvety – 'true naïveness' – has long been impossible for almost all of us, he told me.

Callum, however, had perhaps achieved something like it – but only something like it, Lucas mused. An approximation was the best we could hope for. To watch Callum at work was to be in the presence of something exemplary, said Lucas, looking down at the pavement, as if humbled by the remembered example. Work for Callum was a spiritual exercise, said Lucas. And then he said, not looking at me: 'That is what's wrong with the way I

live. There's no work in it.' The words seemed to constitute the revelation of a secret discontent, yet the tone
was light, almost blasé. This tone was maintained in a
meandering improvisation on the theme of his deficiency,
spoken as though he were speaking of something about
which he had already often spoken. He talked about the
vita activa and the *vita contemplativa*; the terminology –
never used by Lucas before – was intended, it seemed, to
signify some affinity with me and my studies. Centuries
ago, the working day had begun and ended with prayer,
and that was how it should be, he said. The *vita activa*
was imbued with the *vita contemplativa* and vice versa.
He returned to the spiritual labour of Callum, and now
Kathleen was included. 'But there's not enough *activa* to
my *vita*,' he joked.

He halted, and turned back to look again at the sky above
the hills. The fields had become drab; the composition of
the clouds was weaker. Lucas smiled – he saw a metaphor
here, I was perhaps being prompted to think. 'Nothing to
be done now,' he said, and sighed parodically. We walked
on. 'I am such a sentimentalist,' he murmured, with a
shake of the head.

On an evening of heavy rain and thunder, I shared a
bottle of wine with Lucas after a game. The room was at
its most homely: warm, with a fragrance compounded
of old fabrics and burning wood, and the subtle scent
of the *go* board. Beside me, two of Kathleen's bowls, in
the firelight, gave off a murky green glow. Other than the
fire, the old standard lamp was the only source of light.
Encircled by shadows, we listened to the seething of the
rain in the garden.

Observing the drowsily appreciative look I had cast about the room, Lucas remarked, answering the thought that he had intuited, that he was thinking of selling the house. He was attached to the place, he admitted, but he was not rooted in it. He was attached to it in the sense that it embodied his attachment to Kathleen – and to Callum too, of course. But that attachment would endure wherever he might be, and he was beginning to think that life might be more straightforward if he were based somewhere more central than the south coast. Business was brisk, he implied; nonetheless, it would make sense to minimise his travelling time and expenses, and he didn't really need as much space as he currently had at his disposal.

He was a latter-day mendicant, wandering the length and breadth of the land, dependent upon donations from those to whom he ministered, he proposed, albeit not in quite those terms. His home was akin to the order's mother house – he resided here, temporarily, because one had to live somewhere, and naturally a bond of some sort arises when one resides in a particular place. But he was only passing through, as Callum and Kathleen had passed through, as we all were passing through, though we allow ourselves to think that the relationship with our home is one of ownership. 'We own nothing,' said Lucas, gesturing widely, as if the room were the embodiment of nothing. What matters in life is the relationships we construct among ourselves, he felt obliged to instruct me – 'Those are our real roots.' Every week he encountered people who had not taken enough care with their relationships. 'There is so much loneliness,' he sighed, then he said something that seemed to suggest that loneliness might persist into the afterlife, that there were solitary spirits among the numberless throngs of the dead. Surely, I thought, it should be possible to form new friendships beyond the grave, with so many souls to choose from; this was an objection that I left unexpressed. 'Sometimes it's hard,' Lucas confessed, in a melancholy moment. He was not absolutely sober.

But there were, he conceded, good reasons to stay where he was. 'For one, I would miss you,' he said, sternly, replenishing my glass. Then he talked about the case of Katie Burtenshaw.

Within the year, Erin was installed; there was no more talk of relocation.

After the death of Kathleen, Lucas lived alone for two years, give or take a month or two. Then, on a Saturday afternoon, no sooner had I arrived than my mother announced: 'Interesting development. Lucas has company.' Thus Erin arrived. 'A pretty girl,' said my mother; there was some mischievous pleasure in the enigma. The pretty girl had first been spotted five days ago, and was still at the house; she had been seen in the garden that morning. On Thursday she had been observed in the kitchen, carrying an armful of laundry. She might be a relative of whom we hadn't heard, my mother had thought at first. That was before she had seen Lucas talking to the girl, again in the garden. The conversation had been brief, but interesting. The girl, working at a bush with secateurs, had not stopped what she was doing; there was almost no eye contact, and no touching at all. There was nothing in their interaction to suggest a family connection; it was more like an exchange between a hired gardener and the householder. 'Do housekeepers still exist?' my mother wondered. Having a housekeeper might suit the image that Lucas liked to project, we agreed. 'But she is rather good-looking, and very young,' my mother repeated; the youth and prettiness were complicating factors, as the seniority of Kathleen had been before. I stayed that night, but there was no further sighting of the intriguing guest or housekeeper or whatever she was, and no sighting the next morning either.

Three or four weeks later, I was back. In the interim, my mother, in South Street, had passed the pretty girl – she was carrying a heavy bag of shopping in each hand, and had the air of an overworked domestic help. Later that day, she was seen pegging clothes on the line. And then, she had been introduced. At the end of the road my mother had seen Lucas and the girl walking twenty yards ahead, an arm's length apart; the girl was talking with barely a pause, and Lucas, turned towards her, seemed to be listening closely. Hearing footsteps behind them, Lucas looked round, saw my mother, and stopped. 'My neighbour, Monica,' Lucas informed his companion, then: 'This is Erin,' with no further information. 'Pleased to meet you,' said Erin. She was courteous, my mother reported, but not, she thought, particularly friendly; not so much shy as self-enclosed; not a light-hearted person, my mother suspected – it was something to do with the eyes. Erin said nothing else, until she excused herself, politely – she had a packet that had to be posted. She left Lucas with my mother; he made not a single reference to his guest. 'It's all a bit odd,' my mother said to me. Now she was inclined to think that Erin might be a relative after all.

'There she is,' she called to me, that evening, and at last I saw Erin. It was the last half-hour of dusk, so the face could not make its full effect; the long bright hair was what made the impression. She was holding a cat; Lucas had no cat; therefore Erin was in residence.

'Told you,' said my mother, observing my reaction, as if in encouragement.

'You didn't tell me about the hair,' I said. The hair was like something from a shampoo advert, we agreed. There were so many tones in that hair – oak and honey and brass and hay.

☞

My second sighting of Erin, the crucial one, occurred in town. Crossing the street, I noticed first the hair, then that Erin was talking to a fragile little woman, about a foot shorter, and at least fifty years older. Erin was primarily the listener, it appeared; her attention was focused purely on what was being said to her, which seemed to have an element of complaint. The sincerity of this attention was obvious to me, as was the sincerity of her sympathy. This was attractive, but it was a gesture, or a sequence of gestures, that transformed the attraction. The elderly woman, reaching a place to pause, moved closer to rest a hand on Erin's forearm; Erin then put a hand on the woman's hand and smiled, and spoke, very briefly; and at this the woman said something to her – evidently a compliment – that made Erin raise her other hand and cup her neck with it, below the ear. And more than anything else it was the movement of that hand – the grace of it; the modesty it seemed to signify; the vulnerability – that germinated my love of Erin, before I had ever spoken to her. The vignette might be thought mawkish, but there was a truth in it. Struck by the tenderness of Erin, I was overcome by a tenderness of my own; not desire, but an insatiable tenderness.

Only then, as I passed behind the woman and glanced at Erin's face, did her beauty do its work; and here, of course, desire was involved. The eyes, deep-set and dark, transmitted a frankness that was pleasantly unnerving. The perfect symmetry of the arcs above them, and of the angles of the cheeks and jaw, and the pallid complexion – all this was alluring. Small and slightly flattened at the bridge, her nose – and the planes of her cheekbones – gave her the face of an exquisitely pretty boxer; the physique was that of a dancer – or a young woman who had been a dancer, and had softened slightly since relinquishing the discipline, yet retained the posture and the slimness and the strength. And the glorious hair, again. The appearance was wholly admirable; there was, I think, more admiration than desire. I wanted to look rather than hold. I was entranced. It was important to this moment that she did not notice me.

☞

Beauty is nothing other than the promise of happiness.

☞

A few months after Erin's arrival, we were invited for a meal. The invitation was not only an opportunity to meet the new companion – it was an opportunity to enjoy her cooking. 'She really knows how to use a kitchen,' Lucas marvelled to my mother. It was as if an employee had revealed an unexpected and delightful talent, my mother reported.

Lucas welcomed us to the house. The kitchen door was ajar; through the gap, we saw Erin raise an implement in greeting. We went into the living room, where nothing gave any sign that a new person was living there. Watching Erin at work, said Lucas, was like watching a one-woman air-traffic control room. Half a dozen pots and pans might be in action simultaneously, while she chopped and shredded the ingredients for another element of the creation, and all this was done in an atmosphere of perfect calm, he told us. When living alone, he had subsisted on the plainest of diets. He'd had a repertoire of four or five meals. 'I don't care what I eat, as long as it's nothing new' – this had been his position, until now. It was not merely a matter of delighting the taste buds in ways he had not known were possible: considerations of health and of ethics had been impressed upon him. Erin had made him think again about what he ate, and in consequence meat was off the menu, permanently. This was news to my mother; she raised an eyebrow.

Erin brought the plates to the table professionally. At the first mouthful, Lucas led the praise. Closing his eyes, he frowned, like a restaurant reviewer submitting the dish to analysis. 'Stupendous,' he pronounced. 'Very nice,' agreed my mother. But no talent was involved, Erin insisted. It was simply a question of doing things in the right order. Her modesty seemed entirely genuine. Lucas smiled at her, as one might smile at someone who was on probation. It was possible to believe that she had been hired.

Nothing was clarified. All we learned of Erin was that she could cook, and that her mother could not, which was why Erin had taken it upon herself to learn. Just once, in the course of that evening, I glanced at Erin and received a glance in return, a glance that seemed to acknowledge that she and Lucas were objects of speculation, and to dismiss anything that might be thought about them.

She did not speak much; Lucas would have accounted for eighty per cent of the talking. Ten per cent would have been mine – tales from the classroom, mostly. Lucas was over-entertained by my stories. Only one can now be remembered: the boy who had thought that the Beatles and Queen Victoria had belonged to the same period. 'He has a point,' said Lucas. Erin's face at that moment was that of a student in the seminar of an oracular professor. A little nod seemed to signify that something had been understood and put in its place, in the system of Lucas's thinking.

At the end of the meal, Erin cleared the table; it was notable that Lucas made no attempt at assistance; an offer of help from the guests was declined crisply, with thanks; this work was an aspect of her role, it appeared. Before the clearing, Lucas expressed gratitude on behalf of us all. Erin bowed, with a hand placed demurely over her heart. The way Lucas looked at her was interesting: I saw admiration and appreciation; the beauty of the face and form was incontestable, of course, but I saw nothing libidinous in his gaze, and nothing proprietorial; it was not a lover's or a husband's gaze. His pleasure seemed to arise from the good fortune of having found someone of such competence, or so I told myself. The pleasure of patronage was also perhaps involved.

For fully twenty minutes the three of us remained at the table; there was a bottle of wine to be finished. It was a peculiar situation, with Erin at work in the kitchen while we talked, but Lucas made no reference to what she was doing; indeed, as I recall, she was not a subject of the conversation. And when at last she returned, it was only to say that she had enjoyed meeting us, and to wish us goodnight. There was no kiss for her from Lucas, not even a touch of hands. At no point in the course of the whole evening did he touch her. She was going to her own room, I was sure. 'Sleep well,' said Lucas, as though saying goodnight to a colleague at a conference hotel. We stayed for another fifteen minutes or so, and nothing more was said about Erin. I wondered if the purpose of the evening, for Lucas, might have been – in part, at least – to generate perplexity.

Back home, my mother said, right away: 'Well then, what did you make of that?'

'No idea,' I answered.

Erin, my mother proposed, was a 'bit of a cold fish'. Decorative, undeniably, but perhaps with nothing of any substance behind the façade.

'Early days,' I said. And: 'Cool rather than cold, I'd say.'

'Too placid,' she said. She was aware, however, that some men – most men – liked that quality in a woman. She seemed disappointed that Lucas should have turned out to be one of those men.

But I had been captivated. The laugh – a low two-note chuckle, heard twice during this first evening – would always charm me, as would the slight hesitation before speaking, sometimes, as if a moment of self-doubt had to be overcome. The evenness and light timbre of the voice beguiled me, as did the fact that she made no attempt to beguile. I could not imagine her angry, and was never to see her angry, until recently. Her face was fascinating. Again and again I had glanced at her, when she was turned towards Lucas: in profile her eyes and the downward curve of the upper lip – slightly more prominent than the lower – gave a suggestion of sadness and obduracy, whereas her face when fully seen was mild, open, almost ingenuous. The smile too was an element of her attractiveness: the unsudden smile, which seemed to be produced by a rising force of goodwill or contentment or amusement. But to enumerate the visible qualities is to miss the essence; the essence is outside the words, always.

☞

A scene occurs to me. I was at the sink, washing up; my mother alongside, drying. I had become aware that she had been at work on a single plate for longer than could be necessary; staring out of the window, she was rubbing slow circles with the tea towel. A cue was required. 'Something worrying you?' I enquired.

After a pause, as though the question required thought, she answered, in a tone of worry: 'Not worrying, no.'

'Let me try again: I sense that something is on your mind.'

Another plate was taken up, for a protracted bout of wiping. She made a quick soft grimace.

'The suspense, Mother, is killing me.'

She emitted a sigh and disburdened herself: 'I saw Erin this afternoon.'

'Oh yes.'

'Yes.'

'And what did Erin have to say?'

'Not much.'

'This is exciting news.'

After a pause, and a smaller sigh: 'I wish I liked her more.'

'Ah, well,' I said, as though perfectly unconcerned.

'But I just don't trust her.'

To which I answered: 'I have absolutely no idea why you say that.'

'There's something sly about her.' Peering up at the sky, as if something of interest were flying by, she added: 'Nice figure. Nice face. But other than that, I don't know what you see in her.'

'Who, me?'

'Both of you,' she said, like the mother of two sons.

On another day, my mother said of Erin: 'The thing is, I can't imagine her ever saying anything very interesting.' She had decided that 'fey' was the word that summed her up. In a more generous mood, some time later, she decided that 'fey' was not quite the right word after all, and ventured instead that 'dreamy' might be better. 'The dreamy pretty housewife,' she once called her. Having talked to her that morning, in town, she had begun to wonder if Erin might be taking some sort of medication. Lucas was on tour; recently he'd been spending a great deal of time away from home. 'It's not fair on the girl,' she said, but she never invited her to eat with us.

☞

And I remember an encounter, at the top of South Street, one afternoon in summer, before the arrival of Erin. We saw Lucas in conversation with Mrs Dealey, who was always amenable to having Lucas's charm vented on her, and vice versa; a remarkably pert woman, for someone on the downslope of her fifties. As we neared them, Lucas, overcharged with bonhomie, turned to greet us. Pleasantries were bestowed with some gusto. He remarked on how well my mother was looking, but the flattery, as I recall, received no response, pointedly. It did not occur to me that jealousy might have been a factor. In the time between Kathleen and Erin, Lucas was flirtatious with a number of women of Mrs Dealey's age. Some of them returned the compliment; I saw this, several times. With some of them, I wondered, was something more than flirtation happening? With my mother, it was something less: it was a meaningless gallantry. Or rather, that was all I saw.

☞

The first time I called at the house alone, after Erin had moved in, it was she who answered the door. Lucas would be down in a minute or two, she told me; he was upstairs, in the archive. She pronounced 'archive' as though Lucas's filing cabinets constituted a scholarly resource of high repute. Lucas and I had arranged to play a game of *go* that afternoon.

While I waited, she made me a cup of coffee. There was an exchange, very brief, about the meal. 'It came out well, didn't it?' she responded to my praise, as if the meal that she had prepared for us had assembled and cooked itself. She took me into the living room – 'escorted' might be a better word. I received the impression that she had other things to which to attend.

'I'll get out of your way,' she said, when Lucas came into the room, and I did not see her again until the game was over. I did not hear her either, yet no sooner had the game been concluded than she reappeared. It was uncanny. Lucas, defeated, shook my hand, made a remark, and the door immediately opened.

Lucas had a call to make, so Erin led me out. On the doorstep she said: 'Lucas likes you very much.' It was as though she had been deputed to pass on this piece of information, like a personal assistant with a client.

☞

Walking past The Ropemakers one evening in summer, Erin was unambiguously propositioned. The propositioner, more or less her age, was drunk, and it was not the first time this individual had made it clear that he liked the look of her. A week or so earlier, stopping his van to let her cross, he had complimented her on her dress. This time, the aggression was more blatant; she should lose a few inches from the hemline, he suggested. Erin's response was sharp, and the rebuff was taken as an insult. He called after her: 'Say hello to your dad for me.' His companions found the joke hilarious.

It was Lucas, not Erin, who told me about the incident. People were generally more subtle in their disapproval or resentment, he said. When he walked through the town with Erin, questioning glances were sometimes dispatched in their direction; glances of mockery and distaste.

'People are so quick to judge,' said Lucas, without rancour. 'One rarely knows enough to judge correctly.'

☞

References to Erin's youth were infrequent, but Lucas once said to me that he had sometimes wished he were a famous artist, or any kind of famously creative person – not for the fame, of course, but for the immunity that came with eminence. Talent exempts certain men from criticism that an ordinary individual, in a comparable situation, would attract. He had a list of examples, memorised like the details of an alibi. Picasso, of course. Marie-Thérèse Walter was seventeen years old when she became Picasso's lover; he was forty-five. Françoise Gilot, the mother of his two youngest children, was twenty-one when she met him; he was sixty-one. Goethe, sixty-five, fell in love with Marianne von Willemer, thirty. In 1914 Thomas Hardy, born 1840, married Florence Dugdale, thirty-nine years his junior. Lucas knew all of the dates. Alberto Giacometti, born 1901, married Annette Arm, born 1923. (Annette was an 'ingenuous and adoring girl', I later discovered.) Let's not forget Charlie Chaplin: born 1889, eloped with Oona O'Neill in June 1943 (Lucas even knew it was June), just a month after her eighteenth birthday. 'And does anyone care – or even know – about the behaviour of Erwin Schrödinger?' Lucas enquired. In the first six months of 1926 Schrödinger published four papers that constitute an episode that has been described as being 'without parallel in the history of science'. In the previous year, Schrödinger had begun tutoring Roswitha and Itha Junger, twins, aged fourteen. Schrödinger was in his late thirties, and married. When she reached the age of seventeen, Itha Junger became Schrödinger's lover. After an abortion had left her sterile, Schrödinger moved on to other lovers. 'Isn't that disgusting?' said Lucas. 'Despicable. Appalling. And yet, it's ignored, or erased.'

But I was to understand that there were no comparisons to be made. 'I am not in any respect like Erwin Schrödinger,' said Lucas. 'I am not a genius and I am not a creep. I am nothing like Chaplin. I am not like any of them.' The situation was entirely different, and yet people in the town, knowing nothing, thought that they had the right to disapprove. 'Envy, however, I can understand. And forgive,' he said, with a look that might have been forgiving.

Erin reclining, book in hand, then glancing at me, across the room, put me in mind of the wonderful portrait of Madame Récamier. The accomplished and beautiful Juliette Bernard was only fifteen years old when she married the banker Jacques-Rose Récamier, who was some twenty-six years her senior. Announcing his engagement, Récamier wrote to a friend: 'She possesses germs of virtue and principle such as are seldom seen so highly developed at so early an age; she is tender-hearted, affectionate, charitable and kind, beloved in her home-circle and by all who know her.' He also wrote: 'I am not in love with her, but I feel for her a genuine and tender attachment.' It appears that the marriage was not consummated. When David painted his magnificent portrait of her, Madame Récamier was still a virgin. On the afternoon that the similarity occurred to me, I might still have believed it to be possible that the relationship between Erin and Lucas was of this kind.

☞

In his sixties, Guillaume de Machaut composed *Le Livre dou Voir Dit*; its subject is a romance with a beautiful lady, forty years the poet's junior, whose love for him has been ignited by his literary reputation. There may or may not be a factual basis to this Book of the True Tale.

☞

'The soul has no age,' Lucas said to me, on another day; but in what context this was said, I cannot remember.

☞

'She will not be here forever,' Lucas once said to me, watching Erin as she went out of the room. He said it as though, at that moment, she were leaving not just the room but his life. What I was to understand was that he knew that day would come; eventually, he would be abandoned. In that minute I could only admire him.

☞

It had not been 'a condition of Erin's residency' that she should take command of the kitchen, Lucas told me. 'The paperwork is the thing,' he said, and I could not tell if this was a joke. 'I generate an immense quantity of paperwork,' he said, 'and she takes care of most of it. I needed a secretary.' Erin had come into the room, briefly, while we were talking, but she did not react to the remark. A few minutes later she came back. 'Any filing for me to do, boss?' she asked, chidingly, from behind his chair, and Lucas reached back to take her hand. She had been living in the house for nine or ten months by then, and this was the very first time I saw him touch her; I cannot recall ever seeing Erin reach out to touch Lucas.

☞

'You know about my brother?' Erin asked, at the dinner table. They had invited us to eat with them again; now it was late, and my mother had gone home. I knew nothing of any brother.

Erin looked across the table, at Lucas; for her to continue, his permission was required, it seemed. 'His name was Tom. He died,' she said. 'That's how I met Lucas.'

The story was told. When Tom was twenty, and Erin fifteen, he had departed for London, having, in the space of a couple of weeks, quit his job and left – or been left by – his girlfriend, who had been in effect his fiancée. It was not clear what was cause and what was effect, said Erin. Peterborough, the home town (another disclosure; a minor one), quickly palled for him; a place with more life was what he needed. At twenty-four hours' notice, Tom announced that he was going to London 'for a while'. A friend had a friend who had a room to rent in a flat at the end of the District line. This was where Tom would be living while he looked for work. He had no idea what kind of work it might be, but whatever was right for him, he would find it there, because London had everything, said Erin, with a shake of the head for her brother's foolishness. Tom left the next day. He worked in pubs, then hotels, then better hotels. He moved to a more comfortable room, in a less remote zone. There was a girlfriend; she was a singer, Tom said. For three years he stayed in touch; a weekly call or message. He had half a dozen addresses in that time. Then a letter arrived, addressed to the parents. What was in it, Erin never found out, but it upset her mother very much, and angered her father. He phoned his son; the number was defunct. Thus began the silence. Two years later, the visit from the police, telling them that Tom was dead; he had drowned; he had been drinking.

'My mother was mad with grief,' said Erin. 'There was so much she needed to know.'

Having heard from somewhere that families in similar situations had been helped by Lucas, her mother made an appointment. Lucas arrived punctually at midday; his manner was 'completely businesslike', said Erin. 'You'd have thought he was a doctor.'

Here a small laugh from Lucas. All the time Erin was speaking, Lucas looked down at his hands, attending to the story; once or twice he raised an eyebrow, slightly, as if he had forgotten some part of it, or was taking pleasure in a particular phrase. But there was no sense that he was listening to a tale of which he was the subject; no sense that he was being praised.

Erin's father, who had agreed to co-operate only after a campaign of persuasion from his daughters, had insisted that Lucas should not be told the circumstances of Tom's death, nor the place. It would be a test.

And of course Lucas did not need to be told. He saw and heard things that he could not possibly have known beforehand, Erin told me.

At Lucas's request, her mother brought him some items that had belonged to Tom – a book, clothes, a wallet of photos. Closing his eyes, he held a photo sandwiched between his palms, as if his hands were cold and the picture were a source of warmth. It was a picture of a dozen small boys, playing football. Lucas was silent for some time, until, suddenly, he said: 'Vinnie'. Vinnie had been Tom's best friend at primary school; he was one of the children in the photograph. The boy's sister, a very cute girl, was called Amy, and Lucas named her as well. Another photograph prompted him to make reference to 'the lifeboat road'. This gave Erin a shock, because 'the lifeboat road' was the name that Tom, aged eleven, and Erin, six, had used for a particular road in a town where they had once stayed on holiday; Erin had been fascinated by the gleaming lifeboat that perched at the summit of the slipway, and had needed to see it every evening, before going back to the cottage. The photo that made Lucas utter that phrase had been taken during that holiday, but did not show the lifeboat, Erin reported.

Her naivety was radiant.

When the family gathered around the table, Lucas made contact directly with Tom. Through Tom, he saw a scene: an expanse of tarmac; a large area of grass; a lighthouse – specifically, a lighthouse next to something like a fortress, a small fortress; a lighthouse painted with black and white hoops. He didn't recognise the locale, but the family knew where it was, and they knew what Lucas was seeing when he saw a beach of pebbles, in darkness, with an obelisk and another obelisk behind it, a bigger one, some kind of monument – he was seeing where Tom had been found.

But what had Tom said to them, via Lucas? Erin apologised – she couldn't tell me that. The tears informed me that the message conveyed by Lucas had been profound.

It was a significant evening. It marked a new closeness, between us all. The telling of the story was like the opening of a gate.

A month after the death of Kathleen, at home from university for Easter, I spoke to Lucas in the street. Amiable, in no obvious way different from the Lucas of the previous year, he made no mention of Kathleen until, at parting, he said: 'We could play a game. In memoriam.' What this meant, I thought, was that Lucas, now alone, required company for an evening.

In the house, it was as though Kathleen might return at any moment. Nothing was different, other than her absence. By the back door, her gardening shoes stood on a mat of newspaper; a cardigan was draped on the newel post. In preparation for the game, Lucas made a pot of coffee; he assembled a plate of toast. He moved around the kitchen as if being appraised by the spirit of Kathleen, as if the sequence and form of each action had to be precisely as it had always been.

There was some conversation, a little of it about Kathleen, most of that about her work. Mid-game, considering his move, he sat up from the board to turn aside, towards the bowl that still occupied the small round table; it always occupied that table. His gaze rose from the bowl, to roam in the air of the room. 'She's here,' he said, in the tone of a naturalist of greater experience and expertise than his companion, intuiting with absolute certainty the presence of the hidden creature that they have come to observe. Then, with a smile for me: 'Unfortunately, she's not helping me out.' He would lose; he always lost; it was his role to lose to the younger man.

'One day, one day,' he would sometimes threaten, at the end of the game, examining the disposition of the pieces. His demeanour was one of appreciation and bewilderment, like a man in a museum examining a stone that is carved with letters of a beautiful and incomprehensible script. He would play and lose with good humour; the development of the contest, of his disadvantage, intrigued him, as might the inevitable outcome of a complex experiment. But once, having – as I was aware – watched me for some time, as I studied the array of the stones, he said, when I had finally made my move: 'Is victory always absolutely necessary?' He regarded me steadily, for two or three seconds, then laughed, and turned his attention to his failing position.

Lucas was correct. Some of the pleasure of these games was the pleasure of winning. But the ritual in itself was pleasurable: the gloss of the amber wood, the tenuous scent of it, the ticking of the tiny stones, the silences. It gave pleasure, also, to show consideration for Lucas, now that his companion had gone, even if it was not certain that Lucas was in any need of the gift of my company. The invitation to play was always made lightly; occasion-ally I was not free on the suggested evening, and this caused no disappointment for Lucas, or none that I could see. Sometimes, on leaving, I sensed that he thought the game had been more to my benefit than to his; that he had things to do now, which he had set aside for the evening, to please me. From my window I would see him in the garden, seated, not reading, not looking with any intent, not overtly dejected; simply Lucas on his own, in the condition that his vocation entailed; an image of philosophical solitude, which perhaps he wanted me to observe.

With the arrival of Erin, the games ceased for some time; when they resumed, they occurred less regularly than before. A confession must be made: there was a satisfaction in being seen to overcome Lucas, although Erin showed little interest in the contest. Entering the room, she might ask how the game was going. 'The massacre is proceeding,' Lucas answered one evening, and she nodded, and – I remember – gave Lucas a small smile, as though she believed his defeat to be deliberate.

Once I suggested that she might play. Lucas said to me: 'Erin is not one for games.' This meant nothing more than that Erin did not care for this sort of pastime; perhaps there was a slight tone of regret that this was so.

Erin laughed and took up the phrase: 'No, I am not one for games,' she agreed, with self-mocking self-importance. Then added, with a glance that seemed to accuse me of some injustice: 'I just like the pretty patterns.'

One evening, some time before Erin's residence, I was playing badly. 'There's a risk I'm going to win this one,' said Lucas. He looked up from the board and said: 'Something is on your mind.'

A girl was on my mind – a second-year, whose room faced mine across the court. I was dithering over making an approach, I told Lucas, then I gave him her name: Gwendolyn. And at this a semi-smile appeared, and the movement of an eyebrow signified a slight and pleasing surprise.

'Tell me,' I said.

Gwendolyn, Lucas informed me, after minimal reluctance, had been the name of a girl that my father had known, before marrying my mother; it was to be understood that the relationship had not been trivial. Perhaps I was to think that there was some significance to this coincidence, but the coincidence was a matter of indifference to me. What concerned me was that I had never heard of this Gwendolyn, whereas Lucas had. During the time that my father had been with us, Lucas had only been a visitor, occasionally, at the house of Kathleen and Callum; there had never been any reason to think that he had known my father in any meaningful sense. The only explanation, then, was that my mother for some reason had told him about this Gwendolyn; and for some reason had not told me.

'That's strange,' I responded, as if there might indeed be some occult dimension to the recurrence of the name.

There was little more that Lucas could tell me about my father's Gwendolyn, he regretted. He believed that her family had owned a shop and that she had been very attractive. 'I think he was rather fond of her,' he said, as though talking of a broken-hearted friend of his youth. It was not true, obviously, that he knew no more than this.

When, that evening, I mentioned to my mother that Lucas had surprised me, there was no immediate reaction. She nodded, and gave the name some thought, then seemed to see, vaguely, the figure to whom the name had belonged. 'Oh yes,' she said, as the figure became more distinct. 'The sporty girl.'

She had known her only by sight, she told me. A lot of people knew Gwendolyn by sight. The legs were the main attraction, as she recalled. 'Very long, and usually on show. I envied the legs, I imagine,' she conceded. Other than that, Gwendolyn had not left much of an impression. My father had been 'seeing' her for three or four months, at most, and then Gwendolyn had moved to another town – somewhere in the Midlands, possibly. It had not been anything serious.

Gwendolyn, she thought, was not a girl with whom anyone could be very serious. Saying this, my mother's voice, momentarily, had something of a smirk about it. 'He had a few girlfriends before he met me. An attractive man,' she said, wistful, for once. 'And I had a few boyfriends, hard though that might be to imagine,' she added, gesturing at herself with both hands turned inward, descending from shoulders to hips, and her face fixed as though disgruntled with the body that had been allotted to her.

☞

Taking her place at the table one evening, during the Easter break, my mother remarked on the care with which I had presented the food, and the placement of the cutlery and the beaker of water. She was reminded of the way Kathleen had always set the table. The single flower in the slender white vase was a Kathleen-like touch, she remarked. The poise of Kathleen was recalled; the idiosyncratic clothes, which would have looked drab and baggy on anyone else, but on Kathleen were subtle and stylish. My mother would be happy if she could grow old with anything like the dignity with which the elderly Kathleen had carried herself through the last years of her life, she said. There was no mention of the gossip-attracting cohabitation with Lucas. This admiration of Kathleen was an implicit withholding of admiration from the young woman who now occupied the house.

The subject of Kathleen having been exhausted for the time being, a lull ensued. Then my mother smiled, inviting me to enquire as to what it was that had amused her. She was remembering the morning she had thought that the house had been burgled while we slept. The lights were on in the living room and things had been moved from their customary places. But nothing had been knocked over or damaged. The lamp stood a few inches from where it should have been; the bowl of fruit was now on the floor; an armchair was closer to the wall than it had been when she went to bed. In the kitchen, too, the lights were on. Every drawer was open, and open to exactly the same extent. The chairs around the table had all been pulled out a few inches, squarely, apparently with care. And on the tabletop, every knife, fork and spoon had been laid out, in three perfectly straight lines, aligned with the long axis of the table, with the knives uppermost, then the forks, then the spoons, organised by size, diminishing from the left. 'You did it all without waking yourself up,' she marvelled. 'Then you crept back to bed, and I didn't hear a thing.'

I know this incident only through her retelling of it. It seems that I went walkabout several times in the years that followed the departure of my father, but in my memory all that remains of that period of delinquency is a recollection of lying on the floor of the living room, amid saucepans, and another of being carried into the house by a man who was not my father. 'But I remember being found outside,' I tell her.

'Oh my God,' she said, putting her hands to her face, as if in the after-shock of that night. 'How on earth did you stay asleep? You were frozen.'

Once again the traumatic night was revived: the knock on the door, past eleven o'clock; her son, who had gone to bed hours earlier, and whose bedroom door was closed, was now presented to her in the arms of Mr Robertson, asleep. I had been found a hundred yards from the house, heading into town. Mr Robertson had come upon me as he walked home from the White Swan. On catching sight of a small person in the distant gloom – a small person wearing what seemed to be a striped suit – he had not immediately understood that he was seeing a boy in pyjamas. When Mr Robertson had spoken to me, I had answered him with nonsense, and my eyes were half-shut.

'He was a nice man,' my mother remarked.

Now, a new nuance was introduced to the familiar story. An interesting possibility was raised by the slight alteration in my mother's demeanour when she told me this; a suggestion of fondness was to be heard in the phrase 'a nice man'.

I took the plates to the sink; above the sound of the running water I asked, addressing the wall: 'Is there something you'd like to tell me?'

'About what?' she asked.

'About Mr Robertson.'

'What do you mean?'

'Might you care to develop the idea of Mr Robertson's niceness?'

'In what way?'

'In whatever way you choose.'

'He was nice to me,' she said. A game had commenced; she was willing to be teased.

I glanced at her, then reapplied my attention to the dishes. 'I have the impression that there is more to be said.'

'Not really. He liked me.'

'As do many people. You are likeable.'

'He knew our situation. He was kind.'

At no point during that evening did the possibility of Lucas occur to me.

It was shortly before Lucas's birthday, and Erin told us that it was difficult to surprise him, because Lucas, when he put his mind to it, could tell what she was thinking. He would look at her in a particular way, and it was as if he were gazing through a window into fog, and whatever she was thinking was like a person becoming recognisable as she approached the window. For example, a few days earlier, apropos of nothing, he had looked up while they were eating, and told her that she was thinking about Venice, which was exactly what she had been thinking about, only a few minutes earlier. A while ago they had talked about the idea of a holiday in Venice, but she hadn't said anything about it recently – certainly not in the previous day or two. Yet Lucas had known that the idea of Venice had just popped into her head. 'It's a bit creepy, sometimes,' she said, and Lucas glanced at her; he seemed uncomfortable for an instant.

'What?' she demanded, smiling at him. 'Not surprising, is it?'

My mother had listened to her with an attention that had some condescension in it; she might have been listening to a story related by a child who was not quite as enchanting as her parents believed her to be. This was, I think, the last time the four of us ate together. She turned to Lucas and said: 'So can you tell me what I'm thinking now?'

Lucas looked at her studyingly, as if examining a painting that might have been a copy. 'Possibly,' he said. The examination was prolonged for a few seconds more. 'Yes,' he said, becoming confident. 'Yes, I think so.'

'Go on then,' my mother challenged him, in the tone of someone dealing with a boaster, but a personable one.

He shifted forward, put his elbows on the table to prop his head, and directed his gaze, full-force, into her eyes. She held them wide open, as though for the scrutiny of an ophthalmologist.

It was embarrassing. Erin touched my hand to divert me; we should respect the intimacy of the procedure.

'Relax,' Lucas instructed my mother, who was already relaxed. She blinked three or four times, and exhaled, signifying compliance. 'All right,' said Lucas. He urged her to concentrate on what she was seeing with her inner eye. He peered, as if through the chinks in a wall of loose stones, then a smile grew. 'I think I know,' he told her. 'Flowers, yes?'

My mother nodded, frowning.

Further scrutiny was conducted. 'Specifically, peonies,' Lucas decided. 'The peonies by the front door.'

My mother paid him with a gratifying display of astonishment. She rubbed her eyes and shook her head, like a woman waking up. 'Amazing,' she said. Then: 'Try Joshua.'

I demurred, and Lucas was very prompt to excuse me. 'Some other time, perhaps,' he said, whereupon I changed my mind.

We followed the same rigmarole: relax; picture something; concentrate. While my inner vision was appreciating the face of Erin, Lucas trained his gaze into my head. A narrowing of his eyes suggested that, with this one, he wasn't getting a clear view through the gap in the wall. He smiled questioningly, encouragingly, but I was not to be encouraged. 'No,' he said, surrendering. It was not, however, an admission of defeat; it was an expression of disappointment. He could not understand why this young man, his neighbour's son, should be putting up such resistance. 'You don't want me to know,' he explained.

My mother was embarrassed: by me, not by Lucas. Back home, I suggested that Lucas had prompted her in some way. 'He didn't say anything about any flowers,' she pointed out.

'Not that we remember,' I answered. Anyway, the prompting had not necessarily been verbal. The peonies were, after all, rather luscious and conspicuous; she would have taken note of them as we waited for the door to be opened; given her interest in gardening, he would have known that she was impressed; he could have directed her attention to them, without her being aware. 'I could have been thinking of anything,' she told me. 'Why do you have to try to explain it away? It's what you always do.' Rather than discuss what she had just said, and what Lucas had done, she went to bed.

When I left home, for university, Lucas was immensely kind to my mother, she told me. Of course, Kathleen was kind too. Kathleen sympathised, but she could not empathise as Lucas did; she was not a maternal woman. Yet Lucas understood, without being told, that what she was experiencing was a kind of grief. Now alone in the house, she was surprised at the vulnerability that came with the situation. Her thoughts became morbid. At work or out shopping, she would suddenly, with no prompting, find herself imagining catastrophes that would leave her son or herself bereft. As if she had aged two decades overnight, she took elaborate care when crossing the road; she drove the car as cautiously as someone who had passed her test only a week before. Her heart would flutter when the phone rang. To shorten the evenings, she went to bed too early. Time often passed too slowly when she was on her own, and yet there were days when she would panic, because it was as if she had been living for twenty years with a wall around her, and that wall had now been breached by her son's departure, and the days were flowing away too fast.

Lucas's company was beneficial, she told me. Occasionally they would take a stroll together, and she found that something of his 'inner calmness' was transmitted to her wordlessly. He had an aura of contentment that was not the same thing as complacency; it was like the contentment of a monk, she would have me believe.

'Two or three times' he came into the house when they returned from the walk. A disquieting incident occurred after one of these visits. My mother was turning the pages of a photo album, and at a picture of her parents Lucas put out a hand to make her pause. It was the picture taken near Glastonbury Tor, by an unknown person, during their honeymoon; the tandem is propped against a post beside them; the Tor rises in the background. Lucas took the album from my mother, to examine the picture closely; he examined it as if he were a detective and had reason to think that this grainy and colourless image might contain a significant clue. Anyone might have worked out that the woman in the photograph was my mother's mother, and from this it followed that the man was my grandfather. But Lucas somehow extracted from the picture much more information than this. 'You'd have thought he had known her,' said my mother, referring to the detail with which he was able to describe my grandmother's personality. He warmed to her, as people generally had done when she was alive. Her husband did not seem to come into focus to the same degree, but salient aspects were sensed – the erratic temper, for example, and the tendency to moroseness, along with the devotion to his wife.

This character-reading, however, was not the most remarkable thing. The shock came when Lucas said, peering into the face of my mother's mother: 'But there had been someone else, for her, hadn't there?' And this was true. So, now, I learned from my mother that my grandmother's first love – her great love, she had come to understand – had been a young man named Harry Watkins, who had died at Calais in 1940, before they could become engaged. My grandfather, Harry's closest friend, had comforted the bereaved young woman, and the comforting had soon become something else. 'It wasn't a bad marriage. About average. A bit lopsided,' said my mother. 'They were good parents.' But Harry was irreplaceable, as her mother had confessed, some time after the death of her husband. And Lucas had read this in the photograph – not Harry's name, but the essence of the story, the sadness of it, though there was no visible sadness in the picture.

It made her feel queasy, what Lucas had done, she admitted. It was out of the question that she might, in some forgotten conversation, have mentioned my grandmother's first love. After all, she had not told me about it until now.

☞

For many years, Lucas had struggled with disappointment. On going to university, he had imagined that he was 'setting off on a journey' that would make a poet of him. By way of apprenticeship, he had committed Eliot's *Four Quartets* to memory. 'The whole thing,' he impressed upon me. He had written quantities of philosophical poetry – 'What I took to be poetry,' he qualified, in affectionate mockery of the pretentious young Lucas. An obscure and soon extinct magazine had published an excerpt from a work in progress. 'They would have published almost anything,' he told me. The delusion lasted until around the age of twenty, and then he came to see his poems for what they were: anaemic pastiches; impersonations. A few scraps of his writing remained stuck in his memory, but he would not embarrass us both by quoting them. He still knew the entire *Four Quartets* by heart, he said, even though he no longer cared for 'all that sermonising'. He recited twenty or thirty lines in demonstration; it did indeed seem that he could have continued for some time.

Even Callum had been disappointed with himself, Kathleen had once revealed, to Lucas's surprise. Lucas had always envied Callum, as he had envied Kathleen, he told me. Dedicated to his work and to his wife, Callum exemplified the integrity of the true artisan; he had an admirable evenness of temper, and a particular kind of pride – a 'humble pride', to quote Lucas. Yet Callum, like Lucas, had once been ambitious for a different kind of success. From his talent for carving, significant art would in time ensue, he had thought; his talent was the seed – with study, and practice, and encouragement, the art would grow from it, as surely as the growth of a well-nurtured plant. He applied himself; family and teachers encouraged him.

Three years were spent at college, and at the end of those three years Callum knew what he was: he was a carver of stone and wood, and he respected only the old ways of working – giving form, by hand, to resistant and durable materials. A young man of his proficiency, he was told by a sympathetic tutor, would not struggle to find work. So accomplished a figurative sculptor would readily find commissions. But the prospect of earning a living by making likenesses of wealthy people did not appeal to Callum. And there was a more substantial problem: a backward-looking artist, he knew, was a contradiction in terms. He was, then, not an artist in the deepest sense of the word; this was what he had to accept, and he soon came to accept it, with less difficulty than he had anticipated, having taken up what proved to be his true métier – letter-cutting. Once in a while he would undertake something modestly sculptural: the carving of a bird on a slate sign, for example, or a small figure to replace a corroded original above the door of a church. But he was not an artist. He had an eye for the composition of beautiful lettering, and his hand could shape, unerringly, any letters that he could draw. The design of inscriptions, however, was the extent of his vision; he had no ideas.

It irked him sometimes, though, that so many widely lauded artists had no ideas either – or no ideas that merited attention. It could be dismaying that these people had no command of their materials; that they depended on the labour of hired helpers to fabricate the things that bore their name. 'Making their name is more important for them than making the work,' said Lucas, speaking for Callum. It was a summer evening; the sun was no longer visible; we considered the inscription that Callum had cut into the tablet of limestone that was set into the garden wall – *Domi manere convenit felicibus*. The lettering was so fine, it might have been unearthed on the Appian Way, as Lucas remarked.

Having been jemmied out of the wall by Erin's father, the tablet is now an ornament in her sister's garden, I believe.

☞

I remember Lucas in full advice-giving mode; the grandiloquent gestures were augmented by the capacious sleeves of the big blue linen shirt – a birthday gift from Erin, worn on days of recreation throughout that summer. We were in deckchairs in the garden, each with a glass of Erin's special lemonade. I had made reference to my thwarted ambition: I would have become an academic, had it not been for my inability to come up with any substantial ideas of my own, I told them – hoping, I'm sure, to gain credit for not sparing myself from criticism. 'Originality is overrated,' Lucas ruled. Besides, the academic world, though full of very intelligent people ('by definition', he conceded), was a 'world unto itself', a 'small world' in certain ways, 'in the ways that matter'. The limitations of this world, as seen by Lucas, were the customary ones: hypertrophy of the brain, he seemed to believe, necessarily entails some atrophication of the essential human qualities. For every degree of intellectual excellence, there is a countervailing degree of social or emotional incompetence. I lacked much inclination to take issue. It was pleasant to recline in the sunlight, amid the profusion of flowers. There was no doubting the generosity of Lucas; the sincerity of his concern. I surrendered to the voice of Lucas, as I surrendered to the warmth of the day.

Lucas understood the appeal of a life devoted to study. 'I do. I really do,' he said. To continue with his studies would have been the obvious thing to do, in his twenties; it would have been a decision that was in fact no decision at all. 'I was good for nothing else,' he joked. But one afternoon, an afternoon in the spring term, he had been sitting in the café on campus, with some friends, and something had happened that had made him choose a different path. He was seated at a window, and from this window he could look down, across a small courtyard, into the office of a lecturer who had taught Lucas earlier in the year. He was one of those who had encouraged Lucas to consider a postgraduate course. In the centre of the courtyard was a fishpond, shaded by a cherry tree. It was an 'enchanting composition', said

Lucas: the pink blossom, sun-struck; the red fish cruising just under the surface of the green-black water; the white paving stones. The lecturer's desk was positioned against a wall, at a right angle to the window, under shelves on which books had been jammed to fill every last bit of space. Not enough of the sunlight got into the office, it seemed; a lamp was on, and a mess of papers lay in its light. The lecturer, reading one of these papers, put his hands to his temples, forming blinkers; his face was close to the pages. It was like looking down on a hermit in his cave, Lucas told me. Then the lecturer turned to look out at the courtyard. The man's eyes seemed to see nothing delightful there. His face, his posture, his office – it all presented an image of drudgery, of 'non-life', said Lucas. He was aware, he told me, that he was to a great extent the creator of this image. Someone else, seeing the same man at the same time, might have seen instead an inspiring image of concentrated intellect. It was possible that the lecturer was in the process of refining a piece of work that would resound through whatever province of academia he had elected to serve. But Lucas saw what he saw, and it had a great impact. The scene spoke to him, like a fable, and what it told him was that he had to get out into the world. What he would do there was not at all evident, and this lack of clarity, he told me, became, immediately, as he looked down on the cherry blossom and the fish gliding within the water, something like a calling. 'I had to choose the unknown,' he said.

He smiled benignly, appreciatively, in the direction of the apple tree, as if the finches that were frisking amid the leaves were emblematic of everything that the academic is obliged to renounce. 'Do you know what I did, for a while?' he asked; of course, I did not. 'I fitted carpets,' he said, hoisting the eyebrows. 'It's true. I fitted carpets.'

I would have displayed the requisite astonishment. Lucas had needed to 'clear his mind', he told me, and this undemanding work had allowed him to do that. There was a sense of reward in being of use to people – considerably more people than would have benefited from anything that might have come out of his studies. And he had found the work satisfying, in itself. For several years he had fitted carpets, and he had never ceased to get pleasure from the way a room was changed by what he did – not just the appearance of it, but the air, and not just the scent of the fresh material but the way in which sound was muted by the altered room, the way it expired. He was 'acutely attuned to atmospheres', Lucas told me, with no self-praise; he could have been disclosing a not particularly remarkable idiosyncrasy of his body, such as being double-jointed. It was a pleasure, too, to spend time in the houses of strangers, he said. Rooms can be read like faces, like pages of text. Pictures of course tell one a great deal – not just by their subject, but also by where they are displayed, and how they are displayed. Furniture is informative – its style, its age, its placement, its quantity, its condition. 'One can interpret dust and damage,' Lucas pronounced; the poetical phrase had not arisen spontaneously. He talked about a house in which tracks had been worn into the old carpet in the living room, from the door to the armchair that was set squarely in front of the television, and from the television to the window; from every wall, photographs of the husband looked on; the photos had become as pale as old watercolours.

It was 'good for the soul' to learn some sort of skill, Lucas stated. Carpet-laying was a skill, albeit a small one; it had done his soul a small but measurable amount of good. There was, I believe, some mention of 'ivory towers' and 'the real world'. Lucas spoke of his reverence for Callum and Kathleen, for their mastery of their crafts, and their humility; he assumed a voice of humility in talking of them. We admired once more the lettering that Callum had carved into the bar of stone set into the wall. Lucas could hear, as clearly as a song, the sound of Callum at work: three quick taps; a momentary pause; three quick taps; a pause; three quick taps. The rhythm was constant; one could have danced to it. Any mistake would have been irretrievable, but Callum's touch was unerring and light; 'definitive' was a word that Lucas used. Kathleen had likewise possessed this absolute precision and economy of action. 'Such certainty,' Lucas marvelled. This I remember – 'Such certainty,' looking up into the sky, with a sigh that was tinged with envy, which may or may not have been sincere.

Nothing more was said about the uncertain, non-substantial métier of Lucas. Erin came out to us, bearing plates. What she had prepared, I cannot remember. It would have been of restaurant quality, as ever. Lucas thanked her, and the gratitude had force. After Erin had put the plates in front of us, Lucas took her hand and touched his lips to the back of it. In all the years I knew them together, not once, I think, did I see him kiss her face. 'You are a genius, my girl,' he told her.

☙

When Lucas arrived in her life, her 'story suddenly made sense', said Erin. Other people had often told her who she was, but Lucas had made it possible for her to discover her true story for herself. This was said after another meal, and what I remember was that she glanced at Lucas as she said that her story made sense now, but her glance was not that of a lover; neither was the intonation of her voice. She spoke the words not quite as an acolyte, but with respect; not quite as though Lucas were a teacher, but in acknowledgement that she had learned a great deal from him. And Lucas accepted the tribute with a small nod; not with self-satisfaction; simply in confirmation of what Erin had said, as if what she had said was merely something like: 'Lucas bought this dress for me.'

☞

Something I learned from Lucas: a delicious phrase – *Delectatio morosa*. It could be applied to my situation he said; the reference was to my preoccupation with Gwendolyn, and my reluctance to act decisively. Defined by Lucas, it signified the delight one takes in idle imagination. I have found a theologian who, citing Aquinas, writes of a 'complacent dallying' in voluptuous thoughts; a sin is committed if no effort is made to eliminate these delightful imaginings. Elsewhere, *Delectatio morosa* is defined as a pleasure 'in the delay of satisfaction'. Another writer asserts that *Delectatio morosa* entails 'rumination on one's own worthlessness'.

☞

Next time I was home for the weekend, said Lucas, Erin would cook for us again; it was more a notification than a suggestion.

The meal was memorable: crisply fried slices of potato, with roasted onions and garlic, and sautéed spinach, poached eggs, cream and nutmeg, and a slathering of melted cheese. Again, Lucas congratulated the chef at length. Again, Erin was modest: if Lucas were inclined to cook, he would do it just as well, she told us. There was no suggestion that she resented his lack of inclination.

That was simply how things were: Erin took great pleasure from cooking, and Lucas did not.

But what I remember most acutely of that evening is that, by the end, it had become apparent that I had allowed myself to be misled by Erin's apparent placidity. There was an episode of assertion, arising from a conversation – three-way; my mother barely contributed – about Lucas's renunciation of meat. 'Show them the video you showed me,' Lucas said to Erin. After watching this video, he assured us, we would understand. Erin resisted. 'Not now,' she said, and there was a surprising force to the words. Her reluctance was overcome, however; inevitably. She brought in the laptop, and we watched the video. A donkey lay upon a mat of straw, in a corner of a barn; one could readily attribute dejection to this animal. Subtitles informed us that the donkey had for a year shared its stall and the yard with a horse that had belonged to the daughter of the family; when the daughter had left home, the horse had been sold. The horse had been collected by its new owners three weeks ago, and since then the donkey had not left its corner; it had eaten almost nothing; it was in mourning. And so, we read, the horse had been bought back, and we were about to see what happened when it returned to its true home. We hear a truck approaching and stopping, then the unfastening of a tailgate, then hooves on a ramp. At the sound of the hooves, the donkey lifts its head; it listens; it stands up, shakily. The camera follows the donkey to the stable door, so we see, in the moment that the donkey sees it, the horse standing in the sunlit yard, at the water trough, drinking. Slowly the donkey crosses the yard; horse turns, and the donkey trots the last few yards, to press its muzzle to the muzzle of the horse. Minutes later, both are eating, side by side; an hour later, horse and donkey are running together in the paddock.

Erin, having pressed the heel of a thumb to each eye, said to me, as if she were a nurse conducting some sort of health check: 'Do you think this is sentimental?' Before I could answer, she went on: 'OK. You could say it's a tear-jerker. It is. But you have to ask yourself what's going on here.' To dismiss the video on the grounds of sentimentality was to excuse oneself from addressing the issue. 'Only one question matters: Can it suffer?' she told us. The vehemence was new and irresistible. Lucas said nothing, but a small smile expressed something like pride.

At home, my mother professed admiration for Erin's strength of feeling, even if it had not perhaps been entirely appropriate to start 'preaching' to one's guests at the end of the evening. She had things to say about Lucas. As one gets older, there is a general loss of mobility, in the mind as much as in the body. 'Your mind settles,' she said, 'like the contents settling in a sack.' This, she thought, was what the 'thing with Erin' was 'all about' – Lucas needed her to shake him up a bit, she said. 'Just to be clear, though,' she concluded, going up to bed, 'I have no intention of living on potatoes and cheese for the rest of my days. You can forget about that idea.'

☞

'But when were you happiest?' Erin asked. As I recall, I answered instantly, because the question had come from her. There were so many possibilities, I said, scanning the roof, as if seeing there, arrayed like the heavenly host, the images of a hundred days of happiness.

One candidate made itself prominent, a day that was by then eight years old – or, to be precise, fifteen minutes of that day, at most, around 2pm, late July, at the abbey of Le Thoronet. The exactitude was expected of me. With similar detail I set the scene: cloudless sky; temperature in the high eighties; the air scented by heated earth, heated stone, the wood of an ancient olive tree, and a trace of herbs. Already I had spent an hour in the abbey. The building had raised my spirits to a high pitch of receptivity and contentment, or words to that effect. I talked about the perfect severity of the Cistercian architecture – a building of exemplary simplicity, devoid of all inessentials, charged with pure light, et cetera, et cetera. Now I was sitting outside the church, on a low wall. A lizard, ten feet away, crouched motionless in the heat; the ceaseless and unvarying sound of the cicadas augmented a sense of the suspension of time. I was leaning against the pale stone front of the church. The grain of the stone, the slight yet infinite variations of colours in every block – the wall absorbed my attention like a painting, I told my audience. Then, the element that raised the experience to a plane of even higher exaltation: the music. Four men – two quite young, two not – had gone into the church ten minutes before, each carrying a score. Now they were singing. What they were singing I did not know until later – it was a piece written in Paris, in the thirteenth century, to be sung in Notre Dame. I never knew what words were being sung, but the spirit of them – a spirit of serenity and celebration – was, I reported, 'overwhelming'. I corrected myself: the sound was overwhelming. The church itself was, to an extent, the conductor of the music, and a participant: the massive stone walls and the plainness of the interior, I would have explained, created an echo which obliged the singers to keep the tempo slow. From the doorway of the church, out into the heat and sunlight, came the long slow flow of the four indivisible voices – nothing I had heard since that afternoon had affected me so deeply, I confessed to Erin, and to Lucas. Those minutes had been an extraordinary surge of happiness; of joy, even. They had made the day one of those days that makes you want to thank somebody, I said.

I had been verbose; perhaps precious. For a few seconds, nobody had anything to say; one might have thought that I had made a confession of quite a different kind.

Eventually Erin asked: 'Were you there on your own? Or with a girlfriend?'

I had been with my mother, I answered.

Erin nodded; something had been confirmed, she appeared to believe.

Lucas remembered the trip that I had undertaken with my mother. 'They drove all round France, down to the Alps,' he explained to Erin. He even recalled the principal points of the tour.

While I told Erin whatever she wanted to know about our tour of the country, Lucas observed me, as though I were occupying the psychiatrist's couch. Now, when Erin had heard enough, he finally remarked: 'Interesting.' What was interesting was what I had told them earlier, about the afternoon at Le Thoronet. Once again, he said, I had revealed a 'hankering' that I seemed to be determined to resist. Was it not significant that of all the days I could have picked, I had picked that particular one, at that particular place? Why, he wondered, had the music – music of a special kind – been the ingredient that had made the episode one of 'transcendence'? I was of the spirit's party, and did not know it, he joked. I had a yearning for a time when God was still alive.

But Lucas too had misunderstood. The pleasure of that moment at Le Thoronet had been entirely of that moment. The sound and the sunlight and the building had combined to produce a strong reaction, but the state of mind that had been produced by this reaction was not the same as the one from which the music had been created. In my reaction there had been no yearning for a time I imagined to be better than this; I had imagined no such thing. This was the only time possible; there had been no transcendence. The past had become present as nothing more than a ghost. 'A ghost of otherworldly sound,' I said to Lucas.

'Perhaps,' said Lucas. 'Perhaps.' I was to see that he was unpersuaded.

Erin smiled, seeing that Lucas had entangled me. The smile invited me to argue my way out.

Instead, I invited her to nominate her day of maximum happiness.

'The day I came here,' she announced, immediately, with a gesture that encompassed the garden, the sky, the house. Then, looking at Lucas, she said to him, almost in the tone of a parent: 'It's OK. You don't have to join in.'

Lucas nodded his thanks for the exemption.

'But you could, if you wanted to,' she coaxed.

Again Lucas nodded, but this time thoughtfully; he was assessing the possible cost of answering truthfully. 'It would be the same as yours,' he decided.

'He has to say that,' Erin told me.

'Or, maybe,' Lucas went on, considering, 'the day that Laura Henson kissed me.'

Leaning back as though from an unpleasant and sudden smell, Erin asked, blinking: 'Laura who?'

'Henson,' answered Lucas. 'Laura Henson.' He made a wistful cadence of the name.

'And who might Laura Henson have been?' The curiosity had a particle of annoyance in it.

'First love. But it didn't work out. I was too young,' Lucas lamented. He gazed into the sky, in a mist of regret.

'Nine,' he confided to me. 'She was already nine. I was only eight. Too young,' he said, and shrugged.

After a quick examination of his face, she decided, uncertainly: 'You made her up.'

'Oh no,' said Lucas. 'It was a Dante and Beatrice situation, but with an older girl,' he said, raising his head and turning slightly, into a pose of grave nobility, but Erin was not to be amused.

☞

A few days after the day at Le Thoronet, on our way home, we stopped for a night in Bourges.

I stayed in the cathedral some time after my mother had seen enough; we would meet later, at the hotel, before eating at a restaurant that was more expensive than our customary choices – her compensation for being required to accompany me into so many churches. She thought she might take a stroll down to the river; we drew a route onto a map of the town.

An hour later, I came out of the cathedral, into air that was warm and bright; I too would stroll to the river; the afternoon was conducive to meandering. Not a hundred yards from the cathedral, crossing the road, I looked to my left and there was my mother, sitting outside a café, with her back to me, in the shade of an awning, and not alone. On the other side of the table, facing me, was a man of more or less her age, perhaps a little older, casually and expensively dressed, and deeply tanned. He wore a Prussian blue shirt, open at the neck, and white trousers; a sockless foot, in deck shoes, dangled in the sunlight; his hair, thick and grey and quite long, was swept back from an impressive forehead; everything about his style and his manner marked him as a local man. This was strange, because my mother, acutely shy as soon as we arrived in France, had barely spoken to anyone other than her son in the preceding ten days; I had been the spokesman in every social interaction.

Now, however, she was not merely no longer shy – she appeared to be entirely at her ease; in fact, I could not recall ever having seen her in so expansive a mood with someone she did not already know. Seeing these two people in conversation, one would have thought that they had been good friends several years ago, and had encountered each other here, unexpectedly. The man was loquacious and amusing. Lighting a cigarette, he gestured at his belly and said something that made my mother laugh; I did not often see her laugh. She was drinking what I assumed to be water, but then her companion, indicating his glass of wine, raised an eyebrow invitingly; a waiter was beckoned, and a minute later a similar glass was placed before my mother. This was unprecedented – a drink before the evening.

I became conscious that I was spying on my own mother; but what concerned me most, I suspect, was the possibility that she would see me. I continued to the river, passed a pointless fifteen minutes there, and went back to the corner at which I had been standing. The diversion had taken up half an hour, and there she was, still. The man was evidently a raconteur; at no moment of this holiday had my mother seemed as happy as she did now. There were two empty glasses on the table, and two full.

At another vantage point, obscured by trees, I awaited the end of the conversation. Eventually, indicating his watch in apology, the man stood up. Standing almost toe-to-toe, each thanked the other. The handshake devolved into a loose holding of hands, and then the gallant man, after a shrug, and a hesitation, stooped to put a kiss on my mother's cheek; she smiled, and nodded, as the man said something to her that made her smile. The smile implied gratitude.

They walked off in opposite directions; I expected one of them, at least, to turn, but neither did. I followed my mother at a distance, until she turned out of the street. She glanced at every window, and upward, towards the roofs, to left and right. Everything, it seemed, was newly of interest to her.

Only at the restaurant did she say, as if it had slipped her mind: 'I was talking to a very interesting man this afternoon.' He was an engineer, in aeronautics, a local man, with four children: one a pilot; one a fashion journalist; and twins at university in Paris and Oxford. 'Charming,' she said. 'But not very happy.' She suspected that all was not quite right at home; the drinking was a clue.

After the meal, we rambled around the town again. We watched bats flying around the cathedral. At a shop window she stopped to look at the clothes; but what she was looking at, more, was her own reflection, I could tell. Soon I would be leaving home, and I felt guilty for it, that evening.

We were in the second hour of our game, and Lucas was giving protracted thought to his position, and was thus distracted when Erin, of her own accord, brought in two glasses of her lemonade. Glancing up at her, he said, assuming a voice of deferential gratitude: 'Why, thank you, Héloïse.'

This prompted a flash of displeasure, a demi-second's fierce widening of the eyes and a tightening of the mouth – a glare such as I never saw again, just as the name was never heard again. It was not Erin's middle name, I knew, without being told. It was an endearment, a name for private use, and could only have been an allusion to the famous Héloïse.

What did the allusion signify? Perhaps nothing more than beauty of a kind that one might take to be of a spiritual register. And Erin did, that afternoon, have an aura of the beatific. She wore an oversized white shirt, and the hair was pulled severely back; she had appeared beside us soundlessly, almost; I do not think she spoke; there was something of the handmaid of the lord about her, it could be said.

The name might also have been prompted by the seniority of Lucas. Some have maintained that the real Héloïse was still in her teens when Abelard, then in his late thirties, appeared in her life. This is improbable, given that the real Héloïse was esteemed as a scholar of Greek, Hebrew and Latin before she met Peter Abelard, but it's possible that Lucas knew only the version in which Héloïse was a brilliant and lovely adolescent.

Another factor: the antipathy of the family. Fulbert, uncle and guardian of Héloïse, had done his best to ruin her lover's reputation; his cronies then castrated the man. Would Lucas have known that? Possibly. It's widely known. Abelard, gelded, came to regard his relationship with Héloïse as a sin against God. Héloïse had 'preferred love to wedlock', she once wrote. She wondered: 'What man, bent on sacred or philosophical thoughts, could endure the crying of children?' Would Lucas have known this? Was he aware that Abelard had been a proponent of 'understanding through reason', in opposition to Saint Bernard, for whom faith alone sufficed? Our intentions rather than our actions are what will be judged, Abelard had argued. Did Lucas know that? Perhaps he did. But it's more likely, I thought and think, that the endearment signified nothing more than high-toned devotion, both his and hers, and Lucas's image of himself as a man of a metaphysical cast of mind, with a touch of the medieval spirit, as he imagined it.

☞

'He's an encyclopedia,' said Erin. 'I learn so much from him.' We were in the kitchen, washing up. Lucas had retired to the living room. Having driven back from Yorkshire that day, he needed to rest; the kitchen, in any case, was not his domain. Restful music, selected by Lucas, became audible.

That evening, Lucas had discoursed on the subject of Ulysses S. Grant; he had been reading a biography. 'In the entire history of the United States, has there ever been a more remarkable life?' he wondered. Other candidates were proposed by Lucas, and adjudged less remarkable. The biography would have been one of half a dozen books that Lucas was reading that week. He always had several books in progress simultaneously. 'They could be about anything', Erin told me, in admiration.

The restful music, on the evening of Ulysses S. Grant, was a mass by Josquin des Prez, or perhaps Dufay, or Ockeghem. I'm not sure. A bit of Franco-Flemish polyphony was often his way of unwinding at the end of a long or stressful day. It was, in Erin's terms, one of the many things that Lucas knew about. It could be said, however, that his knowledge was not really knowledge of the music. He had his favourite recordings, and what he liked was the sound that the music made. It was a sound that befitted the calling of Lucas. Which is not to say that the pleasure he took in it was not sincere.

It also signified his affiliation with Callum and Kathleen; a trio of elevated spirits. In this respect, though, the affinity with Callum was stronger: whereas Kathleen had always worked in silence (one would never hear music in a Japanese workshop, she had told me; nothing should interfere with the artist's attention), Callum had needed the constant presence of music – this music in particular. One of the first CDs he had ever bought was a recording of Josquin's *L'homme armé* masses; the Agnus Dei of the later mass, he had once told Lucas, was 'the music of eternity'. Lucas was inclined to agree. He often selected it.

One evening – not the evening of the Grant book – I had something to say about the structure from which those wonderful sounds proceeded: the theme of the Agnus Dei was being sung simultaneously both forwards and in retrograde, I explained. Lucas had not known this; he listened again, but could not distinguish the backwards-running line of the music, he admitted. Neither could Erin. One did not need to be able to understand the construction in order to be moved by the music, just as one did not have to be a builder to appreciate the splendour of Chartres cathedral, Lucas proposed; this comparison settled the question for them both. Erin could enjoy this sort of music, but the occasional small dose was enough. For her, she confessed, it was hard to tell the difference between one old mass and another. It was amazing, all those voices singing together, so exactly, so sweetly; she could hear how complicated it was. But before long it all began to wash over her; she needed more variety. The voices became like a perfectly blue sky, she said – 'after a while, you crave a cloud.'

I was tempted to ask Lucas if we might anticipate some clouds in the life to come. Instead, sympathising with Erin, I said something about how, for a long time, I had been unable to imagine the Christian heaven, the choirs of the blessed singing praise to the Creator every waking hour – and in heaven, after all, every hour would be a waking hour. Reading Dante had corrected my imagination – *E'n la sua volontade è nostra pace*, et cetera. I recited that line; I encouraged her to at least look at Dante, knowing that Lucas had not read him. Perhaps I had a notion that she might begin to see that ideas such as those in which Lucas professed to believe belonged to the medieval world. It is certain that I talked too much.

Said Lucas, when I was finished: 'The thing is, Josh doesn't believe in God. He only believes in Dante and Josquin des Prez.'

To which I had to reply: 'Touché.'

☞

The car was a disgrace, Erin complained one evening, after Lucas had brought it back from the garage, where yet more repairs had been carried out. 'It is,' Lucas answered; for him, disgrace of this kind was an achievement.

Erin was not in the mood to indulge him. 'Either it goes or I go,' she said, as if there were no audience. Had the scene been filmed, and ended with these words, the ultimatum might have seemed a serious one. The exasperation was genuine. The car was ten years older than any other car on the street, she protested.

'Indeed,' said Lucas, exaggerating the pride.

'And looks older.'

'Has Baba Yaga been at you again?' Lucas asked – Baba Yaga being the woman at number 7, whose huge Mercedes gave the on-street parking a tone that was severely compromised by Lucas's vehicle. Lucas himself, and his child bride, lowered the tone of the street. Whenever the woman smiled at her, said Erin, it was like the smile of someone being polite, but not quite polite enough, to a host whose food was making her feel ill.

Baba Yaga had nothing to do with it, Erin answered.

Lucas embarked on a solo on the topic of Baba Yaga's husband, whose advice on the cleaning and polishing of one's vehicle he might seek, he told us. On alternate weekends the husband of Baba Yaga could be observed at work on the mighty Mercedes. The procedure required an arsenal of specialised products. Employing one of a number of colour-coded cloths, he would rub away imperfections that nobody else could see. The routine was more than thorough – it was indicative of some deep disturbance of the psyche. In cleaning the car to excess, he was trying to rid himself of something that pained him, Lucas proposed. It is possible that this analysis was correct: one day the Mercedes was missing; the maniacal cleaner was no longer living at number 7, and nobody knew what had brought about his expulsion or flight, not even Lucas.

'It needs more than a polish,' Erin told him. 'It needs to be a different car.'

A new car would send the wrong message, Lucas argued. It would advertise success of the vulgar kind, like those American TV preachers who live in houses that should have film stars living in them.

'I'm not talking about a new car,' Erin snapped. 'I'm just talking about something that doesn't look as if it's waiting to be towed away.'

'I'll think about it,' said Lucas, meaning that he would not. Erin left the room.

This disagreement would have been a few weeks before the kiss.

Within two months of Lucas's death, the old car was replaced with something almost new, on the advice of Chloe, the sister, who knows about cars, it seems.

☞

Before the disagreement about the car – perhaps a month before – there was the afternoon on which Lucas and I walked down to the sea, when Erin was away for a couple of days, visiting Chloe. I was at my desk, and Lucas came out into the garden, took up a position in the middle of the lawn, and then, having gained my attention, made his fingers walk up and down the palm of an open hand, while looking at me questioningly.

'She's with the sister,' said Lucas, right at the start. He made the noun sound like the title of a troublesome person who had some authority over him – notionally, at least. The tone was one I had not heard before. Suddenly I was a confidant, it seemed. He smiled and raised an eyebrow. Something was happening, he implied, that might not be in his best interests; but he was amused by it, as one might be amused by a conspiracy concocted by children, a conspiracy that had been obvious to everyone from the outset. This is what the smile told me, and the debonair flourish of the walking stick.

The sister had a new and superior job, Lucas informed me. 'More money. Bigger office. More underlings. Better view,' he said, listing the achievements weightily, as they warranted. In the past week the sister had posted about a hundred pictures of the London panorama that came with the new office, Lucas reckoned. Had there, he wondered, been a single unrecorded hour of Chloe's waking life in recent years? Erin's 'ridiculous' phone had been bought chiefly, it seemed, to keep track of the sister's 'pathological snapping'.

'She has a compulsion to share every single thing she likes, or "Likes",' he went on. The sarcasm was extravagant. Chloe seemed to like almost everything that passed in front of her. 'Meaningless. Utterly meaningless,' said Lucas. 'Friend' was another word that didn't mean anything any more, he informed me, gathering momentum. 'You gather friends you have never met and will never meet, and about whom you know nothing except that they like you in the same way you like them, and you like each other because you both agreed with something inane that was thrown out into the world by someone else, who is now a friend of both but unknown to either of you. And you tell everyone about all the friends you have and all the things you like, and so you enlarge yourself, and on and on it goes, gathering more stuff and sending it back out, and there is never any end to it.' The narcissism of it all was appalling, Lucas moaned. Never pausing for thought, people passed judgement instantly. With each 'Like' they advertised who they took themselves to be, not understanding that they were in fact becoming nothing. The self, said Lucas, was turning into something like a bloom of algae, getting bigger every day, but with no shape at all, no centre, no real life.

It was a long walk. We had reached the seafront, where a couple of teenagers were sitting on a wall, staring into their phones, as if to give Lucas his opportunity. Each took a picture of the sea, and compared the results. Each took a picture of the other. They kissed, and took a picture of themselves kissing. Then, it seemed, there were messages that demanded attention.

Life is becoming a whirlpool of perpetual distraction, said Lucas, gesturing at the examples who had been set before him. We are surrounded by people who need to ensure that every moment of the day has some form of activity. But all this activity is in truth the opposite of activity – it is a dreadful passivity. 'This is what you have to understand,' he said, though I was not inclined to disagree. He said it urgently, raising his voice, which made the couple turn to look at him. Seeing nothing of interest, they gave a glance to the sea, where nothing of interest was happening either, then turned back to the phones.

'You know where those things are made?' he said. He stopped, so that the couple might overhear what he had to say about factories in China in which tens of thousands of people slave day and night, and every week someone is driven to such a pitch of exhaustion and despair that they jump off the roof. These factories are every bit as bad as the factories of Victorian England, but with a crucial difference: the workers who are suffering for our benefit nowadays are safely out of sight, so we can continue to amuse ourselves untroubled by our consciences. Satisfied that he had been heard, Lucas moved on, to further expound on the perniciousness of these devices. We no longer need to pay attention to the world, because these gadgets – our 'exo-memories' – will remember everything on our behalf. Or rather, record everything, which is not the same thing. The world is being reduced to a pocketful of digital data. It just becomes 'stuff' to possess, along with all the music we can pour into our ears whenever we feel like it. People seem to think that by accumulating all this stuff, by never taking a break from it, they are in some way getting 'more life', he preached. Plenitude is being confused with fulfilment, he instructed me, as two women jogged past us, barely lifting their feet. This was another cue, for the cult of fitness, the obsession with 'activity' and 'well-being', et cetera, et cetera.

On and on he went. We are living in an age of 'hysterical positivity', he stated. It's no longer enough for a company to do or make something – it has to tell the public that it has a 'passion' for it. Only last week, he'd seen a van emblazoned with the words: 'We have a passion for paper.' Could anything be more ridiculous? Another thing that was ridiculous – the assumption, evident every time you open a newspaper or turn on the television – that we all 'love' the same programmes, the same films, the same actors, the same singers. We are in danger of becoming the unresistant consumers of everything, warned Lucas. If one takes a stand against this tide of relentless positivity one is accused of saying 'No' to life.

Some people, he knew, regarded him as a curmudgeon. He was nothing of the sort, but he was quite content to be misperceived, even to be disliked, because dislike is a form of resistance, and thus a good thing. We must not become people who are unable to resist any stimulus. 'Our survival depends upon refusal,' he said, sweeping his stick from side to side, as if clearing a path through undergrowth.

We demonstrated our refusal by coming to a halt, to admire the strange pallor of the sea that afternoon. Then his phone rang. 'This is all you need,' he said, displaying the superannuated device – the thing that was no better than a walkie-talkie, as Erin had said, charmed by Lucas's recalcitrance. It was Erin calling. 'I'm with Joshua,' he told her. 'We're having an interesting talk,' I heard, before he removed himself to a distance of twenty yards, for a lengthy conversation.

On we sauntered, in silence at last, setting an example to all, walking slowly and looking around, taking no pictures.

☞

On the morning of the day that followed my mother's death, Lucas and Erin came to the house, having seen the ambulance. 'How is she?' Erin asked; Lucas, knowing the answer before I spoke, looked at me over her shoulder, steadily. His handshake was only in part a contract of sympathy; it marked my induction into the community of the bereaved, a community that was his domain. As soon as the door was closed, Erin, saying nothing, crying silently, held me; I closed my arms around her, as if taking comfort. Lucas, at a yard's remove from us, waited. When I opened my eyes he was looking at me still; he was assessing what species of grief this would be, and what might need to be done.

There had been no farewell, I told them. By the time I arrived, she had gone. I could not recall the substance of what proved to be the last conversation with my mother. She had not been especially unwell; and then she was dead.

Lucas and Erin spent more than an hour with me, sitting apart, but united in purpose; like compassionate missionaries rather than lovers.

A few days later, after a meal cooked by Erin, during which I had been scrutinised by Lucas less discreetly than he might have intended, he said to me, as I left: 'You are fine, aren't you?' He never offered his services in connection with my mother, and hardly ever spoke of her. In this respect, his conduct was unimpeachable.

Every night, however, for many months, on turning out the light for the night, I would see my mother, the body that had been by mother, in the hospital. I was looking again at the corpse. Suddenly she was no longer in the world; her life was now entirely in the past, and only this thing of flesh remained in the present, for a short time longer. I looked into the pit into which she had fallen, into which I would one day fall. There was no mingling of spirits; there was no spirit at all.

☞

One Sunday, there were fresh flowers on the grave; left by Lucas, I later learned. Certain 'observances' were right and proper, he told me, and I thanked him, while wondering why flowers should be placed on a grave by a man who believed what Lucas professed to believe.

☞

Clearing the table with me, at the end of an evening, Lucas said quietly, with no preamble: 'You were a good son, you know.' I had indeed been thinking, at that moment, of my mother. Then he added, with a dash of eye contact: 'Everything is fine.' I was to understand that he had picked up a signal. He wanted me to know that he knew she was happy. But everything was not fine: she was utterly dead, not happy.

Affronted, I answered: 'Glad to hear it.'

Yet I had to admire him, a little. Even with me, he could not suspend the performance. He had to impart the good news, though I could not be converted. People are so rarely persuaded, Lucas would say. We change our minds not because someone convinces us that we have been in error, but because experience obliges us to change.

Across the table he gave me a smile, a smile that offered some sort of apology, and accepted my resistance, and wanted me to understand that I would one day know what he knew – that all would be well.

☞

Novelist and actress Florence Marryat, in *There is No Death*, a book of which it has been said that it 'has done more to convince many people of the truth of Spiritualism than any yet written', wrote of the medium Bessie Fitzgerald: 'Of course, I am aware that it would be so easy for a Medium simply to close her eyes, and, professing to be entranced, talk a lot of commonplaces, which open-mouthed fools might accept as a new gospel, that it becomes imperative to test this class of media strictly by what they utter, and to place no faith in them, until you are convinced that the matters they speak of cannot possibly have been known to any one except the friend whose mouthpiece they profess to be. All this I fully proved for myself from repeated trials and researches; but the unfortunate part of it is, that the more forcible and convincing the private proof, the more difficult it is to place it before the public. I must content myself, therefore, with saying that some of my dead friends (so called) came back to me so frequently through Bessie Fitzgerald, and familiarized themselves so completely with my present life, that I forgot sometimes that they had left this world, and flew to them (or rather to Bessie) to seek their advice or ask their sympathy as naturally as if she were their earthly form.'

There was a further dimension to the genius of Bessie Fitzgerald. 'She was a wonderful medical diagnoser, and sat for a long time in the service of a well-known medical man. She would be ensconced in a corner of his waiting room and tell him the exact disease of each patient that entered. She told me she could see the inside of everybody as perfectly as though they were made of glass.' Bessie's paranormal examinations took their toll, however. Her gift 'induced her to take on a reflection (as it were) of the disease she diagnosed, and after a while her failing strength compelled her to give it up.'

☞

For a surprisingly modest payment, an investigator traced my father – or rather, found out that my father was no longer alive. He had died, it turned out, a year before my mother, in Castlebar, County Mayo, leaving a widow, Aoife, née Feerick, who had previously been married to one Jack Jennings, proprietor of a Castlebar pub, which Aoife had continued to run, latterly in partnership with her second husband. My father was sixty-three when he married Aoife; she was fifty-six, with two children in their thirties. I can see the pub online, and the streets of the town in which my father lived. It is unimaginable for me; alcohol is absent from my memory of him; no photograph shows him drinking. My investigator did a good job. Now I know even the location of the grave; on my laptop I can follow the route from the centre of town, out along Newport Road, then left; about a mile from the pub to the cemetery gates.

Lucas, on being told what had been discovered, nodded his head at every item of information, as though everything confirmed what he had thought.

☞

When Lucas first talked to me, when I was a child, I saw no resemblance between him and my father. For a long time, I was conscious of no similarity in appearance or character. My father's character was almost unknown to me, it must be said. But then, one evening when I was back from university, I looked at a photograph of my father – taken in Poole, before I was born, on an occasion that my mother could no longer remember, or so she said – and for the first time a small resemblance became apparent: some similarity of posture; something around the eyes – a certain inflection of a sideward glance. The resemblance, such as it is, is not attached to the father whom I remember, who is a figure of no solidity. Rather, the later Lucas, the heavier Lucas, is not unlike my father in this single photograph.

☞

Near the bench of conversation my mother and I once had our picture taken by a man who introduced himself as a professional photographer. For the past few years he had been putting together a collection of images of mothers and sons, he told us. Once a month he would visit a town he had not previously visited, and roam the streets for an hour or two, on the lookout for subjects. By now he had taken hundreds of double portraits; the youngest son so far was only one week old; the oldest was in his seventies. On the day that the photographer spotted my mother and me, I was eleven, Lucas informed me. It seems that I was immediately as impressed by the photographer as he was by us. He was about forty, thin and unusually tall, with black horn-rimmed glasses and soft dark hair that stuck out strangely, as if full of static. He wore a long red scarf wound around his neck, and his companion, a Jack Russell terrier, was tethered by a lead of exactly the same colour. Seeing us walking hand in hand, the man had crossed the road and approached us, smiling with such openness that my mother wondered for a moment if he was someone she should be recognising. The Jack Russell and I established an immediate rapport, and it was then that Lucas passed by, with Kathleen. For the photograph, I knelt on the ground, leaning against my mother's legs, patting the dog.

Lucas first described the scene to me not long after my mother died. The narration came with a plenitude of detail – the weather; the heavy old camera; the coat I was wearing that day; where Lucas and Kathleen had been going. Something began to form in my mind – an imprecise recollection of a tall man and a red scarf, perhaps. On another day, prompted by the sight of a Jack Russell, Lucas again recounted the episode, with other incidentals. This time, I think, I saw more in my memory. There were other occasions in which reference was made to the photographer and the dog with the red lead. At the table, sitting opposite me, he told Erin about the photographer who had been beguiled by the eleven-year-old Joshua and his mother; he made an affecting vignette of it. Now, hearing the story for the fifth or sixth time, I had a glimpse of a man holding a box-shaped camera, standing over me, with a scarf like a huge red collar, which might indeed have been the residue of a scene in which I had played a part as a child.

No picture in my mother's albums corresponds to this scene.

☞

From the garden of their house I could be seen at my desk, hour after hour, day after day. One could draw a line from the centre of the lawn to where I sat, and nothing would impede it. So Erin would have known that she could be seen. She would never sunbathe in the garden when Lucas was at home, as I recall; something could be made of this fact, perhaps. But this is not to say that there was any flirtatious intent. Erin was direct in everything; this was one of her many qualities. Her body was admirable and she was content for it to be admired, as a beautiful dress might be admired. There was no vanity with Erin, no coyness, no affectation. She was not disingenuous. It was a fact that she inhabited a well-made body. One could imagine an artist's model, a professional, regarding herself in the same way.

And it would be dishonest to say that I did not take pleasure from the sight of that body. She would fall asleep in the sunlight and I would look. A woman would have looked as I did. The body of Erin was beautiful. Occupied by any spirit, or soul, or mind, or person, it would have been beautiful. When I looked at that sleeping body, however, I did not see what I loved in Erin, and what I desired. I would be weakened not by the sight of Erin barely clothed, but – for example – when, having dressed, she came back out into the garden to water the plants, methodically, as if in observance of some ritual. The precision and slowness captivated me; the manner with which she executed the task put me in mind of the fastidiousness of Kathleen. It was not possible to imagine either of them hurrying. There was a gesture that Erin often employed when talking – she would turn her hand backwards sharply at the wrist, and swivel it, as if presenting an object for our scrutiny at various angles. Some aspect of Erin was summarised in this gesture; it charmed me, as did the little prance with which she would sometimes step over the threshold to go into the garden.

Fascination rather than charm would be the word for the effect of the veiled look that often came into Erin's eyes – not quite a look of preoccupation, but a slight clouding, produced, I tended to assume, by thoughts of her brother, but not always. She was often not wholly with us. On the other hand, I observed a converse quality: following her, occasionally, I would observe the way she looked at what surrounded her – her entire bearing seemed to signify pleasure, even delight. Another thing that I found alluring: she never gossiped; Lucas would occasionally offer up a rumour that he had heard, but Erin would not join in. She did not squander words; the silence of Erin was a receptive silence, a silence of self-composure. The tone of her laugh was lovely – another banality for this account, but it should be recorded. With the word 'laugh' a scene comes to mind: 'I can spot you a mile spot you a mile off. The white shirt – it's your summer plumage,' she told me, tapping my shoulder; and now I hear that small light sound.

More virtues could be listed; many more. The gentleness, of course; the innocence – an innocence that was implicated, however, in her enthralment to Lucas. The list would not account for the reality of Erin. Her aura would not be explained or depicted. What I loved was Erin, not the qualities of Erin. One does not love a person's qualities.

☞

After the funeral, more than one woman came up to me and said: 'So you are Joshua.' This was unexpected; the meaning was never entirely clear, but some second-hand affection seemed to be involved. A delicate and pretty widow – perhaps sixty-five, with an elegant grey chignon and eyes in which desperation lurked – was one of them; there was a preponderance of widows. This one had been widowed for a year when she called for Lucas, but it was the loss of her mother rather than of the husband that had prompted the call. Clearing out her mother's house, she had experienced some eerie moments, which had made her wonder, and Lucas had been able to set her mind at rest, in ways that were not specified. She told me her name and where she lived, and seemed pleased – but not wholly pleased – to learn that her name, an unusual one, was unfamiliar to me. 'Lucas respected the confidentiality of his clients,' I assured her. The conclusion was unavoidable: this had been another liaison. From what she told me, I worked out that she would have known Lucas at around the time that Erin moved in.

☞

Lucas was consulted by a man whose jealousy, he confessed, had almost destroyed his marriage. His wife, who had died abruptly the previous year, aged only sixty, had been an extremely attractive woman, the widower, seventy-two, told Lucas. Photographs were produced as evidence. Though the client did not say so, it had to be assumed that photos did not do justice to his wife. Even in the wedding photographs, taken in her twenties, this was not a face to make a man look twice, Lucas reported. The figure was likewise in no way remarkable. 'Something of the cylinder about her,' said Lucas. Yet men had found her powerfully attractive, the man insisted, and her attractiveness had been a torment to him. She worked in a library, and thus was on constant display to the public; her husband imagined a procession of admirers.

Sometimes, if she happened to be working on a day when he was not, he would find an excuse to drop by. She accused him of spying on her. On holiday one year, he had awoken to find that his wife was not in the room; he found a note, telling him that she had gone for a swim and would see him at nine, in the breakfast room. He had imagined the worst, and accused her. The following year, she left him. Three years later, she returned. Then he wanted to know everything about the affairs he was convinced had occurred in the interim. There had been only one relationship of even the slightest significance, she insisted. She told him about it as soon as he asked. He interrogated her: he needed to know everything, so she told him everything, and it was too much for him. He had learned, however, that he would lose her if he did not change his ways, and so, finally accepting that there was nothing else to be confessed, he kept quiet. When she took a new job, he refrained from surveillance. He could not say, however, that the torment had ceased; neither could it be said that he had ever entirely believed that his wife had told him absolutely everything about what had happened in the three years of separation. He had never learned to trust her, he told Lucas, and now it was too late. The man wept. Now this man needed to know if his wife was thinking of him, and had forgiven him.

'Your wife loves you,' Lucas could tell him. What the man wanted to ask, but could not, Lucas knew, was: 'And only me?'

Jealousy was unbecoming in an adult, said Lucas, but it was a purgatory through which every young person had to pass. It would be absurd, he said, for him to feel jealousy because there were many young men – and not so young men – who liked the look of Erin. On what grounds could he object to their seeing and admiring in

Erin qualities that he himself saw and admired? Love and jealousy are mutually exclusive, he said. I think I took this as a dismissal; I was not considered to be a rival.

But once, having left an unsatisfactory job, Erin went away for two weeks, to Greece, with the sister. They were 'doing a bit of island-hopping', Lucas told me. He would have liked to accompany her, but his schedule was full for the next couple of months, so Erin had gone with Chloe. 'She needs a break,' said Lucas, in the manner of a benign employer. A few days before her return, visiting Lucas for a game, I noticed a postcard on the kitchen table: small whitewashed domes, violently blue sea, et cetera. Left alone for a minute – I admit this – I turned the card over, quickly. The word 'wonderful' stood out, and this: 'still dancing when the sun came up'. The handwriting was regular and effortful, like the writing of someone rather younger than Erin; it lacked character; it lacked maturity – this is what I tried to think, to negate the jealousy. When Lucas came back, his gaze turned immediately to the card, as if it were an item that had appeared in his absence. He picked it up and put it on the mantelpiece, upright, with the picture outward. For a second or two, in his eyes, there was a suggestion of suffering.

☞

'Oh, the old girls all love him,' said Erin. 'And why would they not?' she said, giving Lucas a sidelong look, and smiling slightly, with something like indulgence.

☞

Four or five weeks after my mother's death, Erin visited me, alone, but as the emissary of the household. She brought

Lucas's sympathy, and an invitation. As yet, no reference had been made to my mother's coolness towards her; there was no need to remark on the fact that the climate of the house had changed. A different air now encompassed us.

I was invited to eat with them when Lucas came back. He was leaving that afternoon, on a tour that would take him to clients in Nottingham, Rotherham, Halifax and Ripon. At the last name, I made a sound signifying familiarity and amusement, and soon I was talking about Lia Seidel, my tutor for a term, who had led a visit to Fountains abbey and Rievaulx. Rievaulx, I told Erin, had been 'one of the great days of my life'. More: I had been 'hopelessly in love' with Lia Seidel. This was not true.

I talked at length about the brilliant Lia Seidel, her eloquence in three languages, the 'seductive creak' in her voice, the sense she gave of having a brain that 'never idled', and the severity of her beauty, a beauty that, as I was speaking, seemed to have had something in common with Erin's – aspects of the profile, perhaps; certainly the colouring of hair and complexion; and the posture, a little. Lia, at the time I knew her, would have been not much older than Erin now. What I had liked most about her, I seemed to realise, in the moment of telling Erin, was that she took no prisoners; she had the appearance of a princess's handmaiden in a kitschy nineteenth-century painting, but her temperament was combative and relentless. So this contrast was a factor too, I decided. The incident by which Lia Seidel had smitten me was a lecture given by a modish young professor, American by birth and residence, but French by intellectual incli-nation. His appearance at our second-tier university was something of an event for us, he evidently believed. In a low drawl, I imitated the suavely provocative style of the glamorous young professor. 'History does not describe reality,' he informed his audience. 'No. Our discourse creates the objects which it purports to study.' At the end of the lecture, I had asked a question, and been crushed. He repeated the simple lesson that I had failed to comprehend: 'A fact has only a linguistic existence.'

Sitting in the row in front of me, Lia Seidel raised a hand and gave it a flourish, as if summoning a waiter. She wanted to be absolutely sure that she had not misconstrued. Was it the case that he was maintaining that the historical record in itself gives us no reason to prefer any one version of its meaning? Was that correct? With evangelical finality, the self-infatuated young professor said it again: 'There is no reason.' Lia nodded, apparently satisfied with this answer. Then, with exquisite timing, as the man was about to take a question from an apparently starstruck undergrad, Lia sighed: 'But that is nonsense.' A thousand survivors of a battle will have a thousand different accounts of what took place; there will be a multiplicity of versions; the relationship between those versions and the realities of the event will be problematical; but each survivor is a fact, as each dead man is a fact. The real might be elusive, but it exists, and it was merely an affectation to maintain otherwise, Lia told our guest. He smirked at her simplicity. Then the argument became heated.

At Rievaulx I had sheltered from a downpour beside Lia Seidel. She had written her PhD thesis on the abbey, on the place of the community of monks within the society of twelfth-century Yorkshire. I could – and still can – picture her face as she gazed over the ruins, as though seeing the whole place reconstituted and inhabited again. For fifteen minutes I had been blessed with the entire attention of Lia Seidel. I could remember some of the things she had said – that we should think of the great medieval cathedrals and churches as 'mass factories', rather than as Bibles in stone. If you look closely, said Lia, you'll find some decidedly un-Biblical things lurking in the stonework. Somewhere – I forgot where – she had seen a carving that was a parody of the Virgin birth, with a dog in place of the baby Jesus. A pregnant woman, seeing something monstrous, or even merely thinking of it, might give birth to a monster, it had been believed, I told Erin.

On and on I talked. The garrulousness was an effect of bereavement, it would have seemed, I hoped.

☞

Some time shortly before the kiss, with Lucas away on a week-long peregrination, I worked at my desk for at least an hour against the distraction of Erin in the garden. She had been reading, then dozing, in the full blare of the sunlight, and now she had returned to her book. She turned a single page, then went back to where she had been; she closed it, keeping her place with a finger, and frowned, and read the page again. She went into the house, and emerged a few minutes later, holding a jug of some deep red drink. At no point, since coming out with the deckchair, had she so much as glanced at my window. Now she looked up, straight at me, and held up the jug in a mime of invitation.

The book had been assigned by Lucas; a project to keep her occupied in her leisure hours while he was away. Poetry with a 'spiritual dimension'. Lucas had thought she might 'get something out of it', she told me; she was not finding it easy, she admitted; then again, 'perhaps that's the point'. She lifted the book and recited: ' ... where from secret springs / The source of human thought its tribute brings / Of waters, – with a sound but half its own'. She presented the book to me, open, indicating the lines in question. 'Do you know what that means?' she asked. 'Why "half"? If it's only half its own, who has the other half?'

I gave the poem some scrutiny, while Erin poured the drinks – an experimental fruit-juice mix. To make sense of the lines, I would have to read the rest, I answered.

'Be my guest,' said Erin, and so I settled on the lawn to read. She sat back in the deckchair; the exquisite feet were exhibited within touching distance. With eyes closed, she smiled into the sunlight. Concentrating less than was required, I proceeded through the lines. 'Well?' she enquired; her voice had the intimacy of a voice on the brink of sleep.

I made some remarks, none of any incisiveness.

'Yes,' said Erin. 'That's what I thought. More or less.' Then she opened her eyes and swivelled in the deckchair, to face me; she took back the book, and there was a touch of fingers, a touch like a spike. We talked about the poem and others in the book, which Lucas had encouraged her to read. She couldn't say that she had enjoyed everything. Some of it had bored her, and she'd often not known exactly what was being said, but she'd enjoyed the confusion, some of the time. Confusion was not necessarily a bad thing, Lucas had impressed upon her; one can understand a poem in a way that is more than rational; putting the words of poetry into other words is a futile endeavour, he had instructed.

We exchanged words that had something to do with this notion. Erin had an image that was hers rather than Lucas's: when reading this book, she had often felt like a woman wandering around an unfamiliar town at night – nothing was perfectly clear, but she soon came to have a sense of where things were, and of the atmosphere of the place, an atmosphere that was like nowhere else.

I joined her in the image of the town, and as we were refining it a disturbance in the tree of the neighbour's house made us look up. A collared dove was flustering there. The pink-brown of its plumage was the loveliest of all colours, Erin said. It was like a cloud in a perfect sunset.

I knew some things about this bird, having worked on a naturalist's memoir the previous year. In just twenty years the range of the collared dove had expanded more than a thousand miles westward from Turkey and the Balkans; no other European species had ever spread with such speed; not until the mid-1950s had it bred in Britain, and now it was common. During the Second World War it had followed the path of the German tank battalions – this is what I was telling her when her phone rang. The interruption was from Steven Greenwood: suddenly short-staffed, he needed Erin to work that evening. Talking to him, annoyed, or apparently annoyed, she raked her hair with her fingers. The boss had other things to discuss, it seemed.

'Back to work,' I mouthed to Erin, and she rolled her eyes and smiled; the smile had a tone that seemed new.

☞

Erin could be seen sometimes in the garden, paused, kneeling at a flowerbed, gazing without focus. More than once I saw her at the window, in the kitchen, looking out at nothing, with the expression of a woman whose convalescence seemed to have become perpetual.

On a Sunday afternoon, after a game, Lucas held forth on the subject of boredom. We sat in the living room; Erin was busy about the house. There had been some evidence of tension on my arrival.

The beneficial effects of boredom were underestimated, Lucas informed me. Boredom was a powerful solvent: even in moderation, it could be effective in dissolving the 'detritus of thought' with which the mind is often clogged; in a stronger dose, it could dissolve much more – the self itself can be reduced to almost nothing by boredom, for a while, and the mind, thereby unobstructed, can become receptive to impressions and ideas to which it has previously been resistant.

Lucas had no appointments, for once. Most of his clients wanted to see him on a Sunday, he told me. This was to be expected: they had more time on a Sunday, and the Sabbath was 'conducive to thoughts of the eternal'. He thought it a shame that the Sabbath was now so widely disregarded. A day of compulsory abstention from work, a day of inactivity and thought, was necessary for the health of the individual and of the community. 'There is not enough boredom in the world,' he said.

Boredom sometimes was nothing but boredom, I countered; it was not always a balm. I was often overcome by a boredom that was only deadening. This was why, I revealed, I had considered removing myself to a town in the depths of France or Spain or Italy, a town with which I had no connection. It would not be picturesque; it would be a place of no immediate charm; only with effort would any attachment be formed, and the attachment could never be strong. Every day I would be learning; I would have to pay attention to everything; I would be freed from habit. I said something about Kathleen's experience of Japan – the exhilarating strangeness of it.

'But Kathleen lasted barely a year in Japan,' said Lucas. 'She was not happy there.'

Now that Kathleen was dead, Lucas was the custodian of her life; if Lucas said that Kathleen had been unhappy, she must have been unhappy. But I could hear her, talking about her time in Japan; I could see her – and still can. 'It was wonderful – I was such a foreigner,' she had said to me, holding out her hands, cupped around an invisible object that made her arms tremble with its energy. Loneliness had been the source of Kathleen's unhappiness, he told me. 'She had uprooted herself,' he said. Yes, she had learned a great deal there; for her art, that year had been of inestimable value; but for herself, it had been difficult. 'She found that she belonged precisely here,' said Lucas. Living in this ordinary little town suited her very well. Life made few demands on her. Its dullness, as some would call it, was nourishing. It allowed her to be free. 'Boredom is the dream-bird that hatches the egg of experience,' he proclaimed, at volume, perhaps for Erin to overhear.

Two months before the kiss, another visit from Erin, authorised by Lucas. We went from room to room, discussing what might be done with the decor. In the doorway of the room that had been my mother's, Erin peered in, as if there were a rope across the threshold. 'You're not going to keep it like this?' she asked; it seemed she thought that I might. She would give me a hand whenever I decided to brighten it up, she told me. A few months earlier, she had helped her sister to give her flat an overhaul.

In my room she scanned the bookshelves, pausing once or twice to look more closely at a title, as one would pause at a family photograph. She picked up the postcard of the smiling head in the York chapter house. 'Who's this?' she asked. I talked too much, again. For centuries only devils were shown laughing or smiling in Western art, I told her; then, around 1200, smiles had appeared on the faces of angels and the blessed. Christ had never smiled or laughed, the church fathers had taught; laughter was indicative of a 'false conscience'. Erin laughed, and looked out at the garden of the house in which she lived with Lucas.

She inspected the row of cards stuck to the wall beside the window: stonework from Chartres, Autun, Moissac, Rouen, Reims, et cetera. 'Why do you like these so much?' she asked. The answer would be of interest to her, it seemed, but I answered too fully. To these artists, I explained, the essence of a person was not something that could be captured by replicating the features of the face. They represented the ideal, not the anecdotal.

Erin considered the face of Jeremiah. 'You know about the heads that Callum made?' she asked. I did not know; she seemed pleased to have an opportunity to educate me.

In Callum's workshop, when Lucas had first been allowed to visit it, photos of half a dozen small stone heads had been pinned to a wall. They looked like museum pieces, but in fact each one was an original, created by Callum, carved in the style of a very specific place, at a very specific time. As Lucas put it, said Erin, it was as though Callum had attuned himself to the spirit of each locality, and expressed that spirit perfectly. They were heads of saints or kings, Erin thought. She was not sure of the dates or localities, but it was something like Paris, a thousand years ago, and somewhere else in France a hundred years after that, and somewhere else some time after that. They were all medieval, definitely. To the untrained eye the heads were very similar, Lucas had said, but you could see the differences when Callum pointed them out. The way the beards were carved was crucial, as Erin recalled.

The heads had been stolen. 'The thief must have thought they were old,' said Erin, now looking out of the window again. She stayed at the window for a while, as if looking at a place where she had lived many years ago. Then she asked: 'Why didn't you stick with teaching?'

'Because it turned out I was a terrible teacher,' I replied.

'How so?' she asked, still not facing me.

'No patience,' I said. 'No authority.'

Erin now turned. With a look of doubt, she said: 'Really?' She smiled, and at that moment a complication of our relationship became imminent, which is why, suddenly, she said she should be going.

☞

A week or so before the kiss, walking past one of the South Street cafés, I saw Erin sitting at a table outside, with the ultra-blonde Polish waitress from Greenwood's restaurant. The conversation seemed to be confidential and intense; their hands were touching. I was on the opposite side of the road, and passed by unnoticed. When I returned, they were still talking – or rather, Erin was still listening. It was obvious that Erin had given whatever advice she could, and was no longer wholly engaged. When she saw me, she smiled. As before, I was on the pavement opposite. I was ready to be invited to cross. But the friend, though she had noticed the smile, could not be interrupted; the point she was making had to be elaborated, with urgency. It was not possible to bring another person into the conversation. So I raised a hand, discreetly, showing that I would not approach. At this point the friend looked down, to rummage for something in her bag, and Erin glanced in my direction, and produced an unusual gesture: first she touched a fingertip to her face, just below the outside edge of an eye; then she pointed the same finger in my direction;

and then, with a grin, she cocked an eyebrow. It was as if she were reminding me of some agreement that we had made, but I did not know what she meant.

☞

Act 2, Scene 2 of *Parsifal*. Kundry – having related to Parsifal the story of his mother's languishing and death, for which Parsifal now blames himself – kisses the remorseful young man, thereby, as she says, bestowing his mother's love upon him: *als Muttersegens letzten Gruss / der Liebe – ersten Kuss!* ('as the last token of a mother's blessing / the first kiss of love'). Parsifal, the pure fool, does not react well. '*Die Wunde!*' he cries, '*Die Wunde!*' – 'The wound! The wound!' Suddenly he is experiencing the agony of Amfortas, king of the knights of the Grail, who is in constant pain from a wound that will not heal. Though the injury was inflicted by a spear (the Lance of Longinus, the Holy Spear itself, no less), the kiss of Kundry enables Parsifal, in his spasm of empathetic suffering, to understand the true source of the king's torment: it is a spiritual anguish, an unbearable guilt caused by the sin that the seductive Kundry led him to commit. It's all the woman's fault, as usual. Kundry is the vehicle of temptation, the agent of corruption.

The kiss with Erin, it occurred to me, some time afterwards, was like the kiss in Parsifal, albeit with the roles reversed; and less ridiculous. The similarity was in the abruptness of what happened.

Lucas was away. I had told her that I was going to watch a film that evening. We watched it together. There was no wine; none of the accessories of seduction; no seduction was intended. The kiss arose from the evening, and was initiated by both of us, in the same instant; we had come to the moment in which it was necessary. I put a palm to her cheek, she put a palm to mine, and we kissed; the kiss went on. It cannot be described; it said everything that had not been said. But then it was as though she had been struck by fear, by panic, in the depths of it. Almost breathless, she fell back. Her eyes were not seeing me. 'I can't', she said, to herself more than to me, dazed. A pause, then she said it again, quietly: 'I can't.' This time the words were spoken with disappointment and a muted kind of wonderment, as though she had unaccountably failed at something for which she had thought herself prepared. The third time, the tone was one of apology. I did not try to persuade her, and she did not attempt to explain. There was no need to apologise, I told her. I took the hand she offered, and held it for a minute. Again she apologised, and I assured her that I understood. She kissed me on the brow; then, having said nothing more, she went home. I knew what it had meant. I would wait.

☞

When Lucas invited me over, a week or so after the kiss, I did not hesitate. There was some guilt, naturally, but it was moderate, and a minor element when I thought about what had happened. A truth had been allowed expression.

I was surprised, however, by how easy it was to conduct myself as if there were no reason why I should not be entirely at ease. Lucas opened the door to me. We shook hands, as always. In the way he looked at me, and spoke, nothing was different; and nothing in my manner was different either, or so I felt. We went into the living room, to the board. Erin was there, in the corner chair, reading a magazine. Her greeting was airy, neighbourly. 'I'll leave you to it,' she announced, rising; on her way out, she exchanged smiles with Lucas. No observer of that scene would have detected any tension.

During the game, though, there were moments at which I wondered what he knew or suspected. Once or twice, considering a move, I was aware that I, rather than the position, was being scrutinised. Glancing up abruptly, I saw Lucas's gaze dip quickly to the board; I thought I saw the vanishing of a smile. It was possible, I told myself, that he was amused by how long I was taking to commit myself to a move; perhaps my decision-making, rarely rapid, was slower this afternoon than usual. And when the game was over, Lucas asked me: 'So, how are you?' The question was part of the routine, but this time the tone, as I heard it, was the tone with which he had asked the same question in the weeks immediately following the death of my mother. His manner, briefly, was again that of a counsellor. 'I'm fine,' I answered, and Lucas gave me a quick checking look, as one might look at a switch to verify that it was off. My answer seemed to be sufficient; no more questions were asked.

Then Lucas needed to go up to the office, to check his emails; a new client was in the throes of a crisis, he explained. He would be back in ten minutes, he said, as Erin entered the room. 'Coffee?' she suggested. She looked me in the eye, and smiled, all with perfectly frank friendliness, under the gaze of Lucas.

I followed her, and now there were signs of some agitation. She found things with which to busy herself, in various parts of the kitchen. Apparently it was necessary for her to keep her back turned to me. Only when I said that we should talk did she stop. She regarded me, frowning, and paused, in such a way that I anticipated a response of some subtlety. But all she said was: 'No.' It was said quietly, unemphatically, as one might answer a simple question of fact.

'Not now, not here,' I said. 'But soon. We do have to talk.'

With narrowed eyes she examined my face, as though the meaning of these phrases was unclear. 'No. We don't,' she said, and here I saw a flash of distress, like a reflection glimpsed in the sudden opening of a mirrored door. She was denying herself as much as she was denying me.

The staircase creaked as Lucas came back down; it was not a ridiculous notion, I later thought, that Lucas had deliberately produced that sound, to signal the end of the time that he had permitted Erin and me for whatever conversation might be necessary. Hearing it, Erin called out to him, with a question that did not have to be asked at that moment; she called out to him as a wife would, as she had never done before.

So I understood that Erin was raising a palisade around herself and Lucas. For the time being, she was enclosing the relationship, in obedience to a principle of loyalty. It was what duty demanded, not love. This was admirable, as of course she knew. I would have to wait; I saw this confirmed in the last glance Erin gave me, as Lucas opened the door.

In the months that followed the kiss, it was never mentioned by either of us. There was nothing more to be said, because what had been said by the kiss was true. Only when Lucas had gone did Erin talk about the guilt. She had always felt this guilt, she said, but now she felt it more strongly than ever. With Lucas dead, she could no longer appease her guilt by subservience. His spirit can see everything, she may believe. I do not doubt that the guilt is real; what I doubt is the cause of it. 'But nothing

happened,' I reassured her. We both knew, however, that
this was not the case.

☞

The kiss – or the evening of the kiss – can be thought of as
a seed; it might lie in dry soil for many years, then grow.

☞

Pietro Bembo, the most loquacious proponent of platonic
love, committed adultery with Lucrezia Borgia; and had
three children, at least; and was a cardinal.

☞

One night, in the small hours, a downpour arrived in
advance of the forecast hour. I was on West Street. Sudden
and extraordinary quantities of water, and thrilling noise.
Above my head, the fabric of the umbrella roared. Rain
from a broken gutter made a clacking racket on the
pavement. The leaves of the nearby elm were seething.
There was so much to hear. Taking down the umbrella,
I closed my eyes. The scene was composed in sound –
without seeing, I could sense the distance to the tree, the
volume of its foliage. I could hear the location of the bus
shelter. The rain drummed on its roof and on the roof of
a van parked close by, and the roof of a car; each timbre
was different. My clothes were becoming saturated, but
the experience was pleasurable – thinking nothing, fully
present. A gush of tyres, moving through standing water,
gave a rich satisfaction. Without traffic, the tarmac and
rain produced a thick white noise. I relished it. The sound
from a storm drain was a gargle. Elsewhere, spattering.

A hiss, a droning. Perhaps ten yards away, the rainwater running over an obstruction was making a sound that was like a small catarrhal cough. My skin, the limit of my substance, was alive with coldness, with water; this body occupied this space, amid all these sounds.

A week later, I was unwell. My sneeze is even more ridiculous than most – an explosive squeak, as if someone has stamped, with all force, on a punctured rubber ball. At the kerb, sneezing, I staggered back a half-step, and a voice behind me said: 'Bless.' Erin, blinking in amazement at the noise. 'That's what comes of getting soaked,' she said. On the night of the storm, she had seen me on West Street. My first thought: if she had seen me standing by the bus stop, with the umbrella down, I would have looked like a mad person. But she had seen me a little later, crossing the road. 'You looked like you'd come out of the sea,' she said. Next thought: how had Erin seen me? Nobody else had been walking on West Street; she must have driven past. Lucas was away. So where had she been, at that hour? Erin looked closely at me – at my eyes, rather than into them, as if examining a minor wound. 'You should not be out in public,' she said. 'You do not look good.' A second sneeze; Erin sprang back, as if from a firecracker, and laughed, alarmed. I remember the look she gave me on leaving: as if she were several years older than me, and hoped that a lesson had been learned.

※

For a short time there was a nightingale in one of the gardens nearby, and one evening – a warm night in June – the bird was singing strongly, and we paused the conversation to listen. The sky was a spectacle: a bright moon, almost full, occluded by small clouds. That was what Erin was watching, when I glanced at her and saw her put a fingertip quickly to the edge of an eye, to stem a tear, it seemed. It is possible that the scene, with the accompaniment of the nightingale, was enough in itself; or a memory had arisen. But earlier, soon after the nightingale had begun to sing, something unusual had occurred. Erin was listening to the song, then Lucas started to speak and Erin interrupted him, cuttingly, with: 'Quiet.' And Lucas obeyed, not jokingly; the rebuke made him turn away from her. Never before had I heard her speak to him in this way, but it seemed, from his reaction, that this was not an aberration. She did not apologise in any way for her sharpness, and the mood of the evening was soon restored; Lucas was re-established in his authority. But there was another observation, a glimpse, later, as I was getting ready to leave. Erin got up from the table and went into the house, and I saw Lucas look towards the doorway through which she had just passed. It was the look, it seemed, of someone whose love was greater than the love he was receiving; and in that moment, I remember, I felt sorry for him, and ashamed. A year later, Kit was born.

☞

'Well, that was quite something, last night,' Erin remarked, two or three days after my terminal argument with Miriam. Smiling, she raised an eyebrow in enquiry. It had been a high-volume altercation, with door-slamming and break-ages; a window had been left open, I discovered after it was over.

'It won't happen again,' I said, as though to a neighbour who had lodged a complaint.

Erin nodded; she had assumed as much.

'She needed a bit more drama in her life,' I explained, with the shrug of a useless specimen.

'I can imagine.'

One Saturday morning, coming back to the house, we had met Erin in the street – the only meeting of the three. Throughout the conversation, Miriam's eyes were doing a lot of covert examination. When Erin touched my arm with a finger, the gesture was noted, I saw. Erin was making the new girlfriend welcome; the questions all came from Erin. Answering, Miriam detailed our plans for the weekend; it seemed that things that we had discussed as possibilities had now been decided. As we parted, Erin gave me a semi-second glance: it intrigued her, pleased her, amused her, that I had taken on the challenge of this woman. In the glance there was also, I am sure, an allusion to what had happened with the kiss; a confirmation that it could now be put aside, if not forgotten.

As soon as we were out of earshot, Miriam laughed: I had under-described my neighbour, she told me. It had struck the dark and aggressive and substantial Miriam – as it had struck Erin, I knew – that each might be seen as the converse of the other. The contrast in appearance was almost absurd, as though a point were being made. What followed was not quite an argument; it was an episode of friction, ending with an exit from the room. 'I need to calm down,' Miriam stated, addressing herself from a distance. Half an hour later she returned, from the shower, transfigured, wearing a towel as a small sarong; the glory of the body of Miriam.

No relationship of hers had ever lasted more than half a year, she had told me, at the outset. This was not to be regarded as failure; she was not in any sense unfulfilled. After a few months the voltage dropped too much for her.

It was not just the intensity of the sex that made those early months the best of life – it was the unruliness, and the acceleration of getting to know the lover. She never wanted to know everything about anybody; life was much too short for marriage.

Miriam knew what Erin had been thinking when they were talking. '"This girl is just not his type" – that's what she was thinking,' said Miriam, who had no patience with any talk of types. 'I'm not that type of person' was a sentence that made her want to scream. It reduced the complexity of the whole individual to a caption. When she was in her teens, and teachers kept singling her out as a disruptive element, her parents forced her to undergo the attentions of a psychologist. Now she had an ineradicable loathing of psychology and its classifications. 'Who knows why people do what they do?' she would ask. 'The point is, they do it. That's all we need to know.' And once, sounding like Lucas, she reminded me that electrons were not entities that existed in themselves – they existed as charges, as relationships. It should be the same with people, Miriam argued. Only in relationships do we fully exist; every relationship changes us; but the charge can never be of prolonged duration.

Erin, in the aftermath of Miriam's departure, said nothing about types, though she did tell me that Miriam might have been what I 'needed' – another word to temporarily put a distance between us. 'You seemed to be having a good time,' she said. 'She was attractive.'

I agreed.

'Great figure.'

'Indeed.'

'And not a pushover.'

'Very much not,' I said, with a ruefulness that was chiefly for effect.

'You shouldn't be in that house on your own,' said Erin.

She seemed more disappointed at Miriam's leaving than I was, as did Lucas. With Miriam, I confessed to him, I had never left the shallows.

'But splashing around in the shallows can be a lot of fun,' Lucas pronounced.

'For a time,' I answered. Erin was in the room too.

Once in a while, at the very least, we should go where our instinct takes us, Lucas instructed. Instinct is spiritual, he said; it bypasses the overcomplications of our intelligence. Only through the plenitude of experience can we arrive at our true selves, he said, sounding like an overwritten Miriam.

I opened the newsagent's door just as Erin was leaving. That morning, the wife was on duty; she would sometimes refer to Erin as 'the assistant', with leaden irony.

This time she said to me, with a micro-dose of tartness: 'Do you notice anything?' She nodded in the direction of the doorway.

'About what?'

'She's pregnant,' the woman stated. She released the words as if releasing a stone over the centre of a well.

'Looks the same to me.'

'Pregnant,' she repeated. 'She's getting the morning sickness. You'll see.' I disliked this woman. 'She seems like a nice girl,' she once remarked, and even that was enough to put a stain, temporarily, on the image of Erin; it was akin to hearing slander.

That night, I remember, Erin appeared in the kitchen, briefly. The dressing gown obscured her shape. For a few seconds she stood at the French windows, holding a tumbler of milk. She looked up; seeing me at the window of my room, she turned away.

☞

This I remember now – the day that the situation became clear. Near the post office, I was on the inside of the pavement and Erin was on the outside, with Lucas's huge umbrella to the fore, held at an angle of forty-five degrees. A gust smacked the umbrella aside, and it was then that she saw me. The first encounter for a week or so; the first sighting, for that matter. The rain had stopped, I pointed out; she presented an open palm to the sky, then brought down the umbrella. Her hair flew out from under the cashmere bonnet, and the wind plastered the coat across her midriff. Her waist was thicker, undeniably. She appeared tired, around the eyes, and the complexion lacked its usual finish. Her manner, definitely, was evasive; she had to be at home for a delivery, she said, no sooner had I spoken. But if what was happening was good news for her and Lucas, why not say? Now, the explanation is obvious – a rapprochement with Lucas had not yet been reached. When the news was announced, it was done with plausible delight all round. Though, again, I remember a strange gesture from Lucas: he put his arm around Erin's shoulders and hugged her quickly, more as if she were his daughter, who had just excelled at something.

☞

Almost as often as I think of the kiss, I recall this moment: walking by the harbour, in the middle of the day, I turned a corner and saw Lucas, sitting at a table outside the Anchor, alone. There was no one at any of the other tables; the day was cool and overcast. He was not reading a book or a newspaper; he was holding a pint glass, and gazing across the water, in the direction of the meadows and the holiday park beyond. It is a familiar and unenthralling landscape, and on the afternoon in question nothing was happening within it to make it any more interesting than usual, that I could see. Lucas did not appear to find anything of interest in what he was seeing. He took a mouthful of beer, and continued to gaze at the tedious view. I had never known Lucas to drink beer, but on this day that is what he was drinking. I had never even heard Lucas make mention of visiting a pub; I could not imagine him in a pub. Why was he there? From his house to the harbour is a distance of a mile and half. Perhaps someone would be joining him, I thought, so I waited. He would have had to turn right around to see me. Sip by sip he drank his beer, never looking away from the water and the meadow. He was an image of stupefied sadness. I watched until the drink was finished. Nobody joined him. For fully five minutes he held on to the empty glass, as if unable to move on. This was some time after the birth of Kit. Erin was away, with the baby, at the sister's, supposedly.

⋈

Other explanations are of course possible. Though Lucas projected the unassailable confidence and authority of a professor, one should not think that he could not be wounded, as Erin once said. He was not thick-skinned, and some of the things that were said about him were hurtful. Melvin and Matthew Dodd had persisted in their abuse for years, and they were not the only implacable malcontents; some of the letters that Lucas received were disgusting, Erin told me.

☞

It is not the case, Lucas believed, that the spirit is breathed into the flesh, as it were, by the all-mighty creator of everything, at the instant of conception; and neither did he believe, as many have believed, that the spirit has an existence that precedes the moment of conception, and that it merely spends an interlude, for whatever reason, in the temporary accommodation of the body. No. Eternity begins in the bedroom, with the fusion of spermatozoon and ovum. That is when the spirit comes into being. This was not an outlandish idea, Lucas pointed out. Many Christians have believed that the individual soul is a hybrid, brought into being by the fusion of the mother's soul and the father's. The mechanics of the process did not concern him; or rather, he did not presume to understand it. Consciousness is likewise a mystery, as he pointed out. None of us – well, none but a few crackpots – has any doubt that we are conscious, yet there's not a person on the planet who can explain how it comes to be that the body can have an awareness of itself. 'How does mere meat come to think?' he enquired, looking down on his hand with distaste, as if decomposition had already begun. No scientist can explain it, but its reality is undeniable, because we have proof of it everywhere, just as Lucas and his clients had experienced proof, many times, of the life of the disembodied spirit.

☞

At first, I saw what everyone else seemed to see. Lucas was an attentive parent. He had never imagined that this would happen, he told me, and he was delighted that it had, though the necessary adjustments would not be easy, for a man of his age.

Years before, I remember, not long after Kathleen had died, he said that Callum had not wanted to have children, that he had been positively averse to the idea, as averse as one might be to something that would severely endanger one's health, and that Kathleen had managed to convince herself that her work and her husband would be enough for her, but she had never – Lucas thought – succeeded in entirely eradicating her regret. Callum's childhood had been bleak, Lucas told me; in what way it had been bleak, he didn't know, but Kathleen believed that the experiences of his early years had made it impossible for him to risk becoming a father. 'Some men do not have what it takes,' said Lucas, and I, detecting a tone of self-deprecation, understood him to mean that he was a man of that kind himself, as I did when he suggested to me that my father too might not have had the right stuff for fatherhood.

Then Kit was born, and Lucas became paternal. Or we should say that Lucas, in my presence – and, we might assume, in the presence of others – was a convincing father of the baby. The greater part of the work was Erin's. The greater part of the work is always the mother's. Many men have little enthusiasm for the messier aspects of the early years of parenthood; his age was an additional excuse. He seemed to be speaking truthfully when he professed to wish that it were not necessary for him to spend so much time away from home. I often saw him playing with the baby, or diverting her. There was some awkwardness, at times, to this play; as if he had been reading books to teach himself how to do it. The intimacy was guarded rather than spontaneous; he seemed conscious always of the child's fragility. He did not often kiss her, and when he did the kiss was extremely delicate, touchingly so. He seemed grateful for her, rather than delighted; he was deferential to Erin; the father was of secondary importance and must deny himself, he seemed to think. Again, I thought his age was much of the explanation. There was no reason to question what I was seeing.

From the start, the baby resembled her mother, and the resemblance quickly became stronger. The form of the chin was Erin's; the brow, and the plane of the temples; the shape and colour of the eyes – even, at times, the glance. She had a watchfulness that was like her mother's. There was little visible trace of Lucas, but this was not remarkable. I've known people whose features were like those of only one parent; I've known some who looked nothing like either. But the nose, one could say, had something of Lucas; the profile might remind you of him. One afternoon, when Lucas was away, coming upon Erin and Kit in the street, I paid my respects to the little one; crouching beside her, I stroked a cheek and, exaggerating, complimented her on the shape of the nose. 'The nose of Lucas,' I said, and at that moment Erin looked away. She smiled, but she could not look at me directly; and I knew then. There was in fact nothing of Lucas in the little girl's face.

It was a shock; it took me some time, I admit, to appreciate what should be appreciated here. How could one not admire the forgiveness that Lucas had immediately offered? He loved Erin and he loved her child, if not to the same degree. Such was his love, nobody could see the truth of the situation. Would any of the gossips and the critics have been capable of that generosity? Could I have done the same? Forgiveness, even now, does not come easily to me. Eventually people will come to understand what Lucas did. Some might think him a fool; an 'old fool', no doubt. But he was not. In this he was noble. That is the correct word. He loved her.

☞

At around this time he said something that, as soon as he had said it, I knew I would always remember, because it was a remark that I could never have imagined Lucas making. It was especially strange, coming from the father of an infant. We had met on the street, near the bench of conversation; the afternoon was warm, and he suggested that we sit for a few minutes. He looked up into the sky, as he had done when he had first talked to me, there, and then, after perhaps ten seconds of silence, suddenly said, while tracking the flight of a pigeon: 'For a mayfly, does a minute feel like a month does to us?' Then: 'Maybe a mayfly, in the course of its one day alive, has time to grow tired of life.' It was said brightly, as though it were a witty proposition that he had encountered in his recent reading, but his eyes were not bright.

☞

Steven Greenwood is the most obvious candidate. I see no resemblance, but that means nothing. I dislike him. Truthfulness requires that this be said. Some envy is in operation here. I admit that too. Though twenty years older than Erin, or thereabouts, he might be mistaken for a man only a decade older. In the gym three or four times a week, I should think. Always a white shirt, to enhance the impact of the five-day beard. Never more than a five-day growth, and never less. Visit the website of his new venture, in London, for monochrome shots of the man in action. The charisma radiates. See him stooping to examine the contents of a pan. Observe the concentration, the dedication, the sheer hard work. Read about his 'passion for innovation', his unceasing 'research'. Customers – 'guests' – can witness the passion in action: the tiny kitchen, the crucible of his art, is visible from the best seats in the house. Amazing what can be conjured in so small a space. Truly, an alchemist of the edible.

☞

The chronology fits – Greenwood's departure for London; the period in which Erin was rarely seen; then her evident preoccupation, for which the loss of employment was taken to be the explanation. Connections are easily made.

☞

I ate at Greenwood's place once, with Miriam; she had heard good things about L'Écume. Her palate is more refined and educated than mine. She is more forthright too. Stirring her debris with a fork, she admitted to disappointment. 'Controversial,' she said, at conversational volume. Seaweed mayonnaise was involved; the rest I forget. Our beautiful waitress, concerned that Miriam's plate had not been cleared, asked: 'Was everything OK?' Protocol required an affirmative or an evasive response. But Miriam replied: 'To be honest, that was really quite nasty.' Word would have been relayed to the kitchen, I'm sure, but the maestro did not come out to demand an explanation, as I feared he would. A few days later, an acerbic review appeared online. Adjectives such as 'pretentious' and 'ill-conceived' were used, and 'overpriced'. This was not the first time a customer had protested at the expense. Miriam did not write this review, and neither did I, but

I have reason to believe that the chef thought otherwise. 'Incandescent, he was,' Lucas reported, gratified.

☞

The waitresses at L'Écume were never plain young women. Steven Greenwood employed no men, as far as I was aware. In addition to Erin, there was the Polish waitress – eerily pale; blazingly blonde hair; slender as a girl of ten, but six feet tall. Something was going on between her and the boss. This was widely known. They were seen together. Miriam and I were served by a remarkable Romanian, of more or less the same dimensions as the Polish sylph, of grave demeanour and catwalk posture. One night, passing by, I saw Erin outside L'Écume, waiting. Greenwood was inside, turning off the lights. After Greenwood moved the operation to London, Erin often seemed anxious; even, sometimes, unhappy. It was not an easy pregnancy, Lucas confided to me.

☞

And Greenwood was in the house, once, when Lucas was away. Erin was no longer working for him. I cannot say I heard an altercation; I heard nothing. All I saw was Greenwood, in the afternoon, in the house, briefly. He appeared at the window, talking. I did not see Erin. Why would he have been there?

☞

At the new L'Écume in London you could pay more, a lot more, for a single meal than a waitress gets paid for her whole evening's work. The original L'Écume was barely cheaper. Lucas thought the prices were scandalous. He threatened to go down there and tell him to pay his staff a decent wage. Erin pleaded with him: it was not as if Greenwood himself was making a fortune out of the business, she argued. But Lucas would have done it, she knew. When Erin had been treated unfairly by the manager of the place where she had worked before joining the Greenwood operation, Lucas had gone to the shop the next morning and 'let him have it with both barrels', in front of the customers, Erin reported. It was embarrassing, but also exciting, in a way, she said, giving him a look that chastised a little and admired a lot.

☞

'Try not to think badly of him,' said Lucas, of my father, after I had made mention of the woman in the green coat. We should refrain from judgement because we can never see anyone in his or her entirety. 'Nobody is transparent,' he said – a strange pronouncement, I thought, from someone who purported to be able to see into the souls of both the living and the dead. Then he talked about his philosophy of forgiveness, a philosophy he had expounded for the benefit of several of his clients.

I should understand that forgiveness was not the same thing as forgetting. People often say that they have at last forgiven a person who offended against then, when in fact all that has happened is that the offence has palled. Forgetting is a perfectly acceptable means of coming to terms with something that has caused pain or distress, but one cannot decide to forget. One cannot cancel a memory by an act of will. Therefore it would make no sense for Lucas to advise me to forget my father. That would be like advising me to be a different person.

Forgiveness is not achieved by cancelling the offence, or writing it off, or 'putting it down to experience'. Neither, Lucas would have me know, was it the same thing as reconciliation. It was not a question of coming to a comprehension of the offender's reasons. If one were to learn the reasons, and offer one's acceptance in return, this would be a kind of exchange, and forgiveness must not be an exchange, Lucas urged. Pure forgiveness, the only true forgiveness, is given without reasons. He had not chosen his words carefully enough, he said, in talking about forgiveness as something that may be achieved. Achievement requires time, and forgiveness is something that one commits, in a moment. Forgiving somebody is as sudden as falling in love, he said. 'I can't tell you how to do it,' he said, 'any more than I can tell you: "Look at that girl over there. Now fall in love with her." It's not a rational decision. It's gratuitous.' The most important things in our lives are not rational, he said. The conversation was taking place in the garden; we looked towards the house; Erin stood at the sink, looking out, as if we were not visible to her.

My mother, I responded, had never seemed to be interested in forgiving my father.

'No,' Lucas conceded. But forgiveness can be immensely difficult, he reminded me.

☞

One evening, soon after his diagnosis, Lucas proposed that, just as only three points in a plane are needed to define a specific form, one's essential self can be represented by means of just three episodes or moments. That is all that is necessary to summarise a life – a mere triad of details. 'What would yours be?' he asked me.

I resisted: the idea of reducing a life to three bullet points put me in mind of the Last Judgement, I told him.

Erin interrupted. It was easy to pick the first: it would be the day that Lucas came into her life. The second immediately followed: the Sunday afternoon on which the family sat down to eat lunch together, and her father put the carving knife into the chicken, and a dribble of watery blood leaked out; though she was only twelve years old, she decided there and then that she would never again eat meat. The third choice was just as obvious: it was 'what any mother would choose'. The smile that Lucas gave her, it seemed to me, had something of approval about it, or even reassurance; not obviously the smile of her daughter's father.

'Now you,' she said to me.

And Lucas coaxed: 'Come on, Joshua. Play the game.'

So I came up with a moment of the expected sort: the proverbial teacher of life-changing influence, who, in a sign of special favour, loaned me a book from his own collection – *The Cheese and the Worms*, which I read in a single sitting (not quite true), because it was like nothing I had ever read before, and inspired me. Then a day with my mother, in an overheated café overlooking a Cornish harbour, on a day of heavy rain, gazing through the speckled glass at the roiling sea; still looking out, she put out a hand, which I took, and she said, with no preamble and no explanation afterwards, 'Thank you', as if I were her one true ally, and an adult. Touched by this scene, as I had hoped she would be, Erin clasped her hands. Finally: a game of tennis, at the end of summer, with a girl who would be moving to another town for the new term; her 'glorious limbs' were made even more glorious by the sunshine of a Caribbean holiday; the family's money was an aspect of her allure, but not a major aspect. Exhausted, we lay under the leaves of a lime tree, for what would be the last conversation. She would miss me, she said; likewise, I said. And she cried, momentarily, barely. This was all too late. We lay in the lime-coloured light, on the hard warm earth; we held hands like lovers who might jump, but there was no kiss. A love gained and lost in the space of an afternoon, I told Erin and Lucas. Enchanted by my own invention, I semi-sang the first two lines of 'Plaisirs d'amour'. Had it been possible to be honest, the third episode would not have been about the girl with the golden legs.

And the choices of Lucas: the day his father died, and their spirits mingled; the day he first saw Erin; and the third was 'coming soon', he said, as though alluding to a surprise that he was planning for us, and which he was sure would impress. No mention of Kit, I noted.

On the subject of his bravery, this should be recorded.

There was no alarm when Lucas decided to turn back before we had reached the seafront. He was breathing heavily, but benign explanations were to hand: symptoms suggested a chest infection; also, he had become too fat. Subsequent walks were shorter; still some shortness of breath, but the cough had gone, and there was no pain, and still no loss of weight.

Then, one afternoon, he beckoned and I went over. 'I have news,' he said, as we went into the living room; the tone was nonchalant. Even when he told me what the tests had shown, one would have thought that he was talking about a temporary inconvenience that had arisen.

It was exemplary, the way he conducted himself on the approach to the terrible last days; again, the word 'noble' would not be inappropriate. He took a disinterested interest in what was happening to his body, the remarkable speed with which it was being overrun. The idea of courage perhaps implies that fear has been overcome; in that case, what Lucas demonstrated was not courage, because there was no fear – only regret that the future years that he had so often imagined would now never be more than imaginary, and compassion for Erin. Some guilt too; an increasing quantity of guilt. 'She's too young,' he murmured, as if she were the dying one. His pity was entirely for Erin.

He was fortunate, he insisted, in that he knew the end of the story. There was time to make the arrangements that had to be made. He saw the path ahead, and beyond. It was not a question of hope; he knew.

☞

Near the end, Lucas told me about an occasion on which he had lied to a client. A woman had needed to know something from her husband, who had died three years earlier. In recent months the widow had come to hear of a rumour about her husband, a rumour that was causing great distress. It concerned something he was said to have done in the early years of their marriage, and if it were to turn out to be true, her memories of all their years together would be blighted. There was no signal, Lucas told me. But the woman was suffering, and he liked her, and he could tell that she had an illness that soon would kill her, and so he had decided to simulate a success – but only a limited success. As a man in the depths of a cavern sees only darkness for a long time, but at last something becomes visible, even if it is nothing more than a patch of lighter darkness, because no darkness on this earth is absolute, so he had detected a minimal quantity of information, the weakest of messages. A denial was what he claimed to have extracted from the air; a fading protest of innocence, from a voice exhausted by the effort of protesting, over and over again, unheard until now.

Lucas seemed ashamed by his duplicity, more ashamed, I thought, than was warranted by the story he had told. Then, for a moment, I imagined a deathbed scene of cinematic grandeur – a total confession. It had all been a pretence, he was about to tell me. I prepared myself to receive it, and in preparing myself I realised that the disappointment would be intolerable, for me almost as much as for Erin. I wanted Lucas to see it through to the finish.

Had there been such a confession, would I, eventually, have told Erin about it? No, I would not. I would have committed that sin of omission, of course, to protect her.

☞

The death room was small and furnished monastically: a narrow bed, a table beside it, two chairs. It could not have been the room in which Lucas usually slept. The bed was set beside the window, from which he could see the sky and a portion of the street. His head, lying in the hollow of the topmost of three or four pillows, was the head of a hermit saint. The beard had been allowed to grow; illness had made pits of his cheeks; his arms rested on top of the bedding, flat and straight, as if in rehearsal for burial; the hands were bloodless and the fingers too long. In just two weeks he had become an old man.

'How have you been?' asked Lucas. His words were barely audible.

As I answered, he moved a hand towards the edge of the bed, and turned it over. Again he smiled, and closed his eyes.

'What are you working on?' he asked.

I was working on a book by a retired businessman who had relocated from London to a village on the Tarn, and there become fascinated by the story of the beast of Gévaudan; it would be self-published, if published at all.

'Go on,' said Lucas.

I told him about the scores of victims, mostly girls and women. I summarised the possibilities: a monstrous wolf or several wolves; a werewolf; a madman; a lion; a hyena.

'A hyena? In France?'

'Escaped from captivity, maybe. The exotic pet of a local lord.'

'I see,' said Lucas.

I told him about the villain of the book, the hunter Jean Chastel, who – the author believed – had mated a mastiff with a wolf to create the beast. Witnesses reported that the monster, whenever it encountered resistance, would retreat from the victim for a while, assessing the situation, before returning for the kill.

'Could have been trained,' Lucas remarked. He was listening closely and understanding, only days from the end.

'Exactly.' And I told him about the hunt of June 19, 1767, when Jean Chastel – using silver bullets, he was said to have claimed – shot a huge animal that was found to have human flesh in its stomach. Thereupon the killings ceased, after more than a hundred grisly deaths; and Chastel's reprobate son – rumoured to be a werewolf – promptly turned to God.

'Suspicious,' Lucas agreed.

'Our author thinks so.'

For some time Lucas did not speak; his breathing was embattled. 'Quite a story,' he said at last. 'I'd like to read it.' Now he opened his eyes; he regarded the nondescript sky. He gathered air deeply into his chest; this provoked a spasm of coughing. 'I'm making progress,' he said, when recomposed. 'As you can see.'

None of the things I had thought to say could be said. I stroked his hand.

'Very interesting,' he said, almost whimsically. Before I could ask him what he meant, he said: 'The next bit.' Then clarified: 'What comes after.'

This seemed to be, on the threshold, an admission of uncertainty.

I said: 'I'll be expecting to hear from you.'

The smile that this produced was expressive more of pain than of amusement. He closed his eyes now, and his face, through some effort, assumed an expression of severe serenity. 'You'll need to look after her,' he said.

'Of course,' I said, and received a look that seemed to be a granting of permission.

Yes, there was some confusion in the last few days of his life; the medication had that effect. But we had this conversation; he followed the story of the beast of Gévaudan. And he knew what he was doing when he gave me the watch.

He asked me to call Erin, and when she came he asked her to bring his watch. She placed it in his palm, then Lucas tipped it into mine. 'No more time for me,' he said; his laugh was like the cracking of a small sheaf of straw. Erin, crying, left us again.

It is a man's watch, a heavy antique thing; I was the obvious recipient. I did not ask to be given it.

Said Cicero: 'to study philosophy is nothing but to prepare one's self to die'. If this is so, then Lucas was a successful student of philosophy, we might decide. Or the creator of something one might term a philosophy.

☞

The final scene began with a call from Erin: Lucas wanted to see me that evening. The call lasted no more than thirty seconds; what the message signified was not made explicit, but it was understood; her voice was quiet and level, as if she were a nurse, speaking in a room in which people were asleep.

On opening the door, she said nothing other than my name. She had been crying, but did not cry. Looking down, she stepped back to allow me into the house. I followed her up the stairs; a silent procession of two.

'It's Joshua,' said Erin, and Lucas turned his head towards me; the movement was slow, of hydraulic smoothness; his eyes were held in pockets of thin grey skin. 'My boy,' he murmured, and smiled; the phrase had never been used before.

Erin withdrew, so quietly that I didn't notice she had left us until I sat on the chair that had been placed beside the bed, and looked to the door.

For the last time, I put my hand in his.

He said: 'In conclusion.' The voice was barely audible, but these words were clear. They had a tone of a commencement, but nothing followed. Sleep was overcoming him. I pressed the hand, and at that he looked at me, and said: 'Speak to your mother.' In his mind my mother was still alive, it seemed. It was hard to make any sense of what he was saying. He talked to me for a few seconds as if I were his brother; he mentioned a woman whose name meant nothing to me, and wanted me to say something to her. He thought Erin was no longer with him. After four or five sentences, or utterances, in which everything was confused, he became quiet, and clenched his eyelids, in a great effort of concentration. 'You and your mother,' he said again, with what I thought was a smile. 'I loved her,' he said, twice, as the smile became a grimace, and he moved his hand towards mine. I lifted it, and his fingers turned into a grip that was stronger than I would have thought possible. There was a sustained look, asking if I knew what was being said, and a nod of the head, very slight, a tremor.

More confusion followed. I became his father, I think. When I placed his hand back on the sheet, there was no resistance at all, and no acknowledgement when I left him.

Downstairs, Erin spoke to me. He would not see anyone else after tonight. She spoke like a doctor to a relative. It would have been wrong to touch her; to maintain this control of herself required the maintenance of distance.

'I'll take my leave on Saturday,' Lucas had told her, a few days earlier, as if talking about a trip that he had been planning. On the Saturday night, Erin rang. She had experienced something extraordinary, she told me, then she reported the wonderful thing that Lucas had said: 'Death has the face of a friend.'

☞

Chloe, the sister, does not like me; this needs to be understood. She was predisposed to hostility. This was apparent at the first encounter, a couple of days after Lucas's death. I had glimpsed her a few times, when she was visiting Erin, while Lucas was away on business, but we had never met. I went to the house and it was Chloe who opened the door. I knew her view of Lucas – or her view of Lucas as relayed by Lucas. Although disreputable and far too old, he did not, as far as she could tell (on the basis of two or three evenings in his company), present a physical danger to her impressionable sibling. The relationship would end within the year, Chloe was sure, and when it was finished, she persuaded herself, Erin would have learned something valuable from the experience. We all learn from our mistakes, as I'm sure Chloe has often remarked.

Chloe had taken charge of the situation, the stance announced; there would be no invitation to enter the house. I enquired after Erin; it would have been apparent that I was a close friend.

'I'm sorry. She's not seeing anybody today,' the sister told me. There was not a grain of apology in this 'sorry'.

'How is she?' I asked, and added: 'I'm Joshua.'

The name made no observable impact. 'As one would expect,' she answered.

'Of course,' I said. The door to the kitchen was slightly ajar; a shadow moved on the panel of frosted glass. Raising my voice by a decibel or two, I said: 'Could you tell her I called?'

'I shall,' she replied. The demeanour suggested that I was some sort of appurtenance to the unhealthy life that Erin had been living here, ensnared by Lucas; I was implicated.

I thanked her. 'You must be Chloe,' I was about to say, when the inner door opened and Erin entered the scene. She was wearing a T-shirt that might have been slept in, and her hair was awry; under her eyes, the skin looked like pencil shading on paper. Her smile was effortful; it told me that I had to accept, for the interim, that she had ceded control to the sister.

'Hello Josh,' she said. Then to Chloe: 'Joshua's the neighbour.' What, I wondered, should I make of the definite article?

A slight movement of Chloe's head acknowledged receipt of the information.

'This is my sister,' said Erin. She stood behind Chloe, as behind a shield.

'Pleased to meet you,' I said, putting out a hand.

'Yes,' is all she said. Her hand was as light and fine and small as Erin's, and a lot of work had gone into its maintenance. The softness of the skin was remarkable, and the coolness – it was like being stroked by water; the nails were opaline.

'We'll talk soon,' Erin promised.

'Whenever you like,' I replied. An embrace would have been appropriate, but for the impediment of Chloe.

'Thanks, Joshua,' she said; there was so much in the way she spoke my name.

'Yes. Thank you,' the sister confirmed. There was nothing but sound in the way she said it. I was no more than ten feet down the path when she closed the door.

☞

It was at Lucas's request that I spoke at the funeral. Erin was present when he asked me to give the speech; he wanted her to witness the moment of commission. He knew I would speak respectfully of him. But I was required to submit the text for approval; this idea, I am certain, was the sister's, not Erin's. For the assessment, I was directed to the damson velvet armchair – Kathleen's favourite. The sisters took the sofa. The distressed leather armchair, Lucas's throne, was occupied by the negative presence of Lucas, as it had once been occupied by the negative presence of Callum. For many months after Callum's death, Lucas told me, neither he nor Kathleen could sit in that chair. It was evident that nobody had sat in it since the death of Lucas; the nest of crushed cushions was a cast of his hips. Elsewhere in the room, however, a new order was already being introduced. The surface of the coffee table was clear; no slew of newspapers and books. No obstructions of any kind on the floor.

When I passed the pages to Erin, Chloe intercepted; she asked me to read it aloud. I went slowly; I was aiming for an effect of mastered emotion, of words well chosen. At the sentence that referred to Lucas's generosity and 'deep interest in people', Chloe glanced towards the window. When I spoke of the kindness that Lucas had shown to me, particularly after the death of my mother, the composure of Erin began to falter. I came to the passage about the house, and 'the love that one sensed in it, immediately'. Here I observed a hardening of Chloe's gaze, but Erin took a deep and trembling breath; tears appeared. Her sister reached an arm around her and pulled her towards the supportive shoulder; Erin did not immediately yield.

'It's lovely,' said Erin, freeing herself. 'Go on.'

More tears at the conclusion: 'I am extremely glad to have known him.' Erin, weeping, smiled at me; she and I were the ones who had known him.

'Thank you,' said Chloe. It seemed that I had passed the audition. She was not sure, though, that there needed to be any mention of Kathleen. The 'Kathleen thing' might be an unnecessary complication.

I asked her what precisely might be meant by 'thing'.

Erin wanted to retain the reference to Kathleen. 'She was important,' she said, to me. And she had one other revision to suggest. She would like me to say: 'He brought comfort to a great many people.'

I would say exactly those words, I promised.

'Because he did,' Erin told me, as though I were one who might doubt it. Then she said: 'I'll show you.'

Her sister watched her walk out of the room, as one might watch a person who is washing her hands for the tenth time in a single hour. Left alone with me, Chloe said not a word. She looked up at the ceiling, tracking Erin's footfall.

Erin returned with a clutch of letters. One by one, she displayed a dozen pages to us: expressions of gratitude – 'boundless', 'eternal', 'heartfelt', 'inexpressible'. There were many more upstairs, she told me. 'Aren't there?' she said, turning to Chloe for verification.

Her sister nodded, not meeting Erin's gaze; her opinion of Lucas was validated by the fact that he had filed all this fan mail. When Erin talked about how difficult it would be to live in the house now that Lucas was gone, her sister's advice was emphatic. 'You'll need to move on,' she said, as though she had made a study of such situations and all the evidence led unequivocally to this conclusion.

I offered, not forcefully, a different view.

☞

I had a sense of loss, certainly, but I would not say that it was grief. Lucas would not be disappointed to learn this. Grief, after all, was what he worked to erase, or at least assuage. After the death of his father, he had overcome his grief more quickly than his sister thought decent. 'What is wrong with you?' she had demanded, distraught, of her dry-eyed brother. So he told me. She could not understand his calmness: he was only fifteen, and had been closer to his father than either of his siblings. 'Exactly,' Lucas answered. His father was with him, he told her. She decided that Lucas was in shock, a diagnosis confirmed when he returned to school more tightly focused than ever; he was still in denial years later, she thought; why else, having gained his first-class degree, would he have taken a job for which no qualifications of any kind were needed? He was continuing to suppress his emotions, she told him, and this was dangerous. But he was suppressing nothing, he replied. His life had been diminished greatly by the physical removal of his father, but he still lived 'in his father's love', and vice versa. His sister, on the other hand, was too attached to her grief. 'She did not want it to end,' he said.

The crematorium chapel was transformed into the church of Lucas; not a single unoccupied seat. The congregation was as colourful as a tinful of wrapped sweets; black had been banned; we were here to celebrate his life. Directly in front of me, Erin sat rigidly upright, attending to the speech keenly, as if she might learn something from it. The sister sat alongside, holding Erin's hand throughout, transmitting dignity. The sister's dress, a luscious shade of blue, was conspicuously expensive and well cut; the most stylish of the mourners, without question. One other woman drew the eye – a handsome and very tall West Indian, sixtyish, wearing an intricate hat with ribbons of magenta and gold intertwined. She appeared to commend what I had to say. When I came to the lines that I had inserted without the sister's prior approval – 'The awful shadow of some unseen Power / Floats though unseen amongst us' – the behatted woman smiled powerfully at me, as if no tribute could have touched her more deeply. I too became moved. While I spoke, my self-accusation was suspended. The speech was not insincere; the words were being spoken sincerely by a version of myself who had come into existence for the occasion.

When it was over, Erin could not speak; we embraced. The sister spoke on their behalf. I had surprised her, it seemed. Then the handsome woman with the complicated hat thanked me; she took me to be a servant of Lucas's mission. We walked back to the house together. Her name was Neriah, she had been born in Trinidad, and had been working as a hairdresser when Lucas helped her, twenty years ago. The salon belonged to her sister, Neola, who had died very suddenly. 'Lucas could tell me so much,' Neriah told me. It was as though he had known Neola for years, and Neriah herself. Lucas was a wonderful gentleman, the kindest of men, a better man in fact than her husband had been. A man of great charity. He could see that she didn't have much money and he would not have taken a penny from her if she hadn't made a fuss about it. He even sent her a present on her birthday. She wept demurely, from recollected happiness, it seemed.

The most beautiful thing that anyone had ever said to her was said to her by Lucas. 'We all walk in mysteries,' he told her. Every day, on waking up, she repeated those words to herself, like a prayer. 'He was a very special person,' Neriah concluded, on leaving me for another conversation, as we entered the garden. 'Just look around,' she said, and I looked around, at the evidence: a company of forty people, perhaps more, and nearly all of them women. The mood was unfuneral – it might have been the audience of a serious-minded film that had just finished, and which everyone had hugely enjoyed. In the farthest corner of the garden, half a dozen people were listening to a woman who had intrigued me, when I was addressing the congregation: the profusion of unfettered russet-and-grey hair had caught my attention, as had the scarlet patent leather boots, and the two young women flanking her – her twin daughters, obviously, with auburn hair as wild as their mother's. The mother had seemed enraptured during the ceremony; her style of narration was ebullient. She ended her anecdote in a crescendo of mock indignation, in which I heard: 'Yes, but her tits are from Brazil!' And everybody laughed, including Erin's mother, who was attending without her husband; her demeanour suggested an unhappiness that had been in place since long before the death of Lucas. She did not spend a great deal of time with Erin; it appeared that she could talk more easily with her other daughter. I did not feel inclined to approach.

The twins, while their mother entertained her audience, were charming Owen, the brother of Lucas, who had commandeered a bottle of wine, from which he overfilled the glasses of all three.

As I passed behind him, a voice on my other side murmured, almost in my ear: 'Nice speech.' It was Gabrielle, sister of Owen and Lucas, also not sober. Chinking her glass on mine, she said: 'I recognised you.' My incomprehension gratified her. She clarified: she had once visited Lucas, during the period when he had lived as 'the potter's lodger', and on a walk through the town, with Lucas, she had been introduced to my mother and me. 'What is your mother's name?' she asked.

'Monica.'

'Yes,' she said. 'That's right.' Her smile was negligible and unpleasant, and might or might not have been intended to mean something. 'You were living there,' she said, waving her free hand in the direction of my house.

I was living there still, I told her.

'Really?' she said. The word should have been garnished with a single upturned eyebrow, but the whole brow, it appeared, had received some sort of treatment; it was like a plate of pale fibreglass. I explained the situation. The fact that my mother was no longer living made no discernible impact on her. In lieu of a response, she took a deep draught of her wine, then said: 'Wasn't a terrifically successful tête-à-tête, that one. More bridges burned than built. Odd set-up, I thought, him and the potter woman. Clammy.'

I had liked Kathleen very much, I told her. 'An interesting person,' I said.

'Yes,' she said, drawling the syllable. She said something about Lucas and his 'old dears'. After another substantial sip, she informed me that she and Lucas had never been on the same wavelength. 'Eight years is a rather large gap when you're young. We never really closed it.' She ascertained that I had no siblings; this, she proposed, had its advantages. Then, with a nod towards the group in which Erin, with the sister at her right hand, was receiving condolences from Neriah and others, she demanded: 'So, what do you think?'

'About what?' I asked.

'I like her,' she said; the implication being that this was a decision that had been reached after prolonged consideration. 'She's very young, but I like her.'

'Who wouldn't?' I responded.

'She says she has some idea about opening a restaurant.'

'She does.'

'Would she take advice from you?' she asked, scanning the garden, as if in readiness for excusing herself.

'Depends.'

'Don't let her do it. Please, don't let her do it. She hasn't a clue. It's the high road to bankruptcy and madness.'

And here Owen stepped in, with: 'This sounds interesting.'

He introduced himself, transferring his glass sloppily to the left hand, for a handshake that was like the yanking of a chain.

'I was just saying how much I like little Erin,' his sister answered.

'Nice young woman,' Owen agreed. 'Very nice. He did well there. Lucky man.'

'And who are the lovelies?' Gabrielle enquired, indicating the twins, with no attempt to make the gesturing subtle. 'You seemed to be enjoying yourself.'

'I was, thank you. I was,' he answered, stroking his cheeks. In silhouette he was similar to his brother – perhaps a stone heavier. The face was likewise a version of Lucas; the eyes, though, were blandly genial; the gaze blunter. The cheeks were as smooth and pale as veal. 'The lovelies are Cyan and Aria. You heard correctly. Cyan and Aria. As in the colour and a song. And that's their Mama,' he said, aiming a finger towards the red-booted woman. Her name was Kate Burtenshaw; it had no resonance for either of the siblings, and I did not reveal that it had a resonance for me. 'The life and soul of the funeral,' he called her, before telling us what the daughters had told him: Lucas had once been of assistance to their mother, and on the anniversary of that happy day Lucas had sent her a card, every year without fail. It seemed that his memory, as Cyan put it, was 'like a computer'. Owen mimicked the star-struck smile of the guileless young woman.

'I'm sure,' said Gabrielle, but Owen was not sceptical. His brother was the cleverest of the family, he told me, perhaps slighting his sister. Lucas's memory, when he was a boy, was 'quite phenomenal'. As evidence, he reminded Gabrielle of what had happened with the school production of Twelfth

Night. The first-choice Orsino had proved to be incapable of remembering his lines, but it was very late in the day when this incapacity was acknowledged to be insuperable. Just a week before the opening night, in fact. So Lucas was recruited as the emergency Orsino, and he succeeded in memorising every line in the course of a single weekend. 'Couldn't act,' admitted Owen, 'but that's not the point.' Lucas was a shy boy, and was not a natural actor. It took a lot of persuasion to get him to accept the part.

'The teacher got him on board by telling him he was a genius,' Gabrielle explained. 'Lucas always thought we undervalued him.'

'Perhaps we did,' said Owen.

'Maybe,' Gabrielle conceded, casting a begrudgingly appreciative gaze over the house that her brother had acquired.

'Strange how things turn out,' said Owen. 'We always thought he would become a lawyer.'

'We did not,' his sister stated. 'For a time one of us thought he might become a lawyer. I didn't. I thought he had the makings of a rogue.'

'Same thing.'

'Don't be a smart-arse, Owen.'

'But a lovable rogue,' said Owen. 'It is in the nature of the rogue to be lovable, isn't it?' He emptied his glass, and, with a grin that one might have taken to be rogueish, offered to replenish mine as well. I declined, as Chloe, looking over her sister's shoulder, directed at me a glance that made me feel like a conspirator. Then one of the widows tiptoed in, thrilled to have the opportunity to meet the brother and sister of Lucas, and I moved away.

That evening, I helped to clear up; I was the last to leave. Alone with me for a moment, in the kitchen,

Erin told me that she had intended to give something to Lucas's siblings, although he had omitted them from the will. They were his family, after all. But now she was not sure what she should do. 'The thing is, I didn't like them very much. Did you?' she asked. 'The sister thinks I'm an airhead, and the brother is grim.'

'You don't owe those people anything,' I advised.

By the next day, she had decided I was right. Her sister had agreed.

☞

Not all of Lucas's female clients had been ladies of a certain age, not by any means. Some were young or youngish, and with some of these – I don't know how many – a relationship 'arose'. Lucas's word: 'arose'. As if the relationship were a thing of its own volition. He talked about a woman he named Stella, who had lost a sister. Stella was 'preternaturally beautiful', he told me, with something like a smirk, a smirk of confession. We were talking man to man, Lucas believed.

☞

Erin's father appeared a couple of months after the funeral. Looking out of my window, I saw activity in the garden – a man wearing jeans and a dirty grey T-shirt, of Lucas's age, approximately, but considerably leaner, attacking the vegetation in the lee of the wall. For some time, the garden had been neglected. First thought: Erin had hired someone for the day. But he did not go about the work as a professional would have done. There was no evidence of method. The aim, it seemed, was simply to reduce the volume of greenery, in the shortest time possible. Without discrimination, he took shears and secateurs to every-thing; he ripped stuff away with his bare hands. Within fifteen minutes he had filled two plastic sacks with debris. Then Erin came out, carrying a mug, which he took from her, with a terse smile; she did not meet his look, and in that moment, though there was no obvious resemblance, I understood who this was.

He indicated the sacks and made a remark that seemed to be intended to amuse; Erin nodded, avoiding his eye. There was a sense of long familiarity, and discord.

When Erin went back into the house, the father surveyed the garden, assessing what destruction still needed to be achieved. Like a drinker at closing time, he tipped up the mug and emptied it in a gulp. He even wiped the back of a hand across his mouth. Refreshed, he seized the shears. In a dozen rapid cuts, he inflicted substantial new damage. His pleasure was obvious. There were moments at which he appeared to be carrying out an assault.

Erin returned, wearing a sweatshirt and tough gloves. She set to work on the honeysuckle, in the corner farthest from the father. She proceeded slowly – editing the plants, rather than hacking. There was no conversation. At one point I looked up from the computer to see that Erin had paused. In one hand she held a pair of scissors, in the other a sprig, at which she was looking, evidently reminded of something. The father, noticing, eased up. He put down the shears, on top of a sack, with care, as if out of respect for his daughter's delicate state of mind. She had her back to him, and did not turn when he approached. As he put his hand on the nape of her neck, she flinched. The reaction was small, but I saw it. And the way he touched her – what were we to make of it? Erin's neck is fine and narrow. The father's thumb slid to one side and the fingers to the other. More a gesture of possession than of love. It could immediately become a grasp, a clamp. The father was re-establishing his claim.

☞

She knew that Lucas had not died, Erin told me. In spirit form, he was still alive, and would always be alive. She knew this. But she knew it, she said, in the same way that she might know that a certain star is so many trillions of miles away, or that this room is filled with billions and billions of particles that cannot be seen. Memories of him were helping her, of course. There was not an hour of the day in which he was not in her mind. Sometimes a memory would burst in as if it came from yesterday rather than seven or eight years ago. But a memory of Lucas was not the same thing as the spirit of Lucas. The only person in a memory is the person who is having it, she said. I very much wanted to kiss her. Wiping her eyes, she looked around the living room. 'His absence is so strong,' she said. In every room his absence was present. It was like the negative of ghost. Every room felt wrong. 'This room,' she said, waving a dismissive hand, felt like a replica of the room in which Lucas was alive. 'The building is what's dead, not Lucas,' she said. She thought she might not be able to stay in the house much longer.

I sympathised. 'It won't always be as bad as this,' I assured her, or some equivalent banality. For months after my mother died I had felt that I no longer belonged to the house. It had become an immense memento. In the morning, the silence into which I awoke was something to be overcome. And so on.

The pain of the separation from the body of the loved one cannot be expunged, Lucas had once said to her, she now told me. He could help to reduce the pain, but he could not eradicate it. Once, at work in a house, fitting a floor, he had abruptly experienced the loss of his father as a shock almost as strong as the grief of the funeral. This grief was in a sense unwarranted, of course, yet it was real. The house in which he was working in no way resembled any place in which he had been with his father, but something – perhaps a sound of which he had not been conscious, or some quality of the light – had bereaved him afresh. He had wept, he admitted. 'I missed him,' Lucas told Erin, and now she smiled at the simple honesty of the statement. The spirit of his father was often present, but the man who had been his father had gone. 'I couldn't touch him. I couldn't see him. And on that afternoon I needed to see him, to touch him,' he had confessed. Bereavement is a perpetual earthquake, Lucas had said, said Erin; the aftershocks go on and on, becoming weaker, but never ceasing.

☞

Erin consulted a woman in Newton Abbot, name unknown. Of all the candidates within a sixty-mile radius, she was the one with most consistently positive customer feedback online, Erin told me. It would appear, then, that Lucas had never spoken highly of any other practitioners in his field, or at least none within sixty miles.

The visit was not a success. The door was opened by a nervy little woman, fiftyish, who seemed to be the live-in assistant; she conducted the client to the room in which the business would be done, then withdrew to the kitchen, to prepare refreshments. The room stank of patchouli, and thin curtains of cheap purple fabric were drawn across the windows. Purple was also the dominant hue of the medium's wardrobe – a kaftan, overlaid with wispy scarves. There was even a double-string necklace of silver beads. 'Everything but the crystal ball,' said Erin. She knew within a minute that this was going to be a disaster. Taking Erin's hand, the woman sandwiched it lightly between hands that were very large and very soft and quite horrible, like two miniature hot-water bottles, overfilled. 'Let's begin,' she said; the manner was patronising. It was as if the oracle had condescended to give an audience.

In the front room's overperfumed, overheated twilight (the radiators were working full blast, to induce a receptive drowsiness, Erin surmised), the spirit of Lucas was invoked. The invocation was something like a summons, said Erin; the woman pronounced his name as though commanding him to step out of the assembled legions of the deceased. With barely any delay, the spirit made its presence known. 'He is here,' the woman announced; one sensed that the spirits were always obedient when she called. Her eyes were closed, her arms folded; taking dictation from beyond, she conveyed the good tidings from Lucas.

The Newton Abbot oracle informed Erin that the spirit of Lucas was both happy and sad, but more happy than sad, because the period of sadness would soon come to an end. He sent messages of love and hope, messages expressed in words that bore no resemblance to the way that Lucas had spoken when alive; this spirit seemed to be taking its script from some New Age bestseller. This was bad enough. Then the spirit invited Erin to tell him how she was faring. 'Why would he do that?' Erin wondered. Lucas would not need to be told what her life was like without him. We are observable to the spirits, for as long as they look at us.

When the woman had finished with the uplifting nonsense, she invited questions on behalf of the spirit. It was ridiculous, Erin told me. The woman was carrying on like some sort of operator on an old-style telephone exchange, facilitating a conversation across the immensity of space. 'But that's not how it works,' Erin insisted. 'You don't have a chat with the dead.' Lucas could connect with the spirits, but he wasn't running a helpline.

As though what I was requesting was simply the clarification of one small aspect of an otherwise coherent dogma, I confessed, after consideration, that this was something I had never quite comprehended: as I understood it, nearly all other mediums undertook to relay questions from the survivors, but with Lucas the interaction with the dead was always an unequal relationship. The dead might make contact and speak to us, through a qualified intermediary, but we, according to Lucas, could not speak to them. This appeared to be a distinctive aspect of what we might term Lucas's practice. For Erin it was a guarantee of his integrity.

She explained: it was a mistake to use the word 'speak' when referring to the dead. The information that arrived through Lucas was not often speech in the everyday sense of the word. Yes, words were sometimes heard, but they were heard in the way that words are sometimes heard in dreams. When people relate what dream-people have said to them in the night, they always misrepresent what was heard: they makes sentences out of utterances that in most cases are not sentences at all – they are fragments, and fragments that are not truly 'heard', but instead arise from within. The 'messages' that Lucas received were not really messages. They were information of a rarified type, like radio waves, which Lucas could 'interpret', just as an astronomer can make sense of the noise that a radio telescope picks up. The metaphor was one to which Lucas had once resorted. Likewise, the dead observe us, but there can be no dialogue, or no dialogue of a talking kind. They pick up our 'radiation', said Erin, but they cannot hear us. 'What would they hear with?' she reasonably enquired.

Upstairs, however, in Lucas's filing cabinets, there were recordings and transcripts of many hours of speech, dictated by the dead, I pointed out.

Again, I had used an inaccurate verb. The words preserved in the archive were not so much dictation as translation. Once more I was invited to think of the analogy of dreams. We all know that dreams, when put into words, lose nearly all of their reality. The experience of dreaming is rich; it is real. Yet a dream, when described, becomes merely a summary, a description of something that eludes description.

To which I said 'OK', in such a way as to imply that the elucidation had been helpful, but there might be further questions. We were taking, I hoped, the first steps towards Erin's liberation.

☞

In the garden, admiring the letters carved by Callum, Erin said to me that Lucas had once told her that Callum was the one man he had ever wholly envied – until, of course, he had learned that his understanding of Callum had been incomplete. He had wished that Erin could have seen Callum at work. His touch was infallible, and as delicate as a surgeon's, Lucas would say. The letters would appear in the stone as if they had always been there and Callum had simply been removing the material that had covered them. Lucas would hear the three quick taps as a statement of three quick words: *This is right. This is right. This is right.* Callum, he would say, had been born into the wrong age: he should have been a mason at a great cathedral, where everyone would have addressed him as Master.

She asked me what I remembered of Callum.

My memory of him was now almost completely abstract, I told her. His name is associated with a tall white-haired man, seen in the garden; one sunny afternoon, cradling an injured dog he had found in the street, he had stood at our front door, talking to my father. 'That's about it,' I admitted.

We observed some silence, contemplating the work of Callum, and Erin told me something I had not known: Callum had signed all of his stonework in places where the signature could not be seen – under the foot of a headstone, or, as in this case, on the reverse of an inscription that was to be set into a wall or the ground.

And when Erin and Lucas had been in Venice, Lucas had remembered a story that Callum had told him, about a sculptor who had been commissioned to make the effigy for an important man's tomb. Because the tomb was to be placed high on a wall near the altar, not all of the effigy would be visible to the people in the church, so the sculptor had economised by carving only the side of the figure that could be seen from below. Callum was outraged.

'Quite rightly,' I said.

'Why?'

'Because one shouldn't try to short-change the Almighty. He can see what you've been up to.'

'You don't believe any of that,' said Erin. 'Don't pretend you do.'

'I'm not pretending,' I protested. 'I'm sympathising.'

'Anyway,' said Erin, 'God would understand. The tomb wasn't meant for him, was it?'

Recalling Callum's indignation, Lucas had wanted to find the offending tomb, but he had been unable to recollect the name of the church in question. A few candidates were found, but from floor level, none of those tombs looked unfinished. The guidebook had been of no use.

'And no guidance was available from Callum?' I wanted to ask; the joke would not have been appreciated. I was a man enamoured of a lovely nun, awaiting the day when sense begins to dawn. But of course there had been no guidance; the spirit of Callum had long been out of range.

Later, at home, I imagined a day in Venice, with Erin, when I would take her into the church that Lucas had failed to find, and point out the shoddy tomb.

And I remembered the evening, after they had come back from that holiday, when Lucas had moaned about the tawdriness of Venice.

'It's so beautiful,' said Erin, to me.

'Historyworld,' said Lucas. 'Too many bloody tourists.'

'As if we're not tourists.'

'Well, I'm not going back in a hurry,' said Lucas.

'I am,' said Erin. One night she'd stayed out until three o'clock, just walking the alleyways. 'It was magical,' she told me. Lucas had gone to bed; he couldn't face another bridge.

At the Rialto market Lucas had encountered a woman who, taking him for a person who seemed to know the place well, had asked him what she should make sure of seeing while she was there. 'How long have you got?' he asked; she would be leaving Venice the next morning. And then there were all the idiots taking pictures of everything instead of looking. 'Taking pictures of paintings, for crying out loud.'

'I'd like to be there for the Carnival,' said Erin.

'God in heaven,' muttered Lucas. It seemed possible that this was not purely a performance for my entertainment. 'All the masks are made in China,' said Lucas. 'Or Albania.'

'Still, I'd like to go,' said Erin.

And Lucas went on, about the terrible restaurants and the pushy gondoliers and the fancy-dress orchestras that play the *Four Seasons* every bloody evening and the inexcusable price of a coffee on the Piazza, et cetera, et cetera.

'It was wonderful,' Erin stated. The discord became discomfiting; I left, but encouraged.

The next day, before opening the curtains, I heard Erin laughing; they were arm in arm in the garden, and might have been talking about the previous evening's amusement.

It is significant that Erin told me, barely three months after Lucas's death, of a dream that had troubled her several times in the preceding weeks.

In this dream she is talking to Lucas late at night, in their kitchen. There is a portentous air to the encounter. It has no prelude: Lucas is facing her, in a room that seems to be lit by something outside the room, as if the house stands on open land and the moon is low in the sky and impossibly close. But she does not see the window; she sees only Lucas. The conversation is reasonable – or rather, it is conducted in a manner that seems reasonable. On waking, she could remember nothing of what was said; within the dream the words do not function as words function in waking life; their meaning does not persist.

Syllables succeed syllables in the way that music proceeds; onward motion is constant. An act of conversation is being performed. It seems to be some sort of ritual – this is what Erin always thinks in the dream. Though she is participating, she is not perfectly sure of the nature of the action in which she is taking part. At one point, in a brief episode in which anger is represented, there is a sense of an audience's presence, as if there were no wall behind them. She does not, though, turn round to see if they are being watched; an implicit constraint makes it impossible to turn away from Lucas. He raises both hands slightly, in a gesture that signifies that he is conceding something. He takes a step forward. It appears that they are about to embrace; the conclusion has been reached. Then Lucas falls back. There is no contact, but he goes down as if struck with violence. He makes no sound as he falls, and the fall is histrionic – his arms fly out and he throws his head back, as if falling onto a mattress. Lying on the floor, he closes his eyes and smiles. 'Look,' he sometimes says, calmly. Always he opens his eyes and looks at Erin, and his smile broadens. 'It's good,' he says, or 'It's OK.' Now, in the space of a second, fear floods into the dream; she sees that Lucas cannot move. 'The face of a friend,' he murmurs. He brings down his eyelids.

This is what Erin told me. She held my arm in a crushing grip.

Mrs Musmari, a medium in Rottingdean, in her capacity as Lucas's spokeswoman, instructed Erin to be happy. 'All is as it should be,' she reported. Words were uttered that could have been spoken by Lucas. And yet, though Erin was with her for most of an afternoon, in all that time Mrs Musmari gave no proof of knowing anything about Lucas that could not have been learned in an hour online. She relayed only words that anyone, knowing Erin's circumstances, would have assumed that this young woman would want to hear. Erin consulted people in Rochester and Oxford. She went as far as Chester and Ely. The woman in Chester asked her in what way Lucas might help her, as though her business were some kind of supernatural customer support. Her intentions were good, though, as were the intentions of almost all of them, Erin thought, but none were credible; none surprised her.

Or rather, only one surprised her: a male medium, middle-aged, formerly a member of some obscure religious order, purportedly, with something of a drink problem, she came to suspect, and a double-barrelled Germanic surname that might even have been genuine; there was the hint of an accent with certain vowels. Having conveyed the good news from the other side, he made a pass at her. Lucas had, after all, urged her to 'live her life to the full' and 'not surrender to mourning'.

These people offered nothing but fake sunshine, Erin complained. She was disappointed by them, but I saw something other than disappointment when she told me what they had asked her to believe. The anguish that I glimpsed was not to be explained by the bad faith of these imposters: it was the anguish of guilt. Lucas, were he to appear, would in some way address the origin of that guilt; that was how she would be able to tell if the presence of Lucas had really been detected. This was obvious to me, as was the cause of that guilt. It was not the kiss; that had been the sin of a moment, or no sin at all.

In Ely the spirit of Lucas had transformed the medium's voice from its customary fluting tone (she was a wispy lady, in her seventies) to a catarrhal rasp, a performance suggestive more of exorcism than of benign communication from the realm of the departed. Erin had broken the spell and irked the woman by laughing, and she almost laughed in telling me what had happened. Encouraged, I said: 'You don't need these people.' I told her that we would always remember Lucas. 'That's enough,' I proposed. But I had misjudged.

'Don't give me that look,' she said, as if I had stopped all pretence and dismissed these frauds for what they were.

'What look?' I protested.

'You know exactly what I mean,' she said, with a stabbing gaze, in which there was also the despair of the confounded.

The door was open, she knew, but she was not yet ready to step through.

☞

Erin had been listening to Lucas's voice. On the table, in the living room, there was a small cassette player. Erin had few photos of Lucas; many of herself, taken by Lucas, but few of him. In the archive, however, there were scores of recordings of Lucas at work, and one of these recordings had been made on the day she first met him, the day he came to help the family. This is the only tape to which she felt entitled to listen; to have played any of the others would have been like reading through a doctor's notes.

It was typical of Lucas that he should have continued to use cassettes long after everyone else had moved on to more modern technology, she said, approvingly. We looked around the room: the cumbrous furniture, the shabby rugs, the lamps. Only the television signified the present decade.

'Lucas wasn't what I had been expecting,' said Erin. We were returning to the story of their first meeting; I encouraged her to talk about it, and she did, at length, willingly; it seemed to help.

It had not seemed possible, she told me again, that the person she saw walking up to the front door could be the renowned clairvoyant: the dark suit and tie and white shirt, the heavy-looking briefcase – it all made him look like a lawyer. He talked like a lawyer, too – 'very precise with his words'. The voice and manner, though, were 'soothing'.

After he had taken all the information that the photos could provide, he was ready to begin the séance – though 'séance' was a term that Lucas had never used, Erin wanted me to know; he preferred the plain 'consultation' or 'meeting'. He went to the table, where he opened the briefcase and carefully laid out its contents: the recorder, a notepad, pens. Each thing was placed as though it had a predetermined and exact place on the tabletop. He asked for a glass of water; he took a sip, and set the glass to the side of the notepad.

The family was invited to come up to the table; the parents flanked him, the daughters opposite. Erin had assumed that they would be required to hold hands, but this was not Lucas's method, on this occasion; it was rarely Lucas's method. Silence and concentration were required, not a physical connection. The silence might be lengthy, he warned them, and it was not guaranteed that anything would come out of it. Communication was not always achieved. Having made a quick note, as though dating the minutes of a meeting, Lucas asked the family to think of Tom, of 'nothing but Tom'. He switched on the tape recorder, then closed his eyes and put his hands, linked lightly, on the table.

For several minutes the only sound was the whirr of the turning tape. Then, at last, Lucas began to talk. He talked to Erin's mother, and the conversation was very strange, Erin told me. For one thing, Lucas did not open his eyes. His voice was altered too – softer than before, and 'blurred'. Everything he said made sense, 'in a way', but he was like a man talking in his sleep. He asked some questions about Tom, and these questions were interspersed with sentences or phrases that were like 'dreamy reminiscences'. Some of these reminiscences seemed to be the speaker's recollections of Tom, as though they had been friends many years ago; others sounded as if they were words that Tom himself might have spoken.

Her ingenuousness, when telling me this, was that of the Erin who was meeting Lucas for the first time.

The strange exchange between Lucas and Erin's mother lasted for a quarter of an hour, maybe. It ended with Lucas opening his eyes. Groggily, he looked from face to face; he seemed not to know immediately who these people were. He scanned the faces again. Nobody knew what to do, but it seemed that the session must now be coming to an end. On the third pass across the faces, the movement of Lucas's head abruptly halted, like a mechanism that had jammed. He was looking at Erin, and as he looked at her the quality of his gaze underwent a change that frightened her, she admitted. Fixing his gaze on Erin's eyes, he frowned, as though he were seeing something that he could scarcely believe he was seeing. 'He looked into me. He made me shrink inside myself,' she told me.

(Another aspect of Erin's character; the absence of vanity. It is no surprise that Lucas, aged fifty-two, should have fixed his attention on the lovely Erin, twenty. Yet she conducted herself as if she had never seen her own image. We can assume that for Lucas too the innocence, or apparent innocence, was appealing.)

Then there was another alteration in the quality of Lucas's gaze; a 'huge kindness' arose; it 'overwhelmed' her. More than that – the object of Lucas's scrutiny seemed to change. He wasn't peering into Erin's soul – his gaze was searching for something else, something that was within her but was not herself. 'It's really hard to explain,' she said. It was as if Lucas were looking down into a cave, through a hole that had just opened in the ground, and he had seen Erin inside the cave; but then, as the darkness in the cave had lightened, he had noticed that there were images painted on the walls, and it was these images that he was now trying to read. Once she had overruled her timidity, she submitted to this 'reading'. She 'cancelled' herself; she made her eyes into windows, so that Lucas could see clearly what he needed to see. This is what Erin told me. This image of the cave is hers.

The inspection, though it was the work of no more than two minutes, seemed to demand a great deal of mental energy from Lucas. Exhausted, he sat back and rubbed his eyes, breathing deeply, as though he had won, after hours of unremitting concentration, a game of chess against a stronger player. Now he was his normal self again. He turned off the recorder, quickly made some notes, and then began a conversation about what had occurred.

But before Lucas left them, Erin told me, he did something else that amazed her. The sister had to be somewhere else, and said goodbye; the father and mother left the room, to fetch the payment. Thus, for a minute or two, Erin and Lucas were left together. The moment the door closed on them, Lucas said something to Erin that made her shiver. Precisely what he said, she could not disclose; just in speaking of it, she was quavering. The essential facts, however, are these: that Erin had for some time been involved with a young man to whom she was by this point not so much attracted as submissive; and Lucas, with no preamble whatever, turned to her and uttered a few words that were sufficient to convince her that he had intuited every nuance of her situation. He advised her, with some force, to reject the boyfriend forthwith; he understood that she had come to feel powerless, but she must overthrow this subjugation, difficult though this would be; and he could absolutely promise her that, were she to do it, she would very soon find herself loved genuinely by someone whom she would in turn come to love. She understood him to be referring to somebody she had yet to meet; there was 'nothing personal' in his manner, she said; he spoke to her like a doctor giving his diagnosis.

At 'love', the tears appeared; she wept soundlessly. I offered a handkerchief, laundered and pressed in anticipation. It was permissible, I saw, to console by taking a hand. She looked at our coupled hands as though they were a gift, but was not quite sure what kind of thing this gift might be. As soon as the tears had been staunched, I released.

Yes, I wanted to hear the voice of Lucas at work. It was not possible, however, to ask if I might listen to that tape. Even had she not been crying, I would not have asked. That evening, I did not ask. Later, just once, I did; and I accepted the refusal immediately.

☞

We leafed through a book that had once belonged to Callum, a hefty volume from which, as I drew it out from the slip-case, a sweet scent of ageing paper was released. At a page that showed the cloister at Sénanque, I paused. No picture could do justice to this place, I told Erin. I waffled about the architecture, the setting, the atmosphere. The air at Sénanque was delicious. I had a lot to say about the air and the light, about how one is changed by the experience of the building, even if only for as long as one is inside it. The experience was a sensual one: it tempts you to believe in God. But the God of Sénanque was not the God of all churches – certainly not the God of, say, a Baroque church in Rome. The God of Sénanque was as severe as the unadorned walls, yet the building was filled with light and scented air, which could be taken to be the light of heaven and the air of love. On the other hand, the God of the Baroque is the extravagant master of the cosmos, the ultimate winner, the glorious One. He overwhelms us with gifts, and at the same time threatens us, I proposed, and then I starting talking about a question that had first interested me after I had spent some time in the church of Santa Sabina, a question that still interested me, and which nobody could answer conclusively, or so I thought. The columns of the nave were what had fascinated me – they had been scavenged from an ancient temple, dedicated to the goddess Juno. How should we interpret them? As signs of the triumph of Christianity over paganism, perhaps. As trophies of war, or captives, imprisoned forever in this huge temple of the one true God.

I became aware that, in trying to advance my position, to secure myself in her affection, I was talking to Erin as Lucas might have talked; I was lecturing. I could not simply stop, however; it was necessary to conclude properly. I went on: the columns may have no symbolic meaning at all. Practicality and aesthetics could be the whole explanation. The columns offered a quantity of ready-made and durable material, and the quality of the handiwork was superior to anything the Christian builders could have produced, so why not just recycle them? They served a purpose, that's all. The supposed meaning was something we were reading into them. It was an intriguing question, I assured her, bringing the monologue to a halt.

Erin looked at me and smiled; the smile confirmed that I had been holding forth. 'Heavy,' she said.

I am aware that I lack lightness at times. So it was not the meaning of the remark that triggered a silent objection: it was the banality of the word, its laziness; and also, perhaps, that the remark had come from someone who had been the companion of Lucas – Lucas, of all people; a man of weighty conversations. I was disappointed by the cliché of that single word, but the disappointment, such as it was, brought some sort of reprieve, for a moment. Mildly aggrieved, I had some respite from the difficulty and unhappiness of loving Erin.

Then Kit woke up, and Erin fetched her, and at the sight of Erin the mother I was captured again.

In the course of an evening's conversation with Maxim Gorky, the renowned mystic Anna Nikolayevna Schmidt discussed her previous incarnations as Saint Catherine of Siena and Saint Elizabeth of Thuringia. Furthermore, she explained how it had been revealed to her that Christ had returned to this world in 1853, taking the form of the scholar-philosopher Vladimir Solovyov, with whom she was destined to beget a heavenly son, by whom this world would be eradicated. Reporting their conversation for the newspaper that employed him, Gorky wrote that Anna Nikolayevna had spoken 'ancient words belonging to the seekers of perfect wisdom and inexorable truth'. Gorky was also impressed by Madame Blavatsky.

Everything in the universe is a form of light, Anna Nikolayevna Schmidt maintained; our flesh is nothing but condensed light. In his *Fragments from My Diary*, Gorky proposed an idea that bears some similarity to Schmidt's: 'At some future time all matter absorbed by man shall be transmuted by him and his brain into a sole energy – a psychical one. This energy shall discover harmony in itself and shall sink into self-contemplation – in a meditation over all the infinitely creative possibilities concealed in it.' He expounded this theory to the poet Aleksandr Blok, 'What a dismal fantasy,' Blok commented.

A fisherman and his wife live in a cottage on the edge of an extensive bog that lies between the house and the bay. This is in Connemara. Each evening, when the husband returns, she sees the light of his lantern a long way off. There is no straight route across the bog: he must pick his way from stone to stone, tussock to tussock. The crossing takes a long time. When it first appears, the light of the lantern shines in the left-hand part of the window; when the wife looks out ten minutes later, the light is in the opposite part; ten minutes later again, it is in the centre, still tiny; the man himself is not yet visible; it will take him another hour to reach his door. When I read it, this appealed as an image for Erin, approaching by an indirect and perilous path, across the bog of nonsense.

I came down to the beach for the last hour of sunlight. The sky at the horizon demanded attention: a long low range of ash-and-iron cloud, with streaks the colour of pomegranate juice. The surface of the sea was gorgeous too: under the breeze and the glancing sunlight, the water was a jostle of violet, black, silver, apricot, white, blue-grey – all of these colours and more. And at the water's edge, two dots of fuchsia stood out – the matching sunhats of Erin and Kit.

Staying on the higher part of the sand, by the fallen rocks, I walked beyond them, and onward for ten minutes. I walked back with the water almost touching my feet. The hats were still there, and I raised a hand as Erin turned. She waved; I was being invited.

I talked to Erin, about nothing memorable, while Kit pranced out of the little waves and in again and out. Then Kit sat down, to let the water flow over her legs. She scooped the sand around her, and on the third or fourth scoop uncovered something; she picked it out and showed it to us. We crawled to take a closer look: a bean of sea glass, pale green, frosted. I rinsed the sand from it, and put it in Kit's palm, and folded her fingers gently over it, to secure the treasure. A few times more she scoured the sand, but discovered nothing else. She made a small mound, and placed the bean of glass on its summit, with great care.

The affection with which I watched Erin's daughter was wholly genuine, but the manner of the watching had an element of artifice. The expression, I hoped, would elicit the question: 'What are you thinking?'

The question arrived, and my answer was: 'Some other time.' But within a minute I was telling her – or proposing – that we should learn from the happiness of Kit. The experience that we were witnessing was immeasurable; it was infinite. Then I stepped over the threshold. 'This is eternal life, right here,' I pronounced. 'Life and death are completely separate things. They do not mix. They cannot mix, by definition.'

'Yes they do,' said Erin. 'Of course they do.'

'No,' I insisted. 'If one lives in the present moment, with the greatest possible intensity, one lives eternally,' I told her, as if the thought were mine, presenting the proof of her daughter.

'I have no idea what you're talking about, Josh,' said Erin. 'You really want to be talking to Lucas,' she said, then she gathered Kit up, and brushed the sand from her legs, too briskly.

☞

At the seafront, one night last year, in weather much like tonight's, a memory of my father presented itself, with the power and suddenness of an apparition. Spray flew up against the darkness and in an instant I saw his face, or I remembered his face as though he had been beside me only minutes earlier. He had been standing beside me, holding my hand as we looked across the water. The wind was making me stagger; my hair was drenched. Over the years, this scene has often come to mind, or elements of it, in various combinations: darkness, noise, waves, my father and I standing together; an atmosphere of thrilling tumult, even peril, but peril at a distance. What is being recalled – or so my mother told me – is a night on which a boat ran aground. We had all walked down to the seafront to see what the storm was doing, she told me. There is no longer any boat in what remains in my mind of that night, and my mother is never there either, though in reality she was. I have a sense only of my father's presence, a presence which, one night last year, became abruptly acute, seconds after it had struck me, with the dash of seawater, that I was standing where my father and I had stood. Momentarily the image of his face was apparent. Against the blackness of the sky his face looked at me – a glance of solidarity, a fortifying smile, as though the storm might worsen but we would confront it together and would see it out. The face was my father's, vividly, but it was perhaps not his face as I had seen it on the night during which the forgotten boat had foundered on the beach. It could have been a face of my imagining, derived from a photo, transposed to the flimsy theatre of my memory. Yet my father in some form had appeared, with more substance than I could make him appear tonight, though the scene was prepared for him, as I stood where we had stood on the night we had all gone down to the beach to watch the waves. The wraith would not be summoned. I had only the memory of having remembered him strongly.

The boyfriend who had preceded Lucas had imagined that he would be famous by the time he reached the age of twenty-five. He was the lead guitarist and vocalist in a band with two ex-schoolmates and a drummer who was a few years older and had been booted out of a couple of bands already, partly on account of his drinking, but mainly, Erin thought, because he was 'a colossal arsehole'. The boyfriend also wrote songs. One of them, inspired by Erin, was called 'Ellen'. It was embarrassing, she told me. Even if it hadn't been embarrassing she wouldn't have liked the song; it sounded like something that any of fifty other bands might have produced; most of the boyfriend's songs sounded familiar. Once in a while the band played a pub gig, and the set always finished with 'Ellen'. She was required to be present at every gig, because she was the main man's muse. 'That was my job,' she told me. In addition to providing inspiration, she was also required to serve as the boyfriend's counsellor and lightning conductor. Acclaim was being withheld from him, while the talentless were prospering wherever he looked. 'Sex was his way of letting off steam, and he had a lot of steam to let off.' She actually told me this. We talked about the violent sex to which she had been subjected, until Lucas had rescued her.

She said to me: 'To tell you the truth, I'm not all that interested in sex.' She was not abashed; it might have been merely an expression of personal taste.

Perhaps, I thought, hearing this, I had not been entirely wrong, after all, in how I had imagined her relationship with Lucas to be. And I would, I suspect, have flattered myself with the idea that I, at some imprecise point in the future, might be the person to make Erin think differently; I would be the gentle corrective, the belated antidote to the poisonous boyfriend. The pleasure of sex was so brief, she said, and so selfish. Assuming a confessor's face, I assured her that I understood what she meant. I hinted that this understanding might owe something to my relationship with Miriam.

The thing one had to know about Lucas, she told me, was that respect for other people was for him a fundamental principle. He respected all the people – or very nearly all the people – who asked for his 'guidance' (this was the word she used), and he had respected her, as the boyfriend had not. 'We're meant for each other,' the boyfriend liked to say; to reinforce the point, he gave her a ring that was made of two interlocking rings. Lucas, on the other hand, 'found nothing more depressing' than couples who were – or wanted you to see that they were – a perfect fit for each other. The 'cult of completion', as he sometimes called it, implied an excessive self-regard, Lucas believed, according to Erin. She was not the 'right person' for Lucas, she told me. 'For a start I was too young, obviously,' she said. 'And I don't have a brain like his. I am not an intellectual person.' This is what so many people had misunderstood: the differences between them did not disprove their love – the opposite was in fact the case. A lot of people are capable of loving only their mirror image, Erin told me. Lucas knew better. Lucas knew what love meant. His life was an example of what love really was.

Again I encouraged her to talk about Lucas. Talking, perhaps, would bring her sooner to a state of mind in which she could begin to free herself. I listened, the hypocrite, like the truest of friends. Recently I had read something for which I thought I might be able to find some use. Now I deployed it, altering the words to take possession of the idea. The relationship with the boyfriend had been a mistake, Erin said, but I replied that no relationship should be regarded as a mistake: our false loves are the necessary preliminaries to the real one; they enable us to recognise it. And I had more to say: there is another kind of love, which, rather than excluding all others as the one real love comes into focus, widens out continually to encompass everything. This spiritual love, I implied, was also what Erin had been talking about, when she talked about Lucas and what love really was.

'Yes,' said Erin. Her gratitude was overpowering; I hated myself, or so I told myself. 'Yes,' she said again, as though I had been revealed as one of the few who could comprehend.

☞

I was at work in my room, around ten at night, six months after the death of Lucas, to the day, when I saw Erin outside, by the kitchen door, mug in hand, gazing into the garden. She looked up, at my window, and nodded; when I waved she smiled, and the smile was an appeal. I went down to ask, over the wall, if she would like to talk.

No sooner had I sat beside her than she said: 'I'm lost'. It was said loudly, to the room, as if appealing to an audience of many people, ranged in ranks around her. Then she told me what had happened that day.

She had gone into town, as soon as the shower had stopped. Overhead, the clouds were coming apart; the mixture of charcoal clouds and bright blue sky was alluring; she stopped to appreciate it. Minute by minute the gaps between the clouds were widening. The edges of the clouds dissolved in the blueness. 'And then it began to go wrong,' she said to me. Something made her feel that it was necessary to wait until the sky had become entirely clear. So she waited and watched. When only a few rags of cloud were left, she became aware that the streets had become busier; there were too many people, and the way that they were moving was not quite right – they were like actors in a crowd scene. A change had occurred. Then, a hundred yards away, approaching, there was somebody she knew. It seemed that he had not yet seen her. Erin did not know what to do. An encounter was imminent. Should she make herself distracted, and allow him to walk past? She had a bag over her shoulder. At this point, should she open it, and take something out? That would allow her to avoid contact. But it was possible that contact was supposed to occur. If that were the case, would there be a greeting, or even a conversation? If they were to talk, what was she to say? She looked around, and everyone she saw was moving with purpose; those who were speaking knew what to say; the listeners knew their part as well. Because she had no words to speak, her feeling was that she should do something with the bag. Opening it, she glanced up, straight ahead, and saw that the man she knew had crossed the street. Now there was no need for any business with the bag. This might have been the moment for her to leave the scene. If so, which way was she to go? The answer did not present itself. It was as if she had yet to receive an instruction. By what means this instruction would be delivered, she did not know. Even more people were on the street now; all knew where they were going. Right in front of her, two people walked towards each other, with arms raised; the embrace happened smoothly. Erin could find no reason to move in one direction rather than any other. There could be only one answer: she had to wait. Through some agency other than her own, the situation would be rectified. 'My head was a mess,' she told me. Some thoughts made a noise in her head, but the thoughts were not hers. A woman was standing in front of her. She placed a hand on Erin's arm, and said: 'Is anything wrong?' And Erin answered: 'It's all right.' And suddenly it was.

'Now I feel better,' she said. We talked for another hour, again about the day she had met Lucas. There was some more crying. I held her hand.

This point must be reiterated: I was invited into the house and Erin spoke to me, at length, about that episode of crisis. I held her hand; she asked me to keep her company.

For Kit's birthday, I bought her some toys – small things – and delivered them in the morning. A strangely warm spring day; Kit was in the garden. One by one I took the presents from the bag. Three or four were examined briefly, then set aside in expectation of the next. The first to hold her attention was a toy pair of sunglasses, with lenses that were interchangeable, in a variety of colours. I held them to my eyes, and laughed for Kit, marvelling at her through discs of yellow-green plastic. Then I handed them to her – they were slightly too large, but she clamped them in place with her hands, delighted by how everything was changed. Looking up at the suddenly plum-coloured sky, she toppled, and I caught her. Her mother's skin and hair were hilariously weird. I fitted the pink lenses; more delight. The violet lenses, however, appeared to give a different order of amazement. Arms outspread for balance, she looked down onto the lawn, as if gazing from a huge height on whole fields and valleys. She knelt, to peer into the magical grass.

Erin wondered if anything of this would remain in Kit's mind for long. 'Maybe, when she's my age,' she said, when Kit had gone indoors to find out how the kitchen would look, 'she'll see a violet glass and suddenly feel happy, and have absolutely no idea why.' For Erin, the smell of seaweed, she told me, sometimes had an inexplicable effect of that kind. Not fresh and wet seaweed – only seaweed of a certain kind, baked stiff in the sun, with the air at a certain temperature, and no wind. A particular intensity of iodine stink, in those conditions – it gave her a moment of elation, which must have something to do with a moment of which she had forgotten everything, so that only the happiness has lasted, locked in a box somewhere in the depths of her brain, and once in a while the box is momentarily unlocked, by the seaweed-key, and a wisp of that happiness is released. The source would be a day from a holiday in Devon or Cornwall, she assumed.

I had something similar to tell her. For me, however, it was not a case of an emotion arising abruptly, for reasons unknown, from a specific thing or things in the world; rather, I sometimes had an inexplicable feeling of well-being that brought with it a memory – or what felt like a memory – of something that could not be traced.

This memory was an image that was barely an image – it was a momentary disturbance, something that seemed to be on the brink of emerging into full sight but then fell back in the same second, barely glimpsed; intuited more than seen. The image, if I could call it that, was of a skim of very fine and very dry sand, over tarmac – a road disappearing under sand. Occasionally, a larger picture was implied: a slatted barrier of grey and heavily weathered wood; beyond, a low dune; beyond it, sensed but never visible, the sea. In that instant, the best of all possible days seemed to be promised.

Now Kit was standing in front of us, ready for whatever else the bag might have for her. When it was empty, a hug was given, without prompting; and a concomitant hug from her mother, plus a cheek kiss, very light. Nonetheless, it had significance, I felt; a new period was beginning.

Later in the morning, while I was at work, Kit came out of the house, leading a trio of children. They blew bubbles towards the garden wall, and Kit watched the bubbles float, through the yellow-green lenses. Trouble broke out, bringing Erin and another mother out. Having restored the mood, Erin looked up at my window, and smiled, raking her hair with her fingers.

☞

The father visited Erin again, not long after Kit's birthday. I observed only the preliminaries to his departure. Erin was in the garden, sitting at the table, with the cat in her lap; she gazed at the clouds; recovering from an upset, it appeared. I did not know that the father was in the house. And then he came out, zipping his jacket; from the way he rubbed his hands, and the semi-sad little smile, it was clear that he was leaving. Erin deposited the cat on the tabletop and stood up. With the back of a finger, her father touched her cheek; he said something to which she appeared to assent. Though the gesture was one of consolation, the father's face was not expressive of love; there was an element of beseeching, yes, but the gaze was primarily that of a man who commands. The smile with which he responded to his daughter's acquiescence seemed to signify approval, and gratification at having secured obedience.

It was time to go. Turning, he put an arm around her shoulder and pulled her closer. Side by side they took a step, and his hand moved down, to her waist. She allowed him to conduct her to the kitchen door, but her arms hung by her side. That struck me. And her gaze was directed at the ground. She might have been a woman being taken home from hospital.

In the light of what was observed, how was I to think of Erin and Lucas? Was Lucas the paternal lover or the anti-father; a lover chosen as a surrogate, or in defiance of the family?

Watching a film in which the husband, the owner of the hotel, passing the pretty chambermaid on the stairs, takes her hand and kisses her, of course I am made aware that a kiss might mean little or nothing, in real life as much as in an Italian film of a certain vintage.

The stair-kiss is not resisted, but it leads to nothing; it does not quite constitute adultery – it is an enquiry as to whether more might be obtainable. The chambermaid indulges the incorrigible boss; she grants this kiss, and that will be all, as we can tell from the look she gives him, over her shoulder, as she strides up the stairs. There are no consequences; within a day, the moment will be forgotten by both. A kiss might be no more than a whim, a misstep. Ours, however, was of a different order. The truth might be revealed in a moment; a brief dialogue of touch, in which more is said than by all the words that went before. I am not making too much of it; I am certain of this. Or think of an old photograph on glass – at first it seems to be nothing but a rectangle of matt smoky grey, but when picked up, and angled into the light, the object changes in an instant, and the image appears; so the truth appears. Some time ago, a woman who intrigued me very much said to me, by way of clearing the path, that she would never kiss a man unless she intended to go to bed with him. She was older than me, by six or seven years. When she said this, I felt even younger; I was made to feel that I was a fool, and I hesitated. So she did not kiss me. Her name was Ursula; this is a regret.

⇞

The woman who moved into number 26 a year ago had again walked past Erin without as much as an acknowledgement. There was no possibility that she hadn't seen her; they almost brushed shoulders. 'She must know the situation,' said Erin. 'Neighbours would have told her.' I have seen this woman a few times; I smiled once, to no visible effect. She seemed joyless, I suggested. Recently divorced with a great deal of ill-will on both sides, I would guess. 'Better than widowed,' said Erin. The people at number 12 – 'Mr and Mrs Ideal Home' – didn't exactly radiate compassion either. She saw them looking at the upstairs windows of the house as if the peeling paintwork told them everything they needed to know. Whenever they came across Erin with Kit they went through the motions of friendliness, but you could see, despite the smiles, that they were passing judgement.

There were people in the neighbourhood who would never accept her, she insisted. People who thought that Lucas was a charlatan necessarily disapproved of her. Others – because Erin was young and pretty, and Lucas was not – thought that she must have ensnared him. She had always wanted the house, some were convinced. Nobody could really accept the relationship. Some blamed Lucas: he dominated the girl; he oppressed her. And then there was the baby: a young mother and an old father – it was just not right. With Lucas gone, some modified their attitude a little. There was some sympathy for the bereaved and solitary parent. But Erin did not want the sympathy of people who had gossiped about her, and about Lucas. Now there was even some gossip about Erin and me, she told me. People were putting two and two together and making five; this is what she'd heard, from sources unspecified. The situation was impossible, said Erin. She was going to sell the house.

'That would be a pity,' I said. 'You have friends here.'

'Not many,' she answered.

And the town would be a good place for Kit to grow up in, for a while at least; not too big, not too small; the sea; the clean air, et cetera. The house was very comfortable too.

She admitted, without speaking, that these points were to be considered.

Then I said: 'And of course I love you. There's that to consider.'

The first reaction: Erin smiled. Perhaps she took it as some sort of joke about the gossips, or thought I was using the verb as it's so often used now, as a synonym for 'like'.

So I said: 'I do.' The words were spoken lightly. What I was saying was that this was a fact, a wholly objective fact. It was not a plea or a declaration; it was simply a statement of who I was.

But tears appeared to be imminent, and Erin asked, perplexed rather than affronted: 'Why would you say that?'

To which I replied: 'For the sake of clarity.'

I could see that a mistake had been made. This was not the right time for the statement. Retraction, however, would be futile; impossible, in fact. A kiss is no sooner shared than it becomes the idea of itself; but words remain words; their half-life is long.

'Well, moving on,' I joked, as if this were a meeting with an agenda to be followed.

Erin gave me an examining look.

'It's true,' I said, and shrugged. 'I'm sorry.'

'OK,' she said, as one would say 'OK' to someone who had confessed to a misdemeanour that might be forgiveable in a week or two.

Several years ago, I was interested in a particular person, and things seemed to be progressing satisfactorily until the evening when she said to me, as if stating one of the maxims by which she lived: 'I have never said "I love you" to anybody, and I never will.' It was a question of respect, both for oneself and for the other person. The phrase was a brand, with which the self-declared lover put his or her mark on the loved one. Disappointed, I took issue; the words might not correspond to a definable state, I agreed, but they were nonetheless valid as an expression. I was saying that, she suggested, because I had hoped to hear her say, one day, to me: 'I love you.' Here, at least, she was right; I knew this at once, though I did not concede the point.

With Erin, however, I did not utter the phrase in the hope of being repaid in kind. She could not yet love me. I knew that.

☞

Another regret: it was an error to raise with Erin the subject of my mother and Lucas. I told her what Lucas had said, near the end.

Erin considered the words. I was misunderstanding what Lucas had meant; he had loved people the way a priest loves people. Lucas loved everybody, in a way.

This was not quite true, I suggested, with examples of people whom Lucas had very much not loved – Steven Greenwood, for example. Father Brabham.

It was impressive that she did not flinch. 'One or two exceptions,' she granted.

Allowing that the crucial word can be taken to mean many different things, I nonetheless thought that Lucas had wished me to hear a particular sense. And it was not only a matter of what was heard: in speaking those words, Lucas had given me a certain look.

'What look?'

Despite the irritation in her voice, I did not stop. 'A look to ensure that I heard what he was saying,' I said.

'He was ill. Very ill,' she answered. If Lucas had wanted to tell me anything, he would have told me straight, she stated. 'And he would have told you before.'

We were in the kitchen; she had found something to do that allowed her to turn away from me. Food had to be prepared for Kit, who was asleep upstairs. 'Perhaps,' I said. Then I speculated about the reasons for my mother's attitude.

'She just didn't like me,' said Erin, having turned to face me. Perched on the edge of the table, she crossed her arms. 'Look,' she said, 'you were close to your mother.' It was not quite an accusation. 'And you never suspected anything, for years and years. That's a clue.'

The answer: a man tends to look upon his mother as a woman apart from other women.

'Some do. Some don't. Anyway, she would have told you, one way or another.'

'But closeness might be a reason not to own up,' I said. It was a question of what might have been lost by telling the truth; the destruction of an image of herself.

'Whose image?' asked Erin, impatient at the obscurity.

'Hers and mine. Shame would be a factor. Guilt.'

My mother had not owned up, Erin told me, because there had been nothing to which to own up. Her arms were more tightly crossed now; she looked at me as a store detective might regard an incompetent shoplifter.

'No,' I said, with the urgency of correction. For the first time we were in conflict, and in this conflict was a new intimacy. 'This is what we know,' I began, and I put things together. Might there not be a connection between the arrival of Lucas and the departure of my father, a connection that I had previously failed to make, having been sure that I had understood the cause of my father's leaving?

'You mean: the one you're now imagining,' said Erin. 'There's no evidence. None whatever.'

'But it's a possibility.'

'Which has only just occurred to you.' Finally the arms were unlocked; her attention was directed wearily towards something in the garden. 'Joshua,' she said, 'there's a good reason it never occurred to you before. It's because it doesn't make any sense.'

'Maybe,' I said. And yet, although I knew it was not in my best interests to continue to the end, Erin's scorn compelled me. 'There's one other thing,' I went on. The question was: why would a man leave his home like that, and never see the child again? One solution would be: if he had come to believe that his son might not be his son at all. The dates could be made to match. 'That would be an explanation,' I submitted. Looking down, I opened my arms, to let the story go. But then I added, thinking – if thinking at all – that this might reduce the pressure in the room: 'Jack Nicholson was in his thirties when he found out that his sister was in fact his mother.'

Erin pressed her hands to her face and kept them there. A significant readjustment had been imposed upon her, I thought. But I had misunderstood. Slowly she dragged her fingers down her face, uncovering eyes that showed only anger. Her voice, however, was quiet and even, as though reading the words from a page. 'It's not that you haven't been able to understand it,' she said. 'It's that you haven't been able to accept it.' I interrupted, but she drove over what I was saying. 'Your father deserted his wife and child. That's what some people do. Men, mostly. Some men are horrible and some of those horrible men have children.'

'Indeed,' I replied. 'I'm not saying—'

In an instant the volume of her voice went up, but the evenness of tone was constant. I surrendered with pleasure. 'It makes no sense, Joshua,' she told me; the name was used like a cosh. 'Absolutely none. Think about it. It's idiotic. You've come up with this stupid story on the basis of what? One word. One word from a dying man. One fucking word. What the fuck, Joshua? What the actual fuck are you talking about?' Never before had I heard Erin talk like this; it was like an undressing.

'All I'm saying is my father might have thought—'

'And Lucas too,' she interrupted. 'But for reasons unknown he never says anything to you. He's living on the other side of the wall for twenty years, and he doesn't say anything.'

It wasn't difficult to explain why that might have been, I said.

'I don't want to hear any more,' said Erin. 'I've heard enough. Just shut up. Right now. Shut up.'

'It's improbable,' I agreed.

'Totally mad is what it is,' she said, but already the anger was becoming just a sediment. 'Bloody hell, Joshua,' she said, as if we had been fighting. 'Apart from anything else, you don't look anything like him.'

'Yes, well—'

'Don't start,' she said, exhausted. 'Please, for God's sake. No more.'

Although apologies can never make good the damage, I apologised.

'Jesus, Josh, how insensitive can you be?' said Erin. 'Go home,' she said, as a woman might say it to a lover. 'For an intelligent person, you are really bloody stupid sometimes.'

It is improbable, of course. Yet it's possible, and the possibility is sometimes like an infection, an infection that might be trivial or might not. And on days when I can almost believe that it is not possible at all, the story is still in my head. Like the idea of God, it can be rebutted by reason, but not refuted.

The questioning was absurd, and it angered me, as it would have angered anyone. 'Routine enquiries,' said officer Boyle; she really followed the script. She was the more congenial of the pair, and the more intelligent, but not intelligent enough. My illuminated window, in the small hours, she informed me, is something of a local landmark. The words 'night owl' were used. I confirmed that I liked to work at night. There was some conversation, briefly, about the nature of the work.

Officer Gardiner, the near-silent partner, made a note.

They 'gathered' that the window of the room in which I work looks over the rear of the house occupied by Ms Paget, formerly occupied also by Mr Judd, deceased.

I confirmed this too.

Was it 'the case' that on 'the night in question' I was at work in the room, at my desk, overlooking the house of Ms Paget?

Indeed it was the case.

'Did you notice anything unusual?' enquired officer Boyle. 'Any activity? Lights going on?'

Had I observed anything unusual I would have reported it, as went without saying, I answered.

Officer Gardiner, writing, made a light intervention: someone answering to my description had been seen in the vicinity of the house at approximately 1.30am.

What, I asked, was meant by 'vicinity'?

Clarification was provided by officer Boyle: directly outside the house was what was meant.

I might well have been passing Ms Paget's house at that time; I had gone out for a walk.

A small quick frown from officer Gardiner. 'At one o'clock in the morning?' he asked; the antennae were twitching.

'Indeed.'

Officer Boyle, solely by means of the eyebrows, requested an explanation.

It is my habit to take a walk at that hour, weather permitting, I told her; I said something about the pleasures of a nocturnal stroll. The landscape of the town is clearer with no people in it. What I had to say seemed to interest officer Gardiner immensely; inspired, he scribbled half a dozen lines.

A question from officer Boyle had to be repeated: I was distracted for a moment, having noticed the hands of her colleague. The fingernails were gnawed; they looked like flakes of cereal. I felt compassion: his job imposes considerable stress. And great tedium, I imagine. Much of his time must be spent on tasks that are a waste of everyone's time, such as this one.

When I passed Ms Paget's house, I told them, the front door was closed; no damage was apparent.

'So you took a good look at the door?' asked officer Gardiner.

The door was shut and undamaged, I repeated.

Then officer Boyle asked: 'How would you describe your relationship with Mr Judd?'

Her colleague looked up from his notes to observe the reaction to the sudden swerve. But the interviewee was not to be thrown off-balance. 'Very cordial,' I said. It is one of the approved adjectives, I believe. Without prompting, I elaborated: I had spent a lot of time with Mr Judd; he was an interesting man, and I had enjoyed many conversations with him, conversations of some length, sometimes with Ms Paget present.

To follow, the inevitable question: 'And how would you describe your relationship with Ms Paget?'

'Friendly,' I decided.

'Friendly,' echoed officer Gardiner.

The intention was that I should wonder what might be implied by the tone. I should be asking myself: 'What do they know? What have they been told?' But I had already imagined what they had been told. That was why they were here. It was disappointing, of course. But I simply said again: 'Friendly.' I asked if anything had been taken.

Officer Boyle regretted that they could not divulge that particular piece of information.

They were welcome to search the premises, I told them.

That would not be necessary, officer Boyle assured me.

I had another question: why would anyone imagine that I would force the door of a house that I could enter easily, at any time. There was no lock on one of the ground-floor windows at the back. And who would see me, if I were to go over the wall in the dead of night? On the street side, however, I would be conspicuous. So the idea was ridiculous. I had urged Ms Paget to improve the security, I told them.

Ms Paget had been given advice to this effect, said officer Boyle. She thanked me for my time.

Rising, officer Gardiner performed a rapid scan of the room. 'Lot of books,' he remarked, as if this in itself were sufficient ground for suspicion.

☞

Seeing Erin in the mid-distance, I caught up with her and asked her what she had said.

An obvious enquiry, but it seemed to surprise her. A long pause followed. It was not that she appeared to be giving the question some thought. Rather, it was as though she had been asked for a piece of information to which her brain did not have immediate access, though she should have known it, such as today's date. Eventually she answered: 'You know why.'

I told her, gently, that I did not know why.

She had explained, she reminded me, that she needed to be on her own, 'for a while'.

But her sister was staying, I pointed out.

'That's different,' she told me.

I said that if she wished to be alone I would not call round. 'But you know where I am,' I said.

She looked straight at me, considering; it seemed that an apology of some sort might be made. 'Yes,' she said. She smiled, but the smile was vapid. It made me wonder if medication might now be involved. She looked down the street, as if something of mild interest had appeared there. From her left hand hung a plastic bag with a dozen tins of cat food in it; her fingers were turning white where the plastic cut in. 'I'll let you get on,' I said.

At the pedestrian crossing she walked out without looking, but on the other side she stopped to look right, then left, then right, then left, as though she had forgotten which way she had to go.

☞

When I went round to the house, on the last day, the sister was standing at the ramp of the lorry, in discussion with a gigantic young man who appeared to be in charge of the operation. She glanced aside and raised a finger, instructing me to wait for a moment, until she had finished; I did not wait. Already the living room was empty, purged of almost every trace of Callum, of Kathleen, of Lucas, of Erin. Here and there, on the walls, lines and shadows of dust marked the location of things that had gone. I walked towards the window; the noise of my footsteps on the floorboards covered the sound of Erin coming in.

When I turned, she was standing in the doorway, the young mother-widow, holding her daughter by the hand. For a moment I could not speak, such was the power of her appearance, a power that was amplified by the bareness of the room. Though I saw that she had been crying, the first thing I said was: 'Are you all right?'

The stupidity of the remark warranted the response, or non-response: Erin looked at me as if I were an object that had been placed in the room for no apparent reason. Her gaze slid to the windows, then back to me. 'What do you think?' she said, after ten seconds of silence. 'No, Josh, I am not all right. How could I possibly be all right?' The voice, the eyes, were those of a woman who needed to sleep, and of someone who knew much more of life than I did.

All I then said was: 'No. Of course.'

Erin did not speak; her face told me nothing.

I said: 'I came to say goodbye.'

She nodded; there was still no smile, but some softening was evident.

Only now did I say something to Kit. She would have come to me, had her mother released her. Confused, she raised a hand, as if I were on the opposite bank of a stream. This upset me.

Overhead, a piece of heavy furniture was being dragged. Someone shouted on the stairs, and at this point the sister appeared. She looked from me to Erin to me and again to Erin, and reached a conclusion instantly. She bent down to whisper in her niece's ear, then carried her off.

'I'll be gone in a minute,' I promised Erin, though what I had to say would have taken hours. I asked if we could go into the garden, away from the noise.

She did not reply immediately, but continued to look at me, reading me. 'There's stuff I have to do,' she said. The situation was too difficult for her.

'I know,' I said, 'I know.' But there were some things I had to clarify, I told her.

'Josh,' she answered, 'this isn't the time, or the place.'

I accepted that this was so. My attitude was one of acceptance; with this, I admit, I hoped to impress. I said a few more words, signifying sympathy. They were inadequate, and should not be recorded. Mid-sentence, I was interrupted by the sister. 'You're needed,' she ordered Erin, from the doorway.

I offered a hand to Erin, and we shook, with a glance that agreed there could, one day, be a time and a place.

The sister lingered by the door, letting Erin pass. The look she aimed at me required a response; I could not let it go.

✍

Last night: a dream of upsetting clarity, but not of Erin. I, or the subject of the dream, was playing in a park, throwing a ball with someone who was intermittently my father. The ball rolled towards my mother, who let it run past her. She seemed to be watching the game with interest, but as though the players were not known to her. The man who was approximately my father was making a great effort to be playful, and became so tired that he could not, in the end, find sufficient strength to lift the ball. It fell from his fingers into the grass, like a lump of iron. My mother was then asleep. She was grinding her teeth in her sleep, and I stood over her, afraid. At a glance from my father, a glance that was affectionate but seemed to suggest that I was behaving oddly, I woke up. Something in this was real, I know. There was much more, and some of that too might have been a rewritten memory, but already it has rushed away from me.

☞

Sigmund Freud, Lucas informed me, was of the opinion that, before homo sapiens had become a linguistic species, telepathy would have been the means by which individuals communicated with each other. With the evolution of language and the ever-greater complexities of conscious thought, our telepathic faculties had become submerged, as it were. Most of us go through our lives unaware that our minds can speak to each other without words, said Lucas. In sleep, however, we might sometimes have an experience that makes us wonder. It is not uncommon, for example, for people to be alerted by a dream to the distress of a distant loved one; many women have learned in a dream of a sister's pregnancy; people have dreamed of friends with whom they lost contact long ago, and then, days later, the friend has returned. The noise of our daytime thinking renders the ethereal messages inaudible, Lucas explained. At night, when circumstances are more favourable, the signal can get through.

Dreams had led a number of people to summon Lucas, and he had been able to confirm that the dreams were communications – albeit blurred communications (the spiritual equipment of the lay person is less finely tuned than the professional's, remember) – from the person whose absence had led the dreamer to contact him. And several of his clients had reported that, during or after their consultations, they had begun to have dreams in which the absent person spoke more clearly to them or appeared with extraordinary vividness. It seemed that as a result of Lucas's attention, the client's unconscious mind had become more sensitive, said Lucas; the process by which this increase in sensitivity sometimes occurs was a mystery. There had been cases in which dreams were shared by client and medium. For example, a man who had once been unfaithful to his wife, and suffered agonies of remorse for many years, a remorse that the forgiveness of his wife had done nothing to assuage, and which had intensified after her death, phoned Lucas to report a marvellous dream, in which he had been looking down on a vast plain of grass, on which many thousands of people were walking, in a procession towards a place that could not be seen, and although he was gazing down from the height of a skyscraper's roof he could see precisely the face of his wife, as she stopped for a moment and looked up, as though sensing that her husband was there – 'and she smiled,' said Lucas, completing the report before the man could finish, because he too had seen the man's wife looking up, in a dream of his own.

The father of the new family has been installing a table and chairs in the paved corner of the garden of the house that was the home of Lucas, the home of Lucas and Erin, the home of Kathleen, of Kathleen and Lucas, of Kathleen and Callum. At last satisfied with the arrangement, he sits in the chair that occupies the last segment of sunlight, and his gaze meanders over the wall of the garden; it pauses momentarily, at the place once occupied by the inscription cut by Callum. There is only an irregularity in the brickwork now; a scar, of no meaning to the new owners of the house. The spirit of Callum has gone from the garden, and the spirit of Lucas. One of the daughters runs out of the kitchen, and her father stands up, to seize her. An upward throw momentarily frees the girl from her father's hands; a squeal of joyful alarm.

I watch them, from the window from which I watched Lucas and Kathleen and Erin, the window of the room that has been mine since I was a child, in the house that is mine, which was my mother's, and where once my father lived too, the father whose spirit is entirely absent, who has become barely a fume of memory. And here is the bowl that Kathleen made, and Lucas presented to me. I hold it, placing my thumb on the thumbprint that was pressed into the bowl when Kathleen held it into the glaze. Closing my eyes, I see Lucas, looking across the room at Kathleen, who is sitting in her chair, with her eyes closed; then her eyes open and she smiles at Lucas, as though in the knowledge that he knows the thoughts from which she has just roused herself. There is a vase beside Lucas's chair; he cups the fat scarlet head of a peony, and examines it for a few seconds, before letting it go, as if it were a highly wrought and expensive item that he might once have been inclined to buy.

Furyū monji, meaning: independent of words or writing; no dependence on words or writing; without reliance on words or writing; not standing on words or letters; not expressed in words or writing. Instead, transmission from mind to mind, as Kathleen explained, forming a bowl of her fingers, supporting the bowl of my fingers, in which rested the bowl that she had made.

Alone, we are like the land in winter, when the earth, denuded, is revealed in its true form; the self, stripped of the vegetation of attachment, the complicating foliage of relationships, is purely itself when alone. We see who we are. Erin will come to understand, or so I hope, when the entanglements of Lucas at last fall away. And life has more urgency like this, when one is exposed. Contentment is often an insulation.

A scene. Every Wednesday, I take my seat at the same small corner table. I arrive on the stroke of 1.15, and what I eat is always the same. The routine has long been an aspect of the character. I am wearing the white shirt, of course. The summer plumage. My table is by the window, so that I can distract myself with the spectacle of the street, such as it is. The invariable choice of dish signifies a certain austerity, perhaps; or a lack of imagination. At 2pm I depart, whatever the weather.

A menu is taped to the window, facing outward, close to my seat. I become aware that a woman is standing outside, scanning the list; I look up, and at that moment a girl, perhaps already a teenager, steps out from behind the woman; the girl is Kit; the woman, Erin.

A mime of astonishment is performed. A minute later, an embrace. It is a tentative manoeuvre; Erin receives me as though taking hold of a parcel of unwieldy dimensions. In her face there is evidence of anxieties of some duration. But the smile, as she reintroduces Kit, is the smile of many years before.

We are walking on the seafront. The loss of Lucas is no longer acute. The sadness has been accommodated. It has become a foundation. We walk side by side. Inevitably, we talk about Lucas. He is with us. We sit on the shingle. Erin has much to say, about Lucas, about Kit. At last she has emerged fully into herself. I will not say that I love her. Words are too precarious. I could place a hand on hers. Everything is forgiven. But the moment must not be momentous. This is important. It must be light, and I must have patience. But things would go from there. It could happen. If not as I have imagined, in another way. Or this may be all I have. I don't know.

ALSO BY JONATHAN BUCKLEY

The Biography of Thomas Lang

Xerxes

Ghost MacIndoe

Invisible

So He Takes the Dog

Contact

Telescope

Nostalgia

The river is the river

The Great Concert of the Night

Steph Fawbert.
31 Vicarage Rd
Hastings
TN34 3LZ

07717 223 997